Descent
Book #2 in The Gallows Hill Trilogy

Katelyn Taylor

Playlist

you broke me first by Tate McRae
Lose You To Love Me by Selena Gomez
Every Breath You Take by Chase Holfelder
Sound of Madness by Shinedown
Elastic Heart by Sia
Sparks by Coldplay
The Death Of Peace of Mind by Bad Omens
I Kissed A Boy by Jude York
Lose Control by Teddy Swims
Cold Blooded by Chris Grey

Copyright

Trigger Warning

There are several graphic and dark elements to this book. Please proceed with caution and review the triggers carefully. This book includes the following triggers but is not limited to:

Violence, Explicit language, Explicit sexual scenes, graphic torture, abuse, murder, dub con, degradation, pain/pleasure play, knife play, torture of an animal (rat), alcohol abuse, spitting, assplay, double penetration

Dedication

Have you ever been in search of a book that takes place in Salem, Massachusetts and revolves around a secret society formed by the men who killed all of the accused witches from the Trials? And then you also wanted it to take place at an elitist university where a woman finds herself with more cocks than she knows what to do with?
Yeah, me too.

Prologue

The Brethren was founded in 1693. With the trials finished, the good townsfolk of Salem were living in terror. Fear ran rampant from people wondering what was to come next. The families of those tried would surely come after the innocent townsfolk. Driven by blood lust and revenge, there was only one thing for them to do.

A society was formed in the ashes of those troubled times. A security was given to those desperate for safety, peace and most importantly, power. The Brethren was born. Safety in numbers, power in those who controlled it. Each family involved in the trials was at risk of the witches who were not discovered and the surviving families of those who were. In such, a member of each family took their place as an Elder. Responsibilities for each Elder differ, the common task – protect those in seek of refuge from the wicked damnation of those witches and their descendants.

Putnam, Parris, Walcott, Griggs, Lewis, Strouhgton, Hutchinson, Preston and Ingersoll.

All Elder families, all essential to the balance of the Brethren. Without one, they all would surely fall. As one we persevere, we prosper, and we punish.

Mors omnibus maleficis – Death to all evildoers

Death to all witches

Chapter One
Asher

Without a word I pull out of Skyla, standing to my feet before grabbing my white robe. I pull it on over my shoulders and tie the sash as I look down to see those watery emerald green eyes staring up at me. I raise an unimpressed eyebrow to her theatrics as I take the white nightgown that's been ripped beneath her, balling up a chunk of the material and forcefully wiping between her legs. Her body bucks at the intrusion but my left hand forces her thigh apart. I continue wiping, smearing her blood and my cum onto the white material, before I yank it out from under her.

She almost falls from the slab at the sudden move, but I maintain my stoic gaze. Once I have the entire thing in my arms, I give her one more cold glance. Her eyes are begging me, pleading with me. For what, though? What does she expect? Doesn't she see this is all we will ever be? All we could ever afford to be? Just because she convinced herself I was capable of being someone else doesn't mean shit. Fuck, for a second there, she had me convinced too.

As I move through the room, I meet Liam's eyes. I've never seen so much hate in my best friend's eyes, and to be honest, it turns my stomach. Of course, I don't let it show as I continue moving through the sacred room. The next set of eyes I land on is Ronan's, who is currently not so subtly holding back a crazed-looking Griggs. Yeah, I'll definitely be sleeping with my door barricaded tonight. Crazy motherfucker looks ready to bathe in my blood.

My father nods to me in approval, casting a disapproving gaze to Skyla before murmuring to me.

"Head to the cemetery. We will follow shortly."

I nod, making my way out of the room, I go through the holding room, where I slip on my shoes before heading down the tunnel. When I get to the church, I realize I'm not alone. A member of the Brethren is there nodding his head in respect as I pass him by.

When I turn right and head deeper into the cemetery, I notice a soft orange glow in the distance. I push deeper into the night, stepping over the occasional tree root or dilapidated headstone.

Finally, I make it to the large bonfire, and I see several members of the Brethren gathered around it, tending to the fire. There are probably only five men here, but it's five more than I expected. I thought these traditions were meant to be kept secret, even from other members. Maybe I'm wrong, though.

We only wait a few minutes before the Elders arrive. Led by my father, they all take their places to form a circle around the fire. My father is beside me, with Henry on the other, before my father steps forward arms raised to the sky as his voice bellows out.

"Christ, we come before you on this night of evil with good. A union holier than thou can imagine has been commemorated. We give you this sacrifice of virgin blood in thanks for the protection you grant us against evil."

"Maleficis esse mori," everyone chants.

Death to witches.

My father continues, begging God to continue protecting us from their evil. That he strikes them down and slits their throats. Of course, I'm not dumb enough to bring up the fact that I'm not sure that's how God works.

I've always known that the Brethren has been a little out there, and by a little, I mean a lot. Tonight, has really opened my eyes, though. The number of steps that was explained to me and told had to be executed to perfection was insane. The ritual, the crazed religious tie to it all.

Maybe Skyla is right; this is seeming more like a cult with each passing day.

Skyla. My wife.

For all intents and purposes, in the Brethren's eyes we are married now. More married than a piece of paper in a courthouse could ever deem us. We are tied to each other for all eternity, or at least for the rest of her life. In case it wasn't obvious, women don't typically last long in the Brethren, especially with an Elder.

Do I feel that I took it a little far in there? Yeah, of course. I had no choice, though. She spoke during the ceremony. She said it was okay, outing that I was remorseful, something that I will not escape unscathed. My father looked ready to blow both of our brains to pieces.

So, I had to sell it. Had to make her and everyone else in that room think that I've been playing her. There is nothing my father hates more than a strong woman, something he knows Skyla to be. That's dangerous enough. If he thought for a second that she had a hold on me, that this love she supposedly has for me would affect my judgment or decision making ...suffice it to say, it would be a bloody end for us both.

The slap to her face hurt something inside me no matter how numb I tried to be, and the spit was the ultimate disrespect. I wanted to make her feel less than, to be ground under my heel until she was nothing. If she believed it, so would they.

I didn't want to break her like that, I didn't want to say a word. We both agreed to stay silent, so why the fuck did she speak? I didn't have a fucking choice! For both our sakes. She should be thanking me, honestly. Though, something tells me thanks won't be the first words she utters to me when we move into our home tomorrow.

Did a small piece inside of me also do it for myself? Maybe. Maybe it wasn't just to keep my father and the Elder's away from her. Maybe a part of me did it to put distance between us. She was too close, too embedded in me. I could feel my whole world shifting and everything started revolving around Skyla. Which is a dangerous thing for me and my heart, when hers is already accounted for.

I don't care what her or any of the guys say. She can't love them all, not equally. In the end, she will have to choose one, and the others will be decimated. I couldn't be involved. We all know I'd never be the choice. So, why would I sign myself up for inevitable hurt?

They can play house with each other for now, convince themselves this thing they have is forever. Eventually, though, this will all be a distant memory until one is left standing...or hell, maybe none. Who knows.

What I do know is that as much as I'd like to believe in fairy-tales and happily ever after's, I'm a realist. Her heart is already too full, too occupied. There is no room left for me anyways.

Chapter Two
Skyla

I lay there numb, in shock, completely naked and broken as Asher slips out of the room with my nightgown clutched in his fist, as he disappears without so much as a backward glance. Fighting back the tears has been hard this entire day, but now? I can't hold them back any longer. I feel the tears begin pouring down my face, a twinge on my cheek from Asher's slap reminding me of the mark.

I don't understand. I don't get any of it. Was it really all for show? A game? That doesn't seem right. Things changed, slowly. It wasn't an overnight shift. We let down our guards; we opened up to each other. We...fell. Or maybe I'm the only one that did the falling. Sure as hell feels that way, as I'm left splattered against this stone slab in front of all these men.

A noise catches my attention, and I see Ronan has Vincent wrapped up in his arms, quickly whispering into his ear. Vincent is seething, and he catches the attention of several curious men around him. My eyes come to Liam, and I find him looking almost as furious as Vincent when my father speaks.

"Ronan, please escort my...daughter to her room."

He pauses on the word daughter, like it's unpleasant on his tongue, before him and the other men make their way out of the room one by one. Everyone leaves until it's just Ronan and me, with Liam and

Vincent purposefully hanging towards the back of the group, probably so it doesn't look suspicious.

Ronan slowly steps towards me, picking up the discarded blindfold before wrapping it around my eyes. He speaks so softly, I almost don't hear him, his touch featherlight as he does.

"Are you okay, baby?"

"No," I whisper, my throat tightening by the second as the building tears continue to fall.

The world goes dark with the blindfold in place, and I feel Ronan's arms slip beneath my legs as he lifts me into his hold.

"I've got you, baby," he says, as he allows his lips to brush against my head.

He carries me out of the room, and I find myself burrowing into his chest as deeply as I can. A chill takes over me, scattering goosebumps across my body before I hear rustling and feel a thin material cover me. I grab onto it, the feel of what I can tell to be a man's shirt now wrapping around me like a blanket.

I take comfort in it, giving a weak smile to whoever gave it to me and whoever can see. It feels like it takes forever before we're back in my room. Maybe that's because we didn't get in a car this time. I'm not exactly sure where we are. Off-campus somewhere I'd assume, though not too far off. Then again, I wouldn't be surprised if they had that creepy ceremony room built somewhere on campus for convenience sake.

My feet touch the ground, and when the blindfold is removed from my eyes, I see Vincent to my left, Ronan to my right, and a shirtless Liam in front of me. We are back in my room already, and when my head whips around again, Liam is the first one to move. He closes the distance between us, burying my head into his chest as a sob I didn't know I was still holding in rips out of me.

"Shhh, shhh. It's okay, babygirl. Let it out. I've got you."

I release my hold on his dress shirt, letting it flitter to the ground as I cling to him for dear life. I feel a warm body press behind me, the familiar smell of Ronan overwhelming me as he wraps me in his arms.

"We both do," he says.

I continue to sob when I blink my eyes open and see Vincent standing several feet away, fists clenched, jaw tight. He looks like a bomb ready to go off, and when I reach for him, desperate for that special brand of comfort that only he's capable of, he jerks away.

It cracks my already bleeding heart, and he seems to be able to tell because he speaks.

"I'm not angry with you, Siren. I'm angry *for* you. I'm ready to tear through every single person that was in that goddamn room and lay their remains at your feet. I *can't* touch you right now," he says, his body shaking uncontrollably as he does.

I reach for him once more and he easily dodges me again.

"P-please," I whisper brokenly. "I-I need you," I say as my words begin to catch, feeling myself on the edge of one of those lovely panic attacks.

He stares at me for several seconds before he reaches out a shaking hand. It comes to cup my face, cradling me surprisingly tender as he speaks.

"I'm here."

My eyes fall closed at that and I sob. I don't even know for how long and I don't even really know why. For the humiliation of tonight? The pain? The hurt? Did any of the bleeding, branding and tearing really hurt compared to Asher's slap and his vile words?

I don't think so.

Ronan slips away for a moment, rustling around in the bathroom before coming back out with a first aid kit. He begins tending to my burnt and bleeding palms. I almost tell him not to worry about it, that my hand isn't the body part that hurts the most right now. Unfortunately, I don't think there is anything in that kit for a shattered heart.

Eventually we make our way onto the bed, my body on top of Liam's, with Ronan and Vincent on either side of me. I feel several pairs of hands running through my hair, rubbing up and down my back, drawing mindless patterns on my hip. The silence is heavy, it's deafening, and I can't take it anymore.

"Why would he do that?" I whisper brokenly, not needing to elaborate.

They are all silent for several moments before Ronan speaks.

"I don't know, baby. But I'm going to find out."

I feel him begin to shift and I cling to him desperately, looking to him with panicked eyes as I shake my head.

"Please don't go. Stay. P-please," I whimper.

Ronan's blue eyes soften on me instantly, and he leans in pressing his lips to mine as he nods.

"Of course. Whatever you need, baby."

Chapter Three
Ronan

It took less than ten minutes for Skyla to fall asleep. When she did, Vincent, Liam and I all exchanged a look. In the next second, we were all moving. I slipped out of bed first, followed by Vincent. Liam carefully pulled her off him, laying her on her side, before pressing a kiss to her forehead.

Liam bent down, picked up the shirt he covered Skyla with and buttoned the bottom four buttons before leaving the rest open.

"Let's go," he said lowly, a look of pure anger on his face as he marched out the door.

Now, here we are, practically rushing our way through the dorm until we stop at Asher's door. I wave my card over the reader, and when it opens, Liam is the first through. We see Asher immediately, peeling off his white robe when he turns to see us.

Liam doesn't hesitate for a second though, practically flying across the room, his fist sucker punching Asher against his temple. We all surround Asher, and when he stumbles from Liam's second blow, I catch him easily. I shove him to the ground before Vincent pulls out his gun, pressing it to the back of Asher's head.

Goddamnit. That kid and his gun, I swear to fuck.

"Siren said that I get to be the one to kill you if you hurt her. Any last words?" he asks coldly, a slight thrill to his voice like he's looked forward to this day for a long time.

Unfortunately for Vincent, Liam rests a hand on the gun, shaking his head as he pulls back his leg and delivers a kick straight to Asher's stomach. He coughs from the impact before Liam does it again and again. For a guy that is normally extremely averse to violence, he seems to be having no problem right now. That's good news for his future in the Brethren, I suppose.

Liam reaches down, grabbing Asher by the throat, as he hauls him up several inches until they are face-to-face.

"You will never speak to her again. You won't touch her. Hell, you won't even fucking look in her direction... Got it?"

Asher sneers, jerking his head away as he spits a glob of blood onto the floor.

"She's my wife," Asher scoffs.

"Hardly," Liam sneers.

"In the Brethren's eyes," Asher counters.

Liam is silent for a moment, his jaw working back and forth as if contemplating what to say next.

"That's all she will ever be now. In the Brethren's eyes and legally sure, but that's the only piece of her you will *ever* have."

Asher scoffs again as he shakes his head.

"Trust me, it's more than I want."

Liam's eyes narrow.

"Liar."

Asher doesn't immediately defend himself. Instead, they stay trapped in a glaring contest while Vincent and I watch. The former looking entirely too trigger happy as he stares them down. It took fucking everything in me to hold Vincent back when Asher slapped her. I'm surprised he remained silent because he raged like a beast that had finally been set free. We got more than a few curious looks, but lucky for him, everyone seemed to be far too interested in the...show.

I can't blame him, though. The whole thing was hard to watch. Fucking miserable, but Asher slapping her? *Spitting* on her? Telling her he basically played her...now I kind of want to shoot the fucker.

Leaning over, I spit in Asher's face, forcing his eyes to come to me as I snarl.

"You're just like your father," I say with a disappointed shake of my head, knowing those are the words that will hurt him the most.

He physically reacts like I've struck him, before all emotion escapes his face and he effectively shuts down.

"We can't all afford to be the Putnam disappointment," he says almost robotically.

The barb is lamely tossed and misses. If he thinks pointing out the obvious would hurt me, he has a lot to learn. I'm a lot like Liam in the way that I've accepted my title as the disappointment, it no longer bothers me. Maybe that's why I like the kid so much.

"I hope breaking her was worth it," I say with a shake of my head. "She will never forgive you, and neither will I."

Asher lets out a hollow laugh as Liam tosses him to the ground, stepping away with a shake of his head.

"So, that's it? Pussy over family? A piece of ass over blood?"

The butt of Vincent's gun comes down on Asher hard. It connects right above his right eye, busting open the skin just below his eyebrow as he falls backwards. Vincent gives me an 'I had no choice' shrug, before I look at my bleeding nephew.

"I'm not even going to dignify that with a response. You and I both know she is more than that. We also know that family isn't fucking shit."

Asher doesn't respond, just sits there and glares as I cross my arms over my chest.

"We're going to move her in tomorrow. Do everyone a favor and don't be around," I say as I turn and head out the door.

I hear Liam and Vincent following close behind; we make our way through the hall and back to our girl. I wish there was a way we could keep her on campus, keep her out of that fucking house. There isn't, though. It's the expectation, and there are enough curious eyes on the four of us right now. We need to blend in, to go along with things exactly as my brother expects. Unfortunately for my baby, that means living with my piece of fucking shit nephew for the time being.

"What are we going to do?" Liam asks. "You have to know Christopher will have the surveillance bugged so he can keep an eye on them."

"The outside, but not the inside," I say.

"How do you figure?" Vincent asks.

I look over my shoulder at him with a raised brow as I continue walking.

"Because I'm the one he had install everything."

"Okayyy, well how will we explain coming through the front door whenever we want to see our girl?" Liam challenges.

"You don't. Tomorrow, I'll be the one to move Skyla in. Then you can come over under the guise of seeing Asher," I say as I point to Liam. "You," I say as I look to Vincent, "will have to figure out your own way in and out, because everyone knows you and Asher fucking hate each other."

Vincent nods, like he's already thought over exactly how he will get in and out undetected. We walk the remaining distance back to Skyla's dorm and are in the elevator when Liam speaks.

"I'm still in shock that he pulled that shit. I thought he was really falling for her."

"He was," Vincent says briskly. "Probably still is. It was a way to brush off her I love you, and probably make him look good in front of daddy."

Yeah, the I love you. Can't say that didn't take me by surprise. Honestly, it shouldn't have. They've been getting closer lately, and with Liam catching them kissing yesterday, it shouldn't have caught me off guard. I think it was more the timing than the words, though. Women are to be seen, not heard, especially during a ritual. Definitely not speaking words of understanding and love. It made Asher look weak and pliable. Though she didn't mean to, she painted a red X on both of their backs.

Maybe Griggs has a point. I'm sure Asher did it partially to appease his dad, prove that he isn't controlled by a woman and that he is the one in power. He was also probably trying to distract from her confession. It doesn't justify what he did, but I have to believe that my nephew isn't all evil. That what he felt, and probably still feels for Skyla, was real. For her sake, at least.

Chapter Four
Skyla

I wake up the next morning, eyes puffy, palms aching, and the sensitive flesh between my thighs is so fucking sore. Last night was what nightmares are made of. It was so much worse than I ever could have imagined for so many reasons. Even with the audience we had, it was a stark contrast to what I imagined it would be like. I didn't anticipate him taking my virginity so savagely, so mercilessly, so heartlessly. I thought maybe he'd try to make it at least a little gentle.

Obviously, I thought wrong on every count because Asher Putnam turned out to be exactly who I always knew him to be. It was my mistake for believing that people could change, that I could see some good in him. In reality, he's just a piece of shit.

"How are you?" Vincent asks from beside me.

I turn to face him, his silver eyes already trained on me.

"Good, you?" I ask with a forced smile.

His brows knit together in disbelief.

"No, I'm actually asking, Siren. Are you hurting?" he questions as his fingers reach out, tracing my palms.

I look down at the bandaged cut, before my eyes come to the branded hand. That one hurts a lot more, for sure. It's a dull, burning pain that won't subside. Honestly, I think it hurts more now than it did last night. The adrenaline and trauma of everything must have helped block some of it, but now? It's terrible.

I only nod, not sure what there is to say. Yes, like hell, but it is what it is? The ugly discolored B, now marred into my palm forever, will never cease to be a reminder of the hell I went through last night. Of the hell that is to come. For a little bit, I was fooled into thinking that Asher and I could have a good life together. Maybe even a happy one. Now I'm beginning to wonder if I would have been better off letting them kill me last night. If more nights like that are in my future...I don't know.

"Here," Ronan says as he reaches over us, handing me two white pills and a bottle of water.

I don't even ask what they are, happily taking any kind of relief that I can, before I pop them into my mouth and take a sip of water.

When I look to my right, I notice that Liam is gone.

"His dad called him this morning to meet with him," Ronan says.

"Is that bad? Is everything okay?"

Ronan scratches his hand against his jaw, where more facial hair than normal is coming in.

"I don't know, baby. I'm not sure if it was about last night or something else. If anyone should be questioned for their behavior, it would definitely be Vincent," he says, as he looks down at my surly boyfriend.

His jaw is tense; he shrugs his shoulders like he doesn't have a care in the world. It takes my eyes another moment to look around my room and notice something. All my stuff is gone. My dresser drawers are slightly ajar, all empty. I can see my walk-in closet from here, all racks looking as empty as they did the day I moved in.

"We took care of it for you while you were sleeping this morning," Ronan says. "Whenever you're ready, I'll drive you over to the house."

The house. My new house. Asher's house more like it.

A sinking feeling churns my stomach at the reminder that today is move-in day. That I'll no longer have my own space. From now on, I'll be in his space, with no way out.

"You're coming too, right?" I ask as I look to Vincent, who gives me a remorseful shake of his head.

"It's not safe right now, Siren. Especially with how I...lost control last night," he says through clenched teeth, spearing Ronan with a heated look.

I feel myself physically deflate.

"So, I'm assuming that means you won't be able to come over for a while to see me?"

"Fuck no," he spits before his hand cups my cheek. "I'll be there tonight, in your bed, waiting to hold you until morning."

"But how? If you're worried about people watching us or—"

His thumb comes to my lips, pausing my words as he pulls my lower lip down, letting it go with a bounce as he speaks.

"You let me worry about that. You just keep yourself safe for now, okay? I promise everything will be alright."

"Okay," I whisper softly, before his lips press against mine.

I'll never not get butterflies when he kisses me. Every touch is filled with so much passion, so much desire. It's as if he's not truly living until he touches me, and when he does...magic.

When he pulls away, he presses a kiss to my forehead, resting his lips for several seconds before pulling back to look me in the eye.

"I'll see you tonight."

It isn't said like a question, it's a promise. A guarantee. Out of anyone in the world, I know without a doubt Vincent is a man that would keep his word, with me at least, or die trying.

I give him a soft smile and a nod before he crawls out of bed and we both get ready for the day. He leaves while I'm in the shower, and once I'm dressed in the outfit Ronan left out for me, I throw my hair into a braid and follow him out of the dorm.

Looking over my shoulder, I cast one more look inside. I wasn't here long, but it had already begun to feel like home. It's sad, in a way, that I'm leaving it behind. Even more sad to think of what lies ahead. I guess the one plus side is that my stalker will, no doubt, have a harder time breaking into Asher's house. At least, I really hope so; I can't really take much more of anything right now.

Ronan walks me out to his car, opening the door for me as I see a black SUV begin to follow us. I give Ronan a questioning glance as he reaches over, cupping my thigh as he speaks.

"That's Wesley, your driver."

"I have a driver?"

He nods. "Now that you're off campus you'll need a ride, so you aren't stranded at the house or dependent on Asher," he says, a sour sound leaving his mouth on his nephew's name.

"He has all of your stuff in the car and will bring it inside for you when we get there. You'll like him, we've been friends for years."

I nod, looking out the window for a moment before I speak.

"Can I trust him? Like, does he know about us? Or the guys?"

I turn to see Ronan go back and forth, like he can't quite decide before he shakes his head.

"If I was going to trust anyone outside of the guys with our secrets, it would be Wesley. But no, don't trust him."

I frown at that. "Why not?"

His bright blue eyes come to me as his hand squeezes my thigh harder.

"Because you're too important, baby. It's not worth the risk. Under normal circumstances, he'd take anything we needed to the grave, but we are all human. We all have our breaking points, our exceptions. I don't want to risk him knowing anything."

"Do you think it would really come to that? That Christopher or my father would find out and..."

"Kill us all?" Ronan cuts me off. "Absolutely. Without hesitation."

I wince, looking back out the window. He couldn't have lied to me or something?

When we get to the house, Asher's cars are all there, and that heavy feeling of dread is alive and well, sinking lower and lower into my stomach. I hear Ronan mutter under his breath as he parks before releasing my leg.

"C'mon, I'll introduce you to Wesley and take care of...that," he says, as he gestures to one of Asher's cars.

I'm not sure what he means by take care of it. He obviously doesn't mean, kill his nephew so that I don't have to look at his disgusting vile face ever again.

Too bad.

Unbuckling my seatbelt, I go to grab my door when it's pulled open for me. A guy dressed in all black is there, his hand outstretched and offering to help me out of the car. I hesitate for a moment before I accept, looking up at the tall blond man with dark blue eyes. Where Ronan's are bright and light like a pool, this man's are deep like the ocean.

His eyes stay on me for a few seconds longer than probably appropriate before he seems to shake himself, giving me a kind smile and a head nod.

"Nice to meet you, Miss Parris."

I nod in return, giving him a polite smile as Ronan rounds the car. He closes the distance between him and Wesley with a handshake that looks more friendly than formal, before they pull each other in for a hug.

"It's been a while," he smiles.

Ronan nods.

"That's what happens when you go off to fight for our country, I guess."

Ronan turns to me.

"Skyla, this is Wesley. We grew up together and he just got out of the Seals."

"Navy, right?" I clarify.

Wesley nods. "Yes, ma'am. I appreciate the job. God knows what I would have been assigned to do, now that my contract was up."

"What? Is it worse than driving a nineteen-year-old girl around?"

His smile stays in place, but a look flashes behind his eyes as he nods. "Much."

My smile slowly falls, and I nod my understanding as Ronan speaks.

"I'm gonna run inside for a moment. Why don't you grab some of her stuff?"

Wesley nods as I step away from the car, he shuts my door before turning back to his SUV. I follow him, wanting to delay any interaction with Asher that I can. He pops the trunk and begins grabbing bags with hangers sticking out the top, my clothes, I assume. He's able to get almost all of them except for one. I reach for it, resting it in my arms before he tries to swipe it from me.

"I've got it," he says easily.

I raise a disbelieving brow at him, which causes him to shrug.

"I need to make another trip anyways. It's not a problem."

"I'm capable , honestly, you're the one that is helping. You're just supposed to be my driver, not my butler."

Wesley shrugs again as we begin walking to the front door.

"I'm whatever they say I need to be for you."

I don't clarify on the 'they' part, that is a no-brainer. Though, I am curious who put him in charge of me. Was it Ronan's decision? Or is this my father or Christopher planting a spy? He seems nice, but I'm not dumb enough to drop my guard just like that. Especially with someone who is very clearly under the Brethren's thumb.

When we step inside, I hear a door slam from upstairs before Ronan appears at the top, a thunderous look on his face that softens when he sees me. He hurries down the stairs, attempting to take the clothes out of my hand when I turn away.

"I've got it. There is a little more in the trunk if you could, please?"

He nods and takes a step closer, as if he were going to kiss me. I send him a panicked look, and he quickly checks himself like he didn't realize he was doing it.

"Of course."

I start up the stairs before I look back casually to see Wesley giving Ronan a curious look before looking back to me. I shrug him off and lead him to the large master bedroom, Asher told me that it could be mine. When I push open the door, I see that it's as undisturbed as it was the other day. Dibs, I guess.

Wesley steps into the room, moving to the closet before hanging up the clothes and undoing the bags protecting them. Ronan follows us, carrying up a few suitcases of my shoes and makeup. It only takes us ten minutes before I'm officially moved in. It's easy to do when I just moved across the world a few months ago. I haven't really had time to collect all that much.

"Thanks, Wes. I'll give Skyla your number if she needs you," Ronan says with a nod.

"I'll probably just hang out here for the day. Maybe if you wouldn't mind giving me a ride to school tomorrow? My first class is at—"

"Seven, I know. I'll be here at six forty, sharp," Wesley says with a polite smile.

"Oh, yeah. Perfect. Thank you."

"My pleasure," he nods before facing Ronan. "What are you up to? Want to go grab a beer and catch up?"

Ronan shoots a quick glance at me out of the corner of his eye like he wants to refuse and stay here. I can already tell that would be a mistake, though. That is, if he really thinks Wesley isn't trustworthy.

"Gosh, I'm kind of jealous. Sounds better than this stuffy place," I tease, subtly pushing him to go.

"You're more than welcome to join us, Miss Parris," Wesley offers.

I smile and shake my head. "It's just Skyla, please, and thank you, but I wouldn't want to intrude. You guys have a good time. Thank you both again."

Welsey nods, turning to head out the door while Ronan hesitates, a frown marring his face before he nods.

"Of course. Call or text if you need anything."

I nod my understanding, and Ronan follows Wesley. I hear the moment they are gone, the large front door closing with a solid thunk. It echoes through the empty home in a final sort of way. Sure, Asher is here, off in one of the bedrooms doing god knows what, but an empty feeling takes up residence inside me and I freaking hate it.

Chapter Five
Vincent

I wait until the sun sets at exactly 5:32 P.M. before I approach the house. I've already studied the building plans extensively. I know that if I park on the next street over, cut through the neighbor's yard that stupidly doesn't have a security system, I can sneak onto their property in the cameras blind spot. From there, it's a quick jog to the west side of the house, up the gutter and over to the master balcony. Easy.

I've had much more difficult targets, with more heavily guarded buildings just last week alone. This is nothing, especially when my Siren is on the other side of this lawn.

Moving exactly as I've planned, I run, duck and climb my way up to the balcony. When I try the balcony doors, I'm irritated that they're unlocked. Doesn't she know that her life will never stop being in danger? That there are plenty of men with skills just like mine who would love nothing more than to take the severed head of the Brethren's princess as a trophy?

Irritation rises inside me as I easily sneak into her room. When I do, I find her in her bed, naked, and her hand between her thighs.

Christ.

I watch as she plays with her clit, her eyes clenched tight as she whimpers and moans. Moving as quietly as I can I cross the room, keeping my eyes on her as she continues playing with herself. She is

31

none the wiser of all the possible monsters that could be in here with her at this moment. Lucky for her, it's just her monster.

She spreads her legs open letting them fall apart, as if she knew that I was desperate for the sight of her. Goddamnit, she is so beautiful.

Two of her fingers trail from her clit down. Before she has a chance to slip them inside, I'm there, slipping two of my own fingers inside her. Her eyes fly open, panicked at first before landing on me.

I begin finger fucking her as I tilt my head curiously.

"What are you doing, Siren? Sprawled out on your bed naked, door unlocked. I could have been anyone."

"But you're n-not," she gasps breathily.

I raise my other hand over her clit, slapping it hard and causing her to cry out in pain.

"I could have been. Do you know how many men and women would kill to be in this room with you right now? To see you like this? Touch you like this? They would take you without a second thought and you couldn't do a thing about it," I say as I slap her clit again.

Her back bows and the yelp that escapes her is a lot more pleasure filled this time.

"You need to lock your fucking door from now on, every time," I say as I continue finger fucking her. "Do you understand?"

She nods her head and I lift my hand one more time, slapping her harder than before as she screams. My fingers press against her g-spot and force her to fall apart on my hand. Her body jerks and writhes beneath my touch, as she shouts out my name over and over again.

"Vincent! Vincent! Oh my god. Yes, baby. Yes," she moans, her chest heaving as she attempts to catch her breath.

I pull my fingers out of her, lifting them to her mouth before smearing her cum against her lips. To no surprise, she opens her mouth quickly, sucking my fingers in as she closes her eyes and groans from the taste. My Siren loves the taste of herself. Who could blame her, she's fucking decadent.

Moving to stand up, her hand stops me, grabbing onto my arm as she pulls me down to her.

"More," she begs.

"More, Siren?"

She nods and I make quick work of sliding out of my clothes, tossing them into a pile on the floor before climbing on top of her. I begin covering her neck with kisses, working my way down to her breasts as I suck one of her nipples into my mouth. My tongue twirls around as she rewards me with a whimper that makes my cock leak pre-cum.

"More," she pants.

I do as she says, flicking my tongue faster while my other hand squeezes her other breast.

"No, Vincent," she says, causing my eyes to come to hers. "I want more. I want...you. All of you."

I hesitate for a moment. She just lost her virginity last night. Savagely, in a humiliating way. There is no way she is ready for me.

"Siren, you've been through a lot. I don't think we should—"

"Please," she whispers. "He was the last person to touch me...like that. He was the first person to do that with me...to me. I don't want him to be the last, I want his memory gone. I want it replaced by someone I love, someone who loves me. Please."

Fuck, how could I ever deny her a thing when she begs so beautifully for me?

"Okay, Siren. Whatever you want but if I hurt you, we're stopping."

She nods as her hands come up to my shoulders, trailing them down my chest, over my stomach before gripping the base of my cock. I jerk in her hand as she strokes me slowly. I continue sucking on her nipple, switching back and forth between the two. She runs her hand up and down my cock until I pull away, kissing my way down her body before settling between her thighs.

Skyla wraps them around my shoulders so easily, and I bury my face into her. The taste of her has me groaning against her pussy. My fingers dig into her upper thighs as my tongue licks through her, circling around her clit before sucking on it.

She buries her hand in my hair as she holds me in place. I'd gladly suffocate in this fucking pussy if she would let me, I'd live down here for the rest of my goddamn life.

"Vincent," she whines. "Please, make love to me."

I wanted to give her another orgasm, to get her as comfortable as possible, but I can't hold myself back another second. Pulling my head up, my eyes lock on hers as I line myself up to her.

"Deep breath for me, Siren."

She does as I say, taking a deep inhale as I begin pushing my way into her. She is so fucking soaked it makes it a little easier, but she is so goddamn tight she's practically choking the life out of my cock. I grit my teeth in an attempt to control myself, while every instinct is telling me to fuck her until we both black out.

"What's wrong?" she whimpers.

"Nothing," I bite out.

"You're holding back, I can tell. I won't break, Vincent. I want all of you, exactly as you are."

"You can't handle me yet, Siren. One day. Soon, but not tonight. Tonight, I'm gonna take my time with you."

She lets out a soft moan when I roll my hips as she nods her head.

"O-okay," she breathes. "Just keep doing that, please."

"This?" I ask, intentionally rolling my hips two more times, forcing her eyes to roll into the back of her head.

"Yes! Oh my god. So good, so so good," she stammers.

Fisting the sheets on either side of her head, I keep my muscles tight, and my movements measured. I don't make love, ever. I fuck hard and rough, and I never speak to the woman again. Of course, that was never a remote possibility with my siren, but it's an adjustment not to fuck her hard and raw.

Each moan and whimper she gives me forces a curse or harder thrust out of me. I try to keep my pace easy, but when her pussy contracts around me, I can only take so much. Her body begins to quiver, and when her breathing becomes choppy I have no choice but to pick up my speed.

I. Need. More.

"Vincent. Oh god. I think I'm gonna...."

"Come for me, Siren. Soak my cock with your cum. Let me hear those pouty lips shout out my name."

She does as I say instantly, as if she was just waiting on my words.

Her screams practically shake the house, and there is no way Asher can't hear us right now. Good. Hope the piece of fucking shit knows what it sounds like to please her now. Fuck knows he'll never get the opportunity himself.

Her pussy clenches down on me hard, and my own orgasm slams into me like a freight train. I growl out my release as I fuck her through it, relishing in the feel of her pussy milking the cum out of me with each thrust until I collapse on top of her.

Our ragged breaths are the only thing you can hear in the quiet room, and after a few moments I lean up to check on her. She has a satiated smile on her face, her eyes dazed and calm as her hand lifts, fingers running through my hair in the way I fucking love.

Sinking into her touch I allow her to play with my hair, waiting for her to speak first.

"Wow," she says softly.

"Did I hurt you?" I ask.

She shakes her head. "No. That was…perfect."

I smile down at her. I don't smile often, honestly, I never do. There used to be running jokes about how I didn't have the right muscles in my face to do so. I've smiled more since I met Skyla than I probably have in my entire life. Which isn't saying much, but fuck it takes some getting used to.

"I love you, Siren."

She practically melts beneath me as I roll off her, dragging her body into my side as I do.

"I love you too, so much."

Pressing a kiss to the top of her head, I blow out a long breath. I haven't felt peace like this in so long. I know it won't last forever, but for now I want to hold onto it with both hands, swim to the depths of the sea and never come up for air.

Chapter Six
Skyla

When I woke up the next morning, Vincent was gone. He told me he would have to leave, but a small part of me hoped he wouldn't. I know that's dumb, but I don't care.

Last night was incredible. It was everything my first time should have been. It's only mildly surprising that it came from, easily, my most broken boy. It makes sense, though. Of course, he is the one who would know how to put my shattered pieces back together. To fix what he never broke.

I'm ready for the day and I step out of my bedroom when I bump into something hard. Correction, someone. Looking up, I see Asher standing before me, his hands gripping my biceps so I don't fall. Though I'm not so sure it's to keep me from falling, because the way he is gripping me feels a lot more like he wants to take the opportunity to hurt me.

It is his favorite past time.

Ripping away from his touch, he lets me go easily as I look up at him. His hair is messier than usual, a lack of fire to those hazel eyes, with deep dark circles surrounding them.

"You look like shit," I say flatly, running my eyes over him.

He just blinks at me, his tone and emotions unmoving as he speaks.

"Couldn't sleep with the porno being made in your room."

I scoff at that and turn on my heel, making my way down the stairs.

Fuck him. Good, I'm glad I kept him up all night. My only regret is that I wasn't louder.

As soon as my feet touch the bottom step, a knock comes from the front door. I open it to reveal a smiling Wesley. He's in another long-sleeved black dress shirt, with the first two buttons undone, and a pair of black slacks. He seems way overdressed for a driver, but looks nice, nonetheless.

Those deep blue eyes lock onto mine as he holds out a coffee cup in offering.

"Good morning, Miss Parris. I wasn't sure how you took your coffee, so I went with a vanilla latte."

"She hates lattes. She prefers apple cider," Asher snaps as he comes up to stand behind me, his eyes raking over Wesley. "And it's Mrs. Putnam. Who the fuck are you?"

I turn around to look at him, disgust hopefully readable on my face before I turn to face Wesley. To my surprise, he doesn't back down. Instead, he levels Asher with an unimpressed stare.

"Has it been that long, Ash? You don't recognize me?"

Asher's eyes squint for a moment before surprise fills them.

"Wesley."

He nods his head. "See you grew up to be the little shit you've always been."

A laugh escapes me, unable to hold it in.

"No truer words have been spoken. Thank you, by the way. I don't hate lattes, I just usually take my coffee black, or lately I have preferred cider, but you don't have to get me coffee in the mornings."

Wesley hands it to me with a nod before handing me a small bag.

"I also figured you'd be hungry, so I got you a couple things. What-ever you don't eat, I will, trust me," he says, as he smacks his hand on his rock-hard stomach.

I smile in thanks when Asher cuts in, yet again.

"Why are you getting her coffee?"

Wesley's brows dip slightly. "Ronan didn't tell you? I'm her driver."

"Since when?" Asher challenges.

"Since yesterday. Ronan said she didn't drive and would need a driver for the foreseeable future."

"And that person is you?" Asher asks dubiously.

"Hence the car and the coffee, yes," Wesley answers flatly.

Oh, I like him.

"She can ride with me," Asher says with narrowed eyes.

"No need. I'm here. Ready, Miss Parris?" Wesley smiles.

I nod, taking a step out of the door before Asher can say something else asinine. Wesley follows closely and I hear Asher call out.

"It's fucking Putnam!"

"Not legally!" I counter, as Wesley opens the door for me.

I hear Asher say something else but can't quite tell what it was, nor do I care. Wesley shuts the door once I'm inside the car, before hopping into the driver's seat and taking off. We drive in silence for a few minutes, me taking a few sips of my coffee and eating half the bagel he brought me before he speaks.

"So, you and Asher are married?"

I hesitate to respond, worried about getting in trouble so I keep things vague.

"We had our ceremony on the thirty first."

His deep blue eyes meet mine in the rear-view mirror, and I don't miss the grimace on his face.

"I'm sorry."

Surprise hits me first, well, he obviously knows what that entails. I nod in response as he continues driving.

"I know he's a little shit, but you could have been paired with worse. He'll protect you."

I let out a bitter laugh as I keep my eyes towards the window.

"Who will protect me from him, though?"

"I can," he says easily.

I give him a tight-lipped smile. It's nice that he thinks that, no matter how wrong he is.

"Or maybe Ronan could."

I jerk at that comment, my eyes flying to his. He's watching me with a careful gaze, like he's testing the waters.

"He's not subtle. He all but gave himself away the moment I saw you two next to each other. Then, speech after speech about how important it was that I keep you safe when you're under my care drove it home."

Fucking lovable idiot.

"I assume Asher doesn't know about his uncle and his wife?"

"Actually, he does," I answer. "No one else does though, so your discretion would be—"

"Life saving?" he guesses. "You don't have to worry about me. With the work I did, I'm used to operating on a need-to-know basis."

I nod, slightly relieved but still very much on edge. I need to talk to Ronan, immediately. I pull out my phone, typing out a message that we need to talk when Wesley continues.

"Wow," he murmurs to himself.

"What?"

He shakes his head. "I'm just surprised Asher is willing to share you. Kinda kinky."

My eyes widen at that, and he smirks.

"Sorry. Intrusive thoughts. Shutting up now."

Thankfully, we're pulling up to Gallows Hill in the next moment and he throws the car into park before opening my door. I slide out, thanking him as he wishes me a good day before I begin making my way through the courtyard.

It only takes me five steps to see Liam waiting for me, his sunshine smile on full display as he sees me. He pulls me in for a hug, releasing me faster than I'd like as he whispers into my ear.

"Good morning, babygirl."

"Good morning. I missed you yesterday."

He pulls away with a sad smile and nods.

"I'm sorry I couldn't be there with you, but I'll come over today. How does that sound?"

"Sounds perfect." I smile as we begin walking to our first class, our fingers brushing against each other every few steps like they always do.

Suddenly, Vincent pops up out of nowhere, falling in step with us as his hand brushes against my other.

"Morning, Siren."

"Morning," I say, heat rushing to my cheeks as I look at him.

His silver eyes are softer this morning, not nearly as cold and sharp. There is the tiniest smile playing at the corner of his mouth and a warmth about him, that has me desperate to bury myself against him. I don't realize how long I'm staring, before Liam murmurs low enough for just the three of us to hear.

"No. Fucking. Way. Did you two fuck and not invite me?" he asks, half in disbelief and half in disappointment.

Vincent and I share a look before he punches Liam in the arm.

"Watch your mouth around my woman, Walcott."

Liam scoffs. "She's not your woman, she's ours, get used to it. Also, she loves my mouth. Don't you babygirl?"

"Occasionally," I say with sly smile.

He clutches his chest dramatically and shakes his head.

"You wound me. Alright, that's it. My turn next. Tell Ronan he can get in line."

"She isn't a goddamn carnival ride," Vincent gnashes.

"Of course not," Liam scoffs. "She's much better, I'm sure. Can you confirm?" he says, holding out an invisible microphone to Vincent.

Vincent slaps Liam's hand away, giving my hip a light squeeze before heading towards his class. Actually, now that I think about it, he doesn't have his first class until ten. I wonder what he does all morning.

When Liam and I make our way into class, we head for the very back, per usual, where Maggie is waiting for us. I slide in beside her and Liam takes the aisle seat next to me. His hand automatically goes to my thigh, gripping it tightly as he smiles down at me. I smile at him before turning to see Maggie watching me with a shit-eating grin.

"So, how was your weekend? I tried to come by your room yesterday, but you weren't in."

My smile falls and my voice lowers as I speak.

"I'm not staying on campus anymore."

She frowns at that. "Why not?"

"Asher and I are living together now."

"Oh," she says, with a knowing smile. "That's nice."

My frown turns bitter as I shake my head.

"No, it isn't."

Maggie's smile drops along with her eyebrows. She looks between Liam and I, neither of us meeting her gaze. I wouldn't blame her for being confused. The last she knew, Asher and I were getting cozy on the Ferris Wheel at the fall carnival, falling for each other hard and fast. If only she knew I was the only one doing the falling.

I can feel Maggie's eyes on me, and she is very clearly not going to drop this, so Liam intervenes.

"He hurt her, bad. We fucking hate him now."

"We? As in, you too, Walcott?"

"As in me fucking three," Liam practically growls. "Motherfucker," he grumbles under his breath.

"Wow. I'm so sorry, babe. I'm with Walcott. Dumb motherfucker," Maggie joins in, heat in her tone in an instant.

I can't help but let out a short laugh as I shake my head.

"I love you, Mags."

"Love you too, babe. No one messes with my girl. Does that mean a spot in your harem opened up?"

"Hmm, what do you think, Liam? Can we make room?" I ask with a teasing smile.

His eyes darken, and he physically adjusts his cock in his pants.

"Don't tease me, babygirl. I'll strip you naked right here and shove Bartlett's face right into your pussy."

"Shit," Maggie huffs. "I'm in. What do you say, Skyla?" she asks, resting her hand on my bare thigh, teasing her fingers on the inside of it before coming to my panty line.

"I say I've got enough boyfriends," I laugh.

"But not nearly enough girlfriends," she taunts as her finger pushes a half an inch further, forcing me to squirm. I'd like to say it's an uncomfortable squirm, but honestly, I can feel my panties becoming wet, so who really knows?

Maggie's eyes stay on mine, a look of intrigue in them as her fingers play with the silky material. I feel Liam's eyes on us, or rather under my skirt, as Maggie continues resting her fingers against me. I swallow roughly and she watches the action before a cocky smile spreads across her face and she pulls away, leaning back into her chair casually.

"Fuck," Liam rasps. "I agree. Bring more girlfriends on."

I scoff, shaking off whatever the hell that just was.

"You are the weirdest boyfriend ever. It's one thing to be okay with sharing, but it's like you want to see me fuck everyone who ever said hello to me."

Liam shakes his head. "I want to see you in pleasure always, baby. I like seeing you be with anyone that can give you that pleasure and take care of you. You know I'm just messing with you. But seriously, I don't share you because I think it's hot, I do it because I literally get off on your pleasure."

My eyes are heavy on his, flicking back and forth between those fields of green. The classroom door shuts, and Professor Corwin grabs the class's attention, effectively breaking our eye contact. I feel Liam's hand squeeze against my thigh, like he's reaffirming that he meant it before Professor Corwin begins outlining our next project requirements.

Chapter Seven
Liam

I couldn't get the hell out of my last class fast enough. One, I hate finance with a fucking passion, and two, I need to find my girl. Ever since I found out that her and Vincent slept together, it's all I've been able to think about.

I'm always the guy up for sharing, encouraging everyone to be as laid back as I am about it all, but I can't deny that in that moment, I was so fucking jealous. Out of all of us, Vincent is the one that she chooses first? Make it make sense.

And yeah, I don't count what happened between her and Asher because, let's be real, that shit was closer to rape than anything. Especially how he did it.

I'm still in fucking shock over it. I honestly can't believe it. I really thought he was falling for her. I was so sure of it. If I'm being real, I think he did, maybe even still does, have feelings for her. I'm sure the shit he pulled had everything to do with his intimacy issues and his dad. Some toxic combination. This isn't one of the times where I will defend him, though. There's no defending him. He hurt the woman that I'm in love with and even if I've always been a firm believer in bros before hoes, that doesn't apply when it comes to the woman you're going to spend the rest of your life with.

Granted, I'm not sure how the rest of our lives are going to look. Shit is messy right now and will be for the foreseeable future. Even if Christopher could magically be accepting of his son's wife being with multiple men, it's just not how things are done in the Brethren. Eventually, they will want to see Ronan, me, and even Vincent married as well. They want all of our legacies to live on as Elder families. I know I speak for all of us though, when I say we couldn't give a fuck about any of that. We just want her forever, or for as long as she will have us.

Speaking of my asshole ex-best friend, he's walking in the opposite direction and our eyes meet as we come closer. He opens his mouth like he's about to say something, but I don't give him the time of day, shoulder checking him as I continue my search for Skyla. He's not even worth my breath.

When I finally make it to Skyla's class, I notice that she isn't where we normally meet up. Frowning to myself, I scan the surrounding area until I see her blonde hair duck around a corner. Heading off in that direction, I turn the corner to see her and Ronan deep in conversation.

"What did you say, specifically?"

"I told him that Asher and I had our ceremony on the thirty-first. He said that he was sorry and then he told me Asher was a decent guy. That he would protect me. When I laughed at that and said who would protect me from him, he said he would...or you would."

I'm on alert instantly, closing the distance between us.

"Who said this?" I ask.

Ronan and Skyla both turn to me, matching frowns on their faces as she speaks.

"Wesley, my driver."

"Your bond brother? He's back?" I ask.

"Wesley is your bond brother?" Skyla asks in surprise.

Ronan nods but ignores the question as he speaks.

"She said he knows about Skyla and me."

"Fuck, babygirl. Why did you tell him?" I say with a shake of my head.

"I didn't! He figured it out. He said he could tell something was up from the way Ronan was acting. I told him he needed to keep the information discreet, and he agreed. I'm just worried."

"Fuck, me too," I agree before I can think better of it.

Skyla's face wrinkles with worry and I take a step next to her, pulling her into my side as I shush her.

"It's gonna be fine babe. Wesley is trustworthy, right, Ronan?"

Ronan is quiet for a few moments before he nods.

"We haven't spoken in a while...a few years ago, I would have said absolutely. Truth is, I don't know what he's been up to all these years, though. I just...fuck, I need to talk with him."

"Is that really a good idea?" Skyla asks.

"We don't have much choice. I'll have him come to my place after he drops you off, okay?"

She nods as I look down at her.

"I'll head over a few minutes later in case anyone is watching the house. It'll look like I'm coming to see Asher."

"Okay," she says, her teeth chewing on her inner lip.

Being the inappropriate comedic relief I am, I decide to break the heavy tension.

"Did our girl tell you her and Vincent fucked?"

Her eyes whip over to me in outrage before she smacks my arm.

"Really?"

Ronan doesn't look surprised as his eyes are on her and he cups her face.

"Did he take care of you?"

She hesitates for a moment before nodding. He looks around us, leaning in for a quick kiss.

"Good, I'm glad. You deserved to have a better experience."

I'm a little surprised that's all Ronan has to say about it. He doesn't even seem a little put out like I was. Maybe I'm not the group's sharing enthusiast. That might go to this big guy right here.

Ronan leaves a minute or so later. Skyla and I walk together until a black SUV pulls up and a guy I haven't seen since I was a little kid steps out of the car.

"What's up, man?" I greet as I pull him in for a quick hug.

He nods and smiles.

"Good to see you, kid. You've grown up."

"What can I say, it's all those Wheaties," I tease as I kiss one of my biceps.

Skyla laughs at me in a pitying way, and I don't miss the way Wesley tracks it. It's as if her one laugh snapped his attention in an instant. It has my smile slipping and my eyes narrowing curiously.

"Where to, Miss Parris?" he asks her.

"Could you please call me Skyla? Just once?" she asks before looking at me, giving me a quick wave goodbye.

It takes everything in me not to haul her into my side and say goodbye properly, even if we will only be separated for twenty minutes.

"Maybe if you're lucky." He winks as he holds open her door.

She smiles at him, though it's not in a flirtatious way. The way he's watching her is definitely flirtatious though, and I'm not sure how I feel about it.

Wesley gives me a wave goodbye and I turn to head for my car. I need to teach Skyla how to drive. That's going to be a priority, immediately. That way, she's not waiting around on a driver to take her places, and it keeps his googly eyes the fuck off my girl. Is this what being jealous feels like? I gotta admit. I'm not a fan.

When I pull up to the house, I see Asher's Maserati is in the driveway, and Wesley's SUV is pulling away. Skyla pauses, waiting for me at the front door, she smiles when I park the car and make my way up to her.

"Hey, what are you doing here?" she asks.

I can't help but laugh, playing along as she opens the door.

"Just came by to see Asher."

She nods, her smile dropping as she steps inside the house. I haven't been here before, so I'm not sure what we're looking at. Skyla's eyes are tracing the foyer, like she's in shock.

"Everything okay?" I ask as I close the front door behind us.

"I can't believe everything is exactly how I described it," she says almost to herself.

"Skyla?" Asher calls out.

I wrap my arm around her shoulders, as his voice begins carrying from what looks like the living room before making its way towards us.

"Look, I know you don't want to talk to me and that's fine. I just wanted you to feel comfortable here. If there is anything you don't like, we'll change it again. Whatever it takes to make you—"

His words die on his tongue when he sees me. His eyes flick between the two of us before landing on her. Her face is impassive as she watches him before she swallows roughly and reaches down for my hand, lacing our fingers together before she's leading me upstairs.

Her eyes stay forward but I can't help but look down at Asher, watching his eyes track her as if he had no choice. When we get to the top of the staircase, he disappears, and Skyla pulls us into a bedroom.

"What's going on, babygirl?" I ask.

She stares at the room for a moment before she shakes her head.

"Nothing just...Asher playing mind games or something. I don't know."

I nod at that, closing the distance between us before wrapping my arms around her.

"Fuck him," I say as I begin peppering soft kisses against her neck. "I missed you, babygirl."

"I missed you too," she says as she winds her arms around me. "Are you going to shower me with all the words of affirmation and devotions of love so I'll put out now?" she laughs.

I don't though, my movements still and I pull back with furrowed brows.

"Is that what you think of me?"

Her teasing smile softens as she looks at me.

"No, I know you love and adore me. I just also know how badly you want to have sex."

"I could give a fuck about sex, Skyla. I want you badly. Just you. We could never have sex for the rest of our lives, and I'd be just fine."

Her brows furrow. "You were really upset this morning when you found out about Vincent and me, though."

"That's because, on occasion, I can be a jealous motherfucker, who knew, right?" I ask with a laugh as I cup the back of her neck. "I never want you to think for a minute, that I need anything but this," I say, as I reach a hand up to cover her heart. "That I need anything but you."

Her eyes begin to water and she practically leaps into my arms in the next moment. I catch her easily as her mouth smashes against mine, tongues tangling together as we fall back onto the bed.

"Babygirl," I say, as she begins kissing my neck and chest. "I'm serious. We don't have to do anything. I'm just happy to be here with you."

"Liam?" she asks breathlessly.

"Yeah?"

"Shut up and fuck me."

Well, fuck. I'm only human.

I flip us in one fluid motion, pinning her onto her back as I kiss my way down her body, her legs open for me, skirt riding up to her thighs before I pull her panties to the side. The same panties I watched Bartlett play with this morning. I really wasn't sure how that was going to go at first.

For a moment, it almost seemed like Skyla was going to let her go for it. You wouldn't have heard a complaint out of me. I could practically see it, Bartlett slipping her finger inside her during class, my head between Skyla's legs, giving her all the praise and selfishly enjoying the view. Find me a man that wouldn't love to watch his girlfriend's best friend finger fuck her, and I'd call that man a fucking liar.

I lick a line through her, stopping on her clit and flicking against it quickly. She pants and moans, her nails digging into my head and shoulders as I continue.

"Fuck, Liam. You're so good at that."

I chuckle, allowing my vibrations to hum against her sensitive flesh and earning myself another moan in reward. I slip a finger inside, curling it up to rub against her g-spot as I use my tongue and finger in unison. She's almost too easy. My babygirl is already right on the edge. All it takes is a few strokes of my finger, a pass or two of my tongue and I'm tasting victory as she comes hard.

I lick and suck every bit of her release until her moans have quieted and her breathing stills. I'm not done yet, though. Gripping her hip in my hand, I flip her onto her stomach, slipping my arm beneath her before pulling her up to her hands and knees.

"Arch that back, babygirl."

She does as I say, that pussy popping out beautifully. My hands run up and down her spine before I'm pulling my cock out and lining myself up to her.

I can't help but pause though, my body is practically vibrating with anticipation.

"Last chance to run, babygirl? Once I have you, there'll be no turning back," I say through clenched teeth.

She looks over her shoulder at me with a lifted eyebrow.

"Was there any turning back anyways?"

Fair point.

Holding eye contact, I begin slowly pushing inside her. She's so goddamn tight, but she takes me surprisingly well. Until my piercings begin to slip inside.

Her eyes widen and her jaw drops.

"Oh my god! Is it supposed to feel like this?"

I smirk as I nod, running a soothing hand up and down her back.

"Yes, babygirl. Ninety percent for pleasure, ten percent to have a decorated cock."

She lets out a laugh, but when I push all the way in and my tip presses against her g-spot, that laugh turns into a moan.

Withdrawing my hips until I'm almost all the way out of her, I pause before pushing myself back inside. Her head turns forward, dropping to the mattress as she moans again. God, that sound alone makes my cock jerk, every fucking time.

I have to pause for a moment because the way she's pulsing around me is so fucking good. Closing my eyes, I take a few slow breaths before I begin thrusting my hips, finding a rhythm that satisfies us both. It isn't hard to find one that satisfies Skyla, though. Her whimpers and moans can be heard throughout the whole fucking house. I have no doubt that Asher is outside the door listening right now, wishing this were him. I don't give a fuck what he did to her, he loves her, even if he doesn't know it yet. Well, fucking sucks to be him, I guess.

My hands grip Skyla's hips tightly, my knuckles turning white as I use her body to pull her in harder and fuck her deeper.

"Fuck! Liam," she whines.

"Yeah, baby? Tell me what you want? What you need?"

"You. All of you. Fuck me, baby," she cries out.

My pace becomes jerky and unstable. I have a one-track mind and the only thing taking up that track is fucking her as hard as humanely possible. My hand comes up to the base of her hair, digging my fingers into her scalp before I withdraw a bit. I wrap a majority of her hair around my fist and I pull.

She gasps as her head is yanked backwards, having nowhere to go but towards me.

"Good fucking girl," I praise. I want to see that beautiful face when you come."

Her mouth is parted into a perfect o, her eyes hazy and lust drunk as I yank on her hair harder, forcing a moan to fall from her lips.

Fuck! I feel my cock begin to pulse, and I know I don't have much longer. Her pussy squeezes and spasms. I know she doesn't have long either. Releasing my other hand's hold on her hip, I reach around, leaning over her as I do while squeezing her cheeks together.

"Open up like a good girl," I demand through clenched teeth.

She does as I say, opening her mouth as wide as she can while I keep my hold on her. Gathering up all the saliva in my mouth, I spit right through her lips and into hers. Her eyes widen in surprise before they shutter close, and she comes. Fucking hard.

My own vision doubles as pleasure runs from the base of my spine all the way to my head and back down. My cock pulses as I shoot my cum deep inside her, forcing her to take every single ounce of my release before we collapse in a heap on the bed. I feel my heaving chest pressed against her sweat dotted back, my cock still buried between her thighs. Would it be so bad if we stayed like this for a while?

Yeah, yeah, I know what you're thinking. UTI central, but goddamnit, I want nothing more than to stay inside her for the rest of my life. Vincent and Ronan can bring me my meals here from now on. Who needs to walk? Or move? I'm good.

Eventually, I do the right thing and pull out of her before forcing her to tuck into my arms. She comes happily, a smile on her face as she looks up at me.

"Wow," she breathes.

"Okay, be honest, I'm better than Vincent, right?"

She scoffs and smacks my chest as she stands up.

"You don't want to go there, Liam."

I frown as I sit up, resting back on my hands.

"Why not?"

"Because you might not like my answer," she says with a cheeky grin, before she takes off running for her bathroom.

I'm on my feet chasing her in an instant because the feisty little thing knew I would. I guess I'm predictable, pretty obvious by now. Wherever Skyla is, I'm there. Even if I have to chase her down, I'm there.

Chapter Eight
Skyla

After Liam gave me two more orgasms in the shower, thankfully not from penetration because, my god, I might need an icepack down there, we curled up in bed and watched a movie. At around one in the morning, I couldn't sleep, feeling restless, so I decided to head downstairs. Maybe a drink and a snack will help.

When I come downstairs, I find Asher on the couch, eyes on the ceiling and a bottle of bourbon on the table–no glass, just the bottle. His gaze comes to me immediately, silently tracking me as I make my way into the kitchen.

I tell myself I'm not going to speak to him, that I'm going to pretend like he doesn't exist. Somehow though, like an addict that gives in no matter how toxic they know the poison is, I engage with him.

"Your bed not comfortable or something?" I ask, as I grab a piece of bread and pop it into the toaster before pouring myself a glass of water.

"Too loud," he answers stiffly. "Hard to sleep."

I turn around, leaning my back against the counter as I cross my arms over my chest. He's sitting up now, forearms resting on his knees as he watches me.

"If you're looking for an apology, you won't find one. Get some noise cancelling headphones or something."

"Not sure even those would drown out my wife's screams as my best friend fucks her into the mattress," he scoffs.

I roll my eyes at him. "I'm not your wife. Just because we did a creepy cult ceremony in front of our parents and practically every fucking man in this society, doesn't make us married. We'd need a marriage certificate for it to even be semi-legal and—"

"Look on the counter," he says, as he nods towards the counter beside me.

There is a folder there that I hadn't noticed before. My brows furrow as I lift it up, my heart coming to a full stop for several seconds as I read the words scrawled across the top.

Certificate of Marriage. Along with Asher's name and signature, then my name and signature.

"What the fuck?" I snap. "I didn't sign this? How did they get my signature!"

"You really don't have a clue how powerful the Brethren is. Do you, Princess?"

I hate that a small part of me still responds to him. That one moment, I have all this anger and hate for him. Then the next, he uses that stupid pet name, and my heart beats out of rhythm. Thankfully, it's back to normal in no time and I'm able to hold on to the anger inside me.

"This is a forged signature. It isn't legal! It'll never hold up in court. I'll fight this and—"

"And what? Take it up to the Supreme Court? Even if you could, guess what? Does the name Chief Justice Eric Hutchinson sound familiar? He is their most senior member . The man that was standing to your father's right in that room, trying to hide his raging hard on. You. Can't. Fight. This."

With every word he speaks, he takes a step closer, until he's mere inches from me. His hands are braced on the counter behind me, eyes hardened and focused, as he leans down until we are eye to eye. Our noses bump against one another for a moment, but he's quick to create just another inch of distance so it doesn't happen again.

For several seconds, all that can be heard in this kitchen is our heavy breathing. My eyes flick back and forth between his, as he does the same. No matter what an asshole he is, there is still...something here and I hate myself for admitting it.

"I did what I did because I had to, Skyla, not because I wanted to. You put me in an impossible situation. I was trying to save us both."

"By hitting me?" I choke, my voice far more watery than I'd prefer. "By spitting on my face, like I was worthless? By calling me a stupid bitch, in a room full of people? Telling me that you could never love me?" I scoff, my voice wavering at the end.

His jaw is tense, but what looks like remorse flashes in his eyes before he shakes his head.

"You were told to be silent. In the moment, I had no other choice."

A humorless laugh escapes me as I shake my head.

"Keep telling yourself that, Asher. Whatever, it doesn't matter. At the end of the day, I was so wrong about you. Or I guess I could say I was right about you all along. You may think you're the next Jesus Christ himself, but you're nothing. You're a coward, you're a follower. You're *weak*."

His nostrils flare, but he doesn't speak, and god help me, I can't stop.

"You sit there and judge me for trying to be happy, for trying to take whatever moments of happiness I can get. When I don't, I'm under my father's thumb, your father's or yours.

When I'm not trying to just focus on the good, I'm worried about a stalker who wants everyone I care about dead. Or I'm worried about one of the guys turning on me, just like you did. I'm constantly worried and afraid, but I don't want to be. So, I'm going to have a lot of sex, loud sex, as often as I can. If you have a problem with that, frankly, I don't give a flying fuck."

"I didn't say you couldn't," he grits out. "I'm just saying..."

His words trail off as he looks at me, indecision and confliction heavy in those hazel eyes.

"What?" I snap.

My word seems to break something inside him; maybe it was patience, or maybe it was compassion, like he had any of that to begin with. Either way, his fists slam down on the counter beside me, forcing me to jump before he spins on his heel.

"Fuck this!" he barks out, before grabbing his keys on the table and swaying a bit in his steps. He reaches for the open bottle of bourbon before heading out the front door.

"Don't you fucking dare drink and drive!" I shout at him as he throws the door open.

I follow him, yelling at him from the porch.

"Asher! Get back here! There are more people on the road than you, you selfish fucking prick! You're gonna kill someone!"

"Don't worry, Princess. If you're lucky, the only dead body tonight will be mine," he says with a bitter sneer, before firing up one of his cars and peeling out of the driveway.

Motherfucker.

Storming upstairs, I grab my phone off the nightstand. I'm still amazed Liam can sleep so peacefully through all of that bullshit. I dial 911 and wait as the phone rings.

"911, what's your emergency?"

"I'd like to report a drunk driver."

I don't know if Asher got picked up by the cops last night or if he slept it off in his car. All I know is that he didn't come home last night, and I wasn't sure if I was relieved or irritated by it. The cops seemed very concerned, until I mentioned his name. Then, in an instant, the seriousness fell away and morphed into a lackadaisical bored tone, assuring me that they'd be on the lookout for him.

One hundred bucks says they didn't even send anyone out for him. They probably just deleted the call log and moved on. God, this town is so fucked up.

Liam had to leave this morning to go talk with some other professors before class. Honestly, with how often he's talking with his teachers, I wonder how well he's doing in school. Does he struggle? I bet his asshole parents love that. We don't talk about them often because Liam can't stand them, and I can't stand the way they treat him. So it's a mutually beneficial 'do not discuss' topic.

Glancing to the chair beside me, I notice that Maggie isn't here yet. She's almost always here before me. Weird.

Pulling out my laptop, I bring up yesterday's notes and begin scanning over them when I feel a presence beside me. A familiar pair of glasses, auburn hair and timid smile greet me. I can't help but smile back.

"Hi, Andrew," I greet.

He nods, his eyes flicking from side to side.

"Hi, Skyla. I just wanted to check on you...after....you know," he says, casting a nervous glance around him.

My smile fades as understanding passes through me. I give him a small nod, my lips smashing together in a flat line.

"Thanks."

"That wasn't right," he continues. "It was disgusting, inhumane. I couldn't believe it, and I wanted to stop it. You know that, right? I would have if I could?" he says, his hand covering my own in what looks like panic.

I tilt my head to the side curiously, unsure why his reaction is so extreme. He acts like I'm about to flip out on him, like everything is his fault, like he has some obligation to my well-being.

"It's fine, Andrew. I'd just like to forget about it."

"How can you?" he laughs, a bitter sound coming from this typically sweet and quiet boy. "I have nightmares about it, every single night. All I can picture is your face twisted up in pain, and Asher..." he trails off, his jaw tightening and fists clenching.

My eyes widen in alarm. I've never seen such sharp mood swings from someone so quickly. I'm thoroughly confused and unsure how to proceed. So, I give him a tight-lipped smile and a soft nod.

"Really, it's okay. I knew what the night was going to entail. It was...

unpleasant, but I'm okay now. Really, thank you for being concerned for me."

His fists slowly unclench, and his jaw softens. What looks like relief seems to pour into his eyes, as he blows out a breath and nods.

"I'm glad. If you need anything, let me know. I'd be happy to leak Asher's text messages to the school, adjust his grades or doctor whatever you'd like and send it to the Brethren."

My brows furrow at that.

"You can do all of that?"

He nods. "In my sleep. My father runs a tech security company. It's the biggest and most advanced on the entire east coast."

"And you're like his protégé?" I guess.

The tips of his ears pink up a bit, as well as his cheeks, as he gives me a bashful nod.

"I've learned a lot, and I'd be happy to make him suffer, at least a tenth of the pain that he has put you through.

Honestly, his offer is tempting. Might not be the worst thing to keep tucked into my back pocket.

"Thank you," I say. "I'll definitely think about it."

He nods happily before plopping down into his usual seat in front of me. My head tilts to the side as I watch him carefully, still more than a little thrown at our interaction when Liam and Maggie walk in together.

Liam gets a dopey grin as he practically jogs over to me, before Maggie takes her seat beside me. Dropping down into the other chair to my right, Liam scoots in as close as he can until I'm practically on his lap.

"What part of this is playing it cool?" I ask, though I can't fight off the grin spreading across my face.

"All of it, I'm as cool as a cucumber, babygirl," he grins with a wink.

A throat clears from the front of the room, pulling my attention from Liam.

"So sorry, Mr. Walcott. Are we interrupting?" Professor Corwin asks with an unimpressed look.

Liam, not having an ounce of shame in his body, shrugs and gives the professor one of his winning smiles.

"A little, but for the sake of education, I'll let it slide."

Professor Corwin lets out an irritated huff before shaking his head and beginning his lecture. He knows that Liam is untouchable, arguing with him is a futile act. He's a Legacy, and clearly, that means everything in Salem. I cast Liam a headshake, and he just gives me a goofy smile, shrugging again before facing the front.

Such a little shit sometimes.

Chapter Nine
Ronan

"C'mon, Ronan. No more blindfolds. It didn't exactly go great the last time," Skyla laughs bitterly, as I wrap the satin tie around her eyes before leading her inside the house.

Since it's not safe for her to be seen out with any of us, I decided to come to her today. I wanted us to be able to spend some time together, just the two of us. I know as the year stretches on, with more legacies beginning to be inducted, my life is about to get a million times more chaotic. Not to mention, my brother's calls about Annie that I've been dodging.

Alone time is difficult enough when your girlfriend has two other boyfriends, but I know that soon any time with Skyla will be few and far between, unfortunately.

We ascend the stairs easily, our footsteps echoing in the empty house. I texted Asher that I was going to come over today, nothing more, nothing less, and he responded with 'K'. When I got here and saw one of his cars was missing, I assumed he took that as a 'get lost.' Not how I intended it, but I'm happy with the result all the same.

He makes Skyla uncomfortable. Not that I could blame her. I think if I was in her position, I wouldn't want to look that man in the eye every day, let alone live with him. So, yeah, Asher can fuck off for the day.

When we finally make it to the top of the stairs, I push open her door before removing the tie. As soon as it's peeled from her face, that hesitant look fades away as her eyes roam around the room.

I lined the perimeter of her room with candles, all varying sizes, and rose petals covering the bed. It's cliché as fuck and something that fell straight out of a romance movie, but with the welling tears in her eyes, I'd say it was just corny enough.

"Ronan," she whispers brokenly.

I cup her face, looking down into those beautiful green eyes.

"You deserve a do-over of that night. You deserve to know what it feels like to be loved and cherished through the whole thing. I'm sure Liam and Vincent did a good job of helping replace the memories of that night, but let me take care of you, baby. Let me heal you."

She nods gently as I lean down, pressing my lips to hers as I cup her face tenderly. Our mouths move together gently, languidly, like we have all the time in the world. I want it to feel that way. I want to take my time with her.

Surprisingly, she's the one to advance things. She pushes against me, softly guiding us backwards until we're falling back onto the bed. I pin her to my chest, spinning us so that it's her back that lands against the mattress. Her eyes are wide and expressive, drowning with want and desire as I begin covering her body with kisses.

My fingers make quick work of her shirt and pants before peeling them down her legs. Piece by piece, I strip away every article of clothing on her body until she is laid before me bare, exposed, and looking like absolute perfection.

My lips trail up and down her thighs, my beard scraping against the sensitive skin gently before she lets out a breathy whimper.

"Ronan."

My eyes come to hers.

"Yeah, baby?"

"Touch me," she begs.

I don't have to ask for clarification, and I sure as fuck don't have to be told twice. I spread her pussy open, admiring how beautiful she is before running my tongue through her. She squirms at my touch before I slip a finger inside, pumping in and out of her a little bit more each time.

"Fuck, yes," she groans.

"Just like that, baby? You like it when daddy finger fucks you?"

Her head whips up at that, making eye contact with me as she moans and nods.

"I love daddy's fingers inside me."

My cock jumps at that. Fuck! She is so goddamn sexy, and she knows exactly what to say to get me so fucking riled up. I love that she has a little daddy kink, it makes my own desires feel validated, understood. It's not some sick game that people twist it into. It's about control, care, and love for my girl.

"Good girl," I rumble hoarsely. "Do you want daddy to eat your pretty little pussy?"

"Yes," she nods quickly, raising her hips and practically shoving her pussy into my face.

I don't waste another second, diving in face first, literally, as I grip her hip in my right hand while the other continues finger fucking her.

I'll never get over how fucking good she tastes. From that first time to now, she has ignited a hunger in me that will never be satiated. I'll always want more. More of her pussy, her mouth, her ass. More of her.

Flicking my tongue against her clit, I push her all the way to the edge before pulling back. She grumbles in displeasure before I do it again and again. Teasing her, edging her, turning her into a sloppy, needy, wanting mess.

"Ronan," she whines. "I want to come. Let me."

Pulling my mouth away from her pussy, I smirk.

"Oh you do? You want to come?"

"Yes," she snaps, sexual frustration clearly taking its hold on her.

I can't help but chuckle before I nod. Standing from my position, I lay down beside her on the bed.

"Come take daddy's cock out and suck it. If you do a good job, I might let you come."

I expect her to argue at that, but instead, she practically leaps for my pants, undoing my belt in record time before shoving the material down to my knees. Her warm, soft hand wraps around my shaft, moving up and down a few times before I feel her wet mouth around the tip.

Not able to hold back my groan, I let out a ragged breath as she takes me deeper, sucking me down her throat the way she's learned I love so fucking much. Winding my fist into her hair, I help guide her motions, keeping them even paced and steady until I'm ready to bust in her sweet little mouth.

"C'mere, baby. Come ride my face," I say. She quickly backs up to me, keeping her mouth on my cock before sitting on my face.

Good. Fucking. Girl.

I'm in fucking heaven. My hands rest on her ass cheeks, squeezing them roughly as I lick my tongue from her pussy to her ass. Every inch of her is fucking delectable. I could spend the rest of my life down here and never get bored.

She's teetering on the edge, so much that all it takes is a hard flick of my tongue against her clit to send her shattering apart. I feel her body spasm as her cum begins leaking down my tongue. I lap at her quickly, intent on not wasting a drop until there is nothing else to lick.

I feel her mouth continuing to suck me, but I don't want her mouth, I want her. Rolling us so that she is on her back again, I turn around and crawl between her legs. I shuck off my pants fully before lining the head of my cock up to her. Her pussy is glistening, and her legs are pulled back wide as I rest my hands on her upper thighs.

"Deep breath, baby," I say, as I begin pushing myself in.

She does as I say, but that doesn't stop her from making a pinched face at first. I take my movements slow, gently pulling out before pushing in a little deeper this time and the next. By my fourth thrust, the tension in her body has eased and she begins to sink into the mattress. Testing her limits, I push myself in all the way, my head actually spinning at how fucking tight she is. It's like I've been drugged with a lethal dose of ecstasy. I feel on the brink of absolution and destruction, all at once.

"Such a good girl, baby. Look how well you take me," I praise as I look between us, my thrusts still slow, as I admire how beautiful her pussy looks stretched for my cock.

"You're so damn thick," she groans, half in pleasure but with a hint of frustration.

"And you're so fucking tight. We're perfect for each other, baby."

"You're just now noticing?" she asks with a half-smile.

I grin at her, closing the distance between us as I press my lips to hers.

"I knew from the moment I met you, that you'd be mine," I say as I push into her all the way, allowing my tip to rub against her g-spot before I withdraw again.

"What I didn't know," I continue as I thrust. "was how meaningless and empty my life had been before you."

"Ronan," she laughs nervously. "You don't have to butter me up, I'm already fucking you."

I snap my hips hard, forcing her mouth to fall open into an o while her eyes come to me.

"Don't ever insinuate that I would ever tell you something or do something just to get you to sleep with me. Don't ever diminish what we have into something as trivial as casual fucking or a manipulative fuck. I'm not a man that says anything that I don't mean. If I don't mean something, I don't speak."

My thrusts aren't as aggressive as the last, but they are a little more punishing than before.

"And I love you, Skyla Parris. I love you so goddamn much it fucking hurts. I love you so much that if I ever lost you, I'd lose myself in the process. My soul would never stop searching for you, never stop craving you. You're my everything, baby. Never forget that."

Tears begin free falling from her eyes as her hands rest on my shoulders.

"I love you too. So much. I don't even remember what life was like before you. I don't even remember what it was like to breathe before you."

"You'll never have to live like that again. I'm here, baby. Always."

One of my hands slips between her thighs, thumb circling her clit in a way that has a shudder running through her.

"More," she begs.

"More, baby?" I ask as I continue the motion, quickening my pace slightly as my thrusts begin to match it.

"Yes. Oh my god! That feels so good. I need—"

Her words break away into a moan as I continue fucking her harder and harder.

"You need, baby? What do you need? Give me your words."

"I need to come. I want it. Please give it to me."

I begin circling my hips, rubbing myself against her in a motion that has her eyes flying open wide.

"Oh my god!"

"You gonna come for me?" I ask.

"Uh-huh," she nods shakily, her breathing becoming ragged.

"Good. Come on my cock, baby. I want to feel that tight little pussy squeeze the life out of me as you come."

"Oh my god," she says, her pussy pulsing at my words.

I can't help but grin.

"You like that? Tell me how bad you want daddy's cock. How bad you need it to make you come?"

"OH! I need it. I need it so bad. I just want daddy to make me come," she blabbers almost incoherently as her orgasm begins to take her over. "Oh my god, Ronan! Daddy! Fuck!" she screams before she's shattering apart.

Wave after wave of her orgasm seems to crash into her, and I'm no different. That tingling at the base of my spine overwhelms me, and I find myself falling over the edge with her. I feel my cock twitch and jerk inside her; it satiates something primal in me as our bodies collapse into a heap on the bed.

We lay there for several minutes, speechless. Our ragged breaths are the only sounds coming from either of us. Eventually I gather up enough stamina to stand, making my way to the bathroom before I turn on the water in the tub. I strip off my shirt and toss it to the ground, before I pour in a generous amount of lavender bubble bath and come back out for her.

She's in the middle of the bed, her legs spread, my cum seeping out of her. Before I can help myself, I lean forward, gathering the leaking mess between my fingers before pushing it back inside. Her eyes come to me in surprise, but I don't stop. I continue finger fucking my cum back into her as deep as I can.

Despite knowing she's on birth control, a small part of me hopes it's ineffective. I hope that she gets pregnant from this, from me. I'd love nothing more than to see her round with my baby. Goddamnit, I need that to be a thing immediately.

Without a word, I pull my fingers out of her and scoop her up into my arms. I take her into the bathroom before slowly climbing in the bath with her. We sink down into the warm water, some sloshing over the side as we do before she nuzzles herself into my lap.

I'm not sure how long we lay there, until the water has long run cold, and our bodies begin to shiver. Neither one of us is ready to let this moment go, though. Each craving just a little longer. A little more. I'll never have enough of Skyla Parris, and I hope to fucking god that she will never have enough of me.

Chapter Ten
Asher

I thought that if I stayed out until well past midnight that I'd avoid hearing them. Fuck, was I wrong. Despite us all having class in the morning, it's currently 1:23 A.M. and Skyla's screams are echoing through this house. I've slept on the couch the last several nights; I finally got sick of it and used noise cancelling headphones in my own bed.

It's not enough to drown her out. The sound of her orgasms play over and over in my head, like a taunting loop. A reminder that it's something I'll never get.

Fucking hate how much it's been bothering me. After our ceremony, I told myself I wouldn't allow her to get to me. I'd distance myself and that would be enough. I can't, apparently. So, I do the only thing I know how to.

Reaching for my phone, I scroll through the string of messages I've left unanswered for weeks. I pause on a name I know is a no-strings hookup.

Me: Unlock your door. I'm coming over.

It takes a minute or so for her to respond before she shoots back her reply.

Mercy Cock Gobbler Lewis: Okay! See you soon.

That was easy.

Rolling out of bed, I throw the blankets to the side, pulling on a pair of sweats and tennis shoes. I run my fingers through my hair before spraying on a little cologne. My keys, wallet and phone are all in my pockets and I'm heading out the door in the next minute. I do everything I can to breeze past Skyla's door without an ounce of hesitation, but I'm fucking weak.

I linger by her door, listening to her soft mewls.

"I love you," she moans. "I'll always love you."

Something about those words stabs me right in the fucking chest. Maybe because the soft breathiness to her voice stirs the memory of her saying those words to me. It brings back the feeling of shock that I felt when she uttered them, followed by fear that she said it in front of everyone. It took half a glance towards my father, the outrage in his eyes and the disappointment to know I didn't have long. I had to make her look like a lovesick, silly little girl.

Christopher Putnam doesn't believe in love. He believes in lust and advantage. He believes that if you fall in love, or think that you have, that you are weak, easily controlled and a liability.

I did what I had to do for her and for myself. I'd do it again, not matter how much it fucking hurt.

None of that shit matters, though. In the long run, Skyla and I would have hit some other crossroad. It's better that we not go down that path. We can stay neutral, co-habitants. It's for the best.

The drive to Gallows Hill is quick, and I weave my way through the Parris Dorm before stopping on the second floor. I glance at Mercy's contact info, taking note of her dorm room number before I grab the handle. It gives way easily, and I find her laying in her bed, full red lingerie set wrapped around her silky smooth skin. It looks fucking good on her. Suddenly, my unsureness about this helping to get Skyla out of my system fades away.

I cross the room, kicking the door shut before I strip off my shirt and shoes. I push down my sweats and freeing my cock before I come to her. Her brown eyes look up at me eagerly as she sits up onto her knees and opens her mouth. I push inside her without hesitation; her tongue expertly twirls around my cock. I don't have her saved in my phone as

Mercy Cock Gobbler Lewis for nothing. The woman knows how to suck a fucking cock.

For a moment, I contemplate just using her mouth and hitting the road, but something in me wants to hear her moans tonight. I want to replace the track in my mind that has Skyla's screams and groans on repeat, to record over it.

Pushing her to her back, she bounces softly, her breasts spilling free of the carefully placed strappy lingerie. I take full advantage of it, climbing on top of her as I cup her tit in my hand and suck that milk chocolate nipple into my mouth.

Her raspy moan is nothing like Skyla's and it's exactly what I need. Suddenly, my entire objective is to make this woman moan as loud and long as possible. While my mouth works on her nipple, my hand slides between her thighs, her cunt absolutely dripping wet. Two fingers slide into her easily as I begin thrusting them in and out quickly. Mercy always likes a rough and hard fuck. The way that she shouts when I hit her g-spot tells me that hasn't changed in the last two months.

I feel her orgasm coming before she begins chanting my name, shouting and screaming as her cum leaks down my fingers. I'm not done with her yet, though. Tearing my mouth away from her nipple, she looks up at me with want, dragging my head to hers. Usually, I don't like to kiss women on the mouth. It leads to messy feelings and unwanted attachments. But the last pair of lips that were on mine were Skyla's, and just like everything else, I need it gone.

Her full lips feel good against mine; our tongues tangle together as I line my cock up through her crotchless panties. Her back arches into me and I wrap my arm under her, pressing her chest against mine as I thrust inside, loving the sound she makes as I do.

"Asher! Fuck. I've missed this dick," she groans.

"Missed this cunt," I lie as I push deeper into her.

"Really?" she asks, her movements pausing as she looks up at me, like I make her world go round.

Damn, I never got these vibes from her before. I always thought she was down for a casual fuck. She never tried to play it as anything more than that. I guess she was just playing the long game, though. I know if I tell her the truth, she'll kick me out. She isn't a doormat, like Bridgette or some of the other girls. So, I turn up the charm and give her my most convincing act.

Cupping the side of her face I smirk down at her, letting my eyes twinkle in a way that makes her melt.

"Of course, baby. You're my number one girl. You know that, right?"

Her perfect white teeth sink into her lower lip, batting her lashes up at me as she nods.

"Now be a good girl, and let me hear you moan for me," I say, as I begin fucking her hard and rough.

And fuck does she deliver. Her moans and screams are loud, if not a little forced, but they do the trick. Her pussy grips my cock nicely, and I rub at her smooth ass cheek before cracking my hand against her skin. That soft color changing with a nice pink hue to it that spurs me on. She whimpers a little at the pain and I can feel her ready to tell me stop. She's too dedicated to pleasing me or too lost in the moment to do so, so I don't.

I spank and fuck her raw, as I milk every ounce of pleasure I can out of her. This was the best way to spend my night. I haven't had sex in well over a month, and my left hand is not the same as a wet and willing cunt.

My cock begins to throb, and I know she doesn't have long either. Lifting one of her legs up to rest on my shoulder, I fuck her deeper as I press my lips against hers, savoring the feel of her lips on mine before I pull back. When I look down at her though, she's changed.

Her beautiful brown locks have been replaced with long blonde strands. Those deep brown eyes have shifted into bright green gems and her face...it's all Skyla. I close my eyes, shaking my head before looking down at her again. Still Skyla.

I don't know if it's wishful thinking, I'm tripping balls or I'm about to stroke out. Either way, I do something I really shouldn't. I keep going.

"Asher," she moans.

It doesn't even sound like Mercy anymore. All I see, all I hear, all I feel is Skyla. I fuck her harder, unable to stop myself as I moan.

"Yeah, say my name, princess."

"Princess?" she giggles stupidly, ruining the fantasy.

"Say it," I grit through clenched teeth.

"Asher. Fuck, you fill me up so good."

Fuck, yes, I do, princess.

"Oh, Asher. I want you so bad. I always want you."

"Me too, baby. Me too," I pant as my eyes stay on hers, those emerald colored eyes staring up at me like I'm her everything.

"Asher! Asher! Asher!" she moans, as her pussy begins to pulse.

"Skyla!" I roar, as my orgasm tears through me.

I cum hard, so hard I see stars. My thrusts don't stop as I fuck her until I have nothing left to give.

When I open my eyes, I look down to see a pissed off looking Mercy.

"Skyla?" she asks with a huff, before shoving me off her.

I land on the ground with a hard thunk, before she covers herself with her blankets.

"Get the fuck out, Putnam, and lose my fucking number."

Well, honestly, can't blame her. I get dressed quickly and slip out of the room; her soft cries hit me as I shut the door. I'm not a total monster. I don't like making people cry and it was an accident. I didn't say it to hurt her; it slipped out. Trust me, I think I'm more upset that it came out than she is.

Chapter Eleven
Skyla

Last night was absolute perfection. Ronan and I made love all night. I'm not even ashamed to be walking with a slight limp this morning from the delicious ache between my thighs.

I sit down at a table with my lunch, Liam by my side as he takes the seat beside me. Maggie sits across from us, and I don't miss how Asher slows by our table, making eye contact with Liam and me before continuing towards a corner table alone.

The pang inside my chest pisses me off. I shouldn't be feeling sympathy for that asshole. Turning away from his penetrating gaze, I smile at Liam. He squeezes my thigh, a teasing lilt to his voice.

"How you holding up, babygirl? Ronan do some damage?"

I scoff, shoving him to the side as I shake my head.

"Seriously? Don't be crass."

Maggie chuckles from across the table, but quiets immediately when I level her with a look. She smashes her lips together, concealing her laughter as she stares down at her plate. I turn back to Liam when two figures catch my attention. Bridgette and Mercy are whispering to each other, shooting me lethal glares before Bridgette stands, walking across the dining hall with her nose in the air.

I track her carefully, unsure of what exactly she is going to try to pull this time.

"Christ, here we go," Liam grumbles under his breath.

"So, what's the deal? Asher isn't good enough for you? You're trying to go after Liam too?" Bridgette says, loud enough for the entire room to hear.

All eyes turn to us, Liam and I make quick work of separating.

"What are you going on about?" Liam scoffs in a casual way, that is honestly pretty damn convincing.

Bridgette turns her eyes to him, her aggressive posture softening slightly.

"I'm just worried about you. She's a master manipulator. The way she is obviously playing Asher, then dragging you into it."

"How about you stop talking about things you know nothing about and go back to your lunch?" I offer.

Her venomous eyes shoot in my direction, her black hair flipping over her shoulder as she closes the distance between us.

"How about you stop whoring yourself around my school and go back to where you came from?" she says, before a hard crack of her hand slaps against my cheek.

Honestly, it's impressive how much it hurts. I didn't think she had it in her. Liam yanks me out of my seat, protectively shoving me behind him before another body darts across the room. Asher is behind Bridgette in a flash, grabbing Maggie's silver fork before plunging it into the back of Bridgette's hand. It effectively pins her hand to the table, and the scream she releases is unlike anything I've ever heard.

An ear piercing shriek fills the room, as several people grimace in disgust. Bridgette tries to pull her hand free but the fork is jammed in so deep, I have no doubt it is there to stay unless someone pulls it out.

Maggie's face is full of panic as she watches Bridgette, her eyes darting to Asher like she's not sure who he will strike next. Asher doesn't pay the screaming banshee any mind, though. Instead, he takes the opportunity to hop up on the table and address the room.

"I thought that we had learned this lesson a while ago, at this very table no less, but perhaps we need a refresher. Skyla is off-limits, period. You will not whisper about her, you will not glare at her and you will most definitely not put hands on her," he says, looking down at Bridgette like the worm she is.

"The next person that even breathes *my wife's* name, will be leaving this school in a body bag. Clear?"

There is a hushed shock that rolls through the room at the word wife. Honestly, I feel it too. I stare up at an infuriated Asher as he looks down at me, only for a moment. He stomps on the table hard, causing Bridgette to scream in pain.

"I said CLEAR?!"

"Yes!" The room answers in unison.

"Better," he says. "One more thing, you would all do well to keep my bond brother's name out of your fucking mouths as well. Anymore bullshit rumors about my wife, or my brother being unfaithful to me, and you will receive the same treatment."

With that, he jumps off the table, crouching down beside me as he examines my cheek.

"You good?" he asks in a soft tone.

I nod as he does the same, helping me to my feet as he jerks his head to Liam.

"C'mon, let's go."

We both follow him. I can't help but turn my head to see Maggie whispering in Bridgette's ear, petting her head soothingly before she yanks out the fork. Bridgette screams before a sob rips through her. Maggie gathers her into her arms, hushing her softly.

My eyes widen as understanding clicks. Holy shit. The girl from this summer was Bridgette. The girl that Maggie can't get over is Bridgette? Her step-sister? If I had even a smidge of doubt, the look on Maggie's face when our eyes connect solidifies everything I need to know.

I don't have time to do or say anything before Asher is tugging me out of the dining hall and out into the courtyard. We continue moving at a brisk pace. When we are around the side of a building away from prying eyes, Asher releases his hold on me, allowing Liam to gather me into his arms.

He peppers my face with gentle kisses as he shakes his head.

"I'm so sorry she hit you, babygirl. I should have intervened sooner."

"It's fine. At least it wasn't a plate this time," I smile softly, forcing a snarled breath out of Asher.

"I think, if anything, this was a reminder that at school...we need distance. People are suspecting and I...none of us can risk that," I say, hating the pained look on Liam's face as he pulls away from me and nods.

"You're right."

"You should be the only one that she's seen with right now. Keep an eye on her." Liam says to Asher.

Asher's body language is rigid, his arms crossed. He nods but doesn't speak as Liam continues.

"You will keep her safe, right? Please," Liam says, a hint of pleading in his words.

Again, Asher nods, his deep voice taking on a gruff tone.

"I will."

Asher's little display made it around school by the end of my next class. Everywhere I went, everyone kept a large distance between me and them. I heard several people talking about how they didn't know Asher and I were already married, how crazy it is that a legacy got married before induction or graduation. I also heard that Bridgette's hand is fractured, and she had to be taken to the hospital to have surgery on it. Does it make me a bad person that I don't really care?

When news hit Ronan's ears, he pulled me out of class and had Wesley take me home early. He said that he would meet me there as soon as he could. When I got to the parking lot, Wesley was there with a compassionate smile on his face as he held the door open for me. Before we left, I saw Asher climbing into his car and following after us. Guess he's taking Liam's request seriously.

"You want to talk about it?" Wesley asks as he merges lanes.

"About what?" I ask.

"The altercation," he says easily.

I shrug. "At least I don't need stitches this time."

"Stitches?" he frowns.

I nod. "She hit me over the head with a plate. A ton of blood. Super gross," I say, as I wrinkle my nose up in disdain.

Wesley's tone becomes cold and stiff.

"And she wasn't dismissed?"

I turn to look at him with a tilt to my head.

"Dismissed? Like expelled?"

He nods.

"No, I don't think she even got in trouble," I laugh. "Besides Asher choking her, I suppose that was punishment."

"He choked her?" Wesley asks with raised eyebrows.

"Yeah, and he stabbed her with a fork today."

He makes a face before looking out the driver's window.

"What?" I ask.

"Hm?"

"That face. What was that about?"

"It's nothing," he says, with a shake of his head and a fake smile.

"Wesley," I say with furrowed brows.

He lets out a slow breath, as he shakes his head again and keeps his eyes forward.

"I just hope that doesn't reach Christopher's ears. He won't like his son getting violent with a daughter of the Brethren. Not a good look."

I hadn't even thought of that. I'd imagine that would be a very bad look for Asher, for all the Putnam's...shit.

We pull up to the house, a heaviness inside the car as he opens the door for me.

"Thank you," I murmur.

"My pleasure," Wesley says, as Asher parks his car.

I begin walking up the steps when I get to the front door and pause. No. Not again.

A white envelope is resting against the doorstep– no name, no return address. Just blank and foreboding.

"Skyla?" Wesley calls out. "Everything okay?"

I don't respond or even move a muscle. I feel a body come up behind me before I smell Asher's cologne. He reaches down, lifting it up before opening it.

"Fingerprints," I say as he tears into it.

His hazel eyes are hard and filled with anger.

"He has yet to make a mistake. I doubt he has this time."

He has a point.

I watch over his shoulder as he opens it, pulling out a photograph. I feel another body come up behind us and I glance to see Wesley, watching us with a deep frown.

"What's going on?"

Turning back to the picture in Asher's hand, my heart stills as I stare at it.

It's a picture of us from today in the dining hall after he stabbed Bridgette, when he was holding my face. It has sharpie drawn over it, a noose around Asher's neck and a veil over my head. There isn't a letter this time, though. Instead, his words are written across the bottom in bold, chunky letters.

HIS WIFE?!

How did he possibly take the picture, print it, draw on it and drop it off before we got here? How is he always one step ahead, one move faster? I swallow roughly as my eyes come to Asher's.

"He knows where we live," I say.

Asher nods as he glances to Wesley.

"The stalker?" Wesley guesses.

I watch as Asher's eyes narrow. "What do you know about it?"

"I know what Ronan deemed necessary to keep Skyla safe."

Asher watches him for several seconds, like he's assessing if Wesley is a threat. He turns back to me, crumpling up the photo and pulling a lighter from his pocket. He sets it on fire, holding on to it until the very last second before letting the charred pieces flutter to the ground.

"Fuck him. I'm not scared," Asher says, as he practically stomps his way into the house.

He might not be, but I am.

Chapter Twelve
Skyla

Before Wesley left, he insisted on sweeping the house. Honestly, I was relieved he offered. Did he go inside? Or did he just leave the photograph on the doorstep? Who knows, but I sure as hell didn't want to find out at night that he was hiding under my bed the whole time.

Thankfully, the house was clear. Wesley even offered to stay behind until Ronan got there. The way he said Ronan's name confirmed my assumption, that he suspects something is up with him. But it's not like I'm going to be the one to out us. I told him it wasn't necessary and before he could even argue, Ronan was calling me, demanding I tell him everything.

Now, Ronan and Liam are both at the house and we are sitting downstairs in the living room. Asher is in the kitchen, pouring himself his third drink of the day. I never noticed how much he drank before. Probably because we didn't live together, but honestly, it's a concerning amount. I'm surprised he's not already drunk with how full those scotch glasses are.

No one says anything as we sit in silence, until the front door is practically blown off its hinges and a furious Vincent storms inside. He's dressed in black from head to toe, his hair wet from sweat when he turns to face us. Scratch that, not wet with sweat. Blood.

There is blood splattered across his entire face and arms, his eyes practically bulging out of his head as he screams.

"Why the FUCK am I the last to know about anything? I leave town for half a goddamn day, and everything goes to shit?" he shouts at no one in particular, before he turns his eyes on Asher.

"Putnam, I swear to fucking god if you don't bring that bitch to heel—"

"Trust me, one more misstep and that fork is going straight in her fucking neck," Asher practically bites out before tossing his drink back.

Vincent seems surprised by Asher's cooperation. He was clearly looking for more of a fight. Unfortunately, that leaves him without a target, and he sets his eyes on me. He closes the distance between us, anger still boiling just under the surface as he crouches down in front of me.

"Siren, why the fuck didn't you call me?"

"I did," I say softly.

"You called me when your fucking stalker showed up at the house. Why didn't you call me when she assaulted you?"

I shrug my shoulders and shake my head.

"She slapped me, it's hardly assault."

"Not in the law's eyes," Vincent interjects.

Asher snorts. "Yeah, 'cause you know all about the law don't you."

Vincent doesn't even look at Asher as he continues staring at me. Past the blood-splattered face, I see an unmasked hurt and I hate that I put it there. Vincent wants me to need him, to rely on him, desperately. I think he believes that's the only good he is to me. That he's only here as a protector and if he's not doing that...

"I was okay. I was safe. I knew you were busy, and I didn't want to—"

"I swear to Christ if you say bug me, I'll kiss you until your lips are bruised," he groans in irritation.

I can't help but give him a small, sad smile. That's what he promised me the other day, in Ronan's yard after he grabbed me a little too hard. He promised that from then on, the only bruises he'd leave on me would be on my lips. Good to see he's attempting to make good on his promises.

"I'm sorry," I say dejectedly, not having it in me to fight with him.

He blows out an angered breath, nodding his head as he stands up.

"Go clean yourself up and we'll talk," Ronan offers.

Vincent wordlessly nods and walks to the downstairs guest bathroom. Several minutes go by before there is a knock at the door. I frown at the sound, my body instantly tensing as Ronan stands to answer it. The living room is tucked out of view from the front door and Liam holds me closer than before. His hand running soothing circles on my back as the sound of the door opening echoes through the house.

Some murmured words are exchanged before Maggie meekly walks into the room. She looks around at the guys, not meeting Asher's eyes as she looks to me.

"Hey, Sky."

"Hey, Mags," I say softly.

She stands there stiffly, twisting her hands together before she speaks.

"Can we talk?"

I nod, standing up and moving towards her. I feel all the guys follow me with their eyes, but I ignore them as I lead her upstairs. When we get to my room, I take a seat on my bed and she does as well.

We sit there in silence for several minutes, her eyes on her twisting hands in her lap before I speak.

"So, you and Bridgette?" I ask.

Her eyes come to mine, regret and sadness in them as she nods.

"Kinda. Not really. I mean, not anymore, you know," she says, as she runs a hand through her thick red hair.

"As soon as she realized people were watching me console her in the dining hall, she shoved me to the ground. She called me a nasty lesbian and ran away crying," Maggie scoffs, sinking her teeth into her bottom lip as she looks away.

My heart hurts for my friend and I reach my hand out, resting it on her leg as I squeeze. Her watery eyes come to me, full of shame and disappointment.

"What's wrong with me? Why does it have to be her? She's mean and vindictive and a fucking cunt. So, why the fuck do I still want her?"

A tear drips down her face, and I close the distance between us, pulling her in for a hug as she begins to cry into my neck. I hold her and let her release all the pent up hurt inside. Truthfully, I couldn't tell her what the reason is for her not being able to get over Bridgette Brenton. Besides being beautiful, she has virtually nothing going for her. She's a nasty bitch, and my best friend is one of the kindest humans you'll ever meet. She deserves someone a hell of a lot better than Bridgette. Especially if that's how she's going to treat her.

"I'm sorry I was even worried about her today," Maggie says as she pulls away from me, sniffing and wiping away her tears. "She attacked you. I should have been checking on you, not the other way around."

I give her a sympathetic smile and a nod.

"It's okay. Maggie. You like her, you saw her hurt. If that was one of my guys, I'd have felt the same way."

"You're not mad at me?" she asks.

I shake my head. "I'm just sorry she's putting you through the wringer like this."

Maggie lets out a sarcastic laugh and shakes her head.

"It is what it is. She's just so afraid of being labeled, she can't get out of her own way to realize how happy we were this summer. We had the house to ourselves while our parents were out of town; we spent all day together and every night in bed. It was...perfect."

I listen intently, only she doesn't continue. She trails off before shaking her head.

"Whatever, though. I need to be done. After the plate thing, and then today? I can't have that kind of toxicity in my life, any more than required."

I twist my mouth down in sympathy and nod.

"Well, for what it's worth, I think you can do much better."

Maggie gives me half a smile.

"If this is the part where you admit that you've been in love with me this whole time and want me to join the harem, you have to let me fix myself up first," she says, as she waves her hand over her face.

I throw back my head and laugh.

"You caught me. I'm down bad."

"Psh, they always are," Maggie says with a roll of her eyes, her spark coming more to life by the minute. We hang out for another twenty minutes or so before she stands.

"I should probably get going. I'm massively behind in econ."

I grimace at that and nod.

"Luck be with you," I say as I stand with her, walking her down the stairs and out the front door.

When she's gone, I turn to find the guys murmuring to themselves in the living room. As I crest the corner, all eyes swing to me, though Liam is the first to speak. He gives me a heartwarming smile as I move around the couch.

"Hey, babygirl. Everything good?"

I nod, not choosing to air out Maggie's dirty laundry before I glance at where to sit. I could take up my old spot between Liam and Ronan, but a freshly showered Vincent is sitting on the other side of Ronan, looking broodier than normal. Ronan catches my eye, gesturing to Vincent with his head and a nod.

"Yeah, give Vinny some love. He's had a hard day," Liam teases, as Vincent flips him off.

I slide into Vincent's lap, and he welcomes me happily, scooting myself until I'm completely on top of him before pressing a kiss to the top of my head. I turn to see Asher is still in the kitchen, nursing a new drink.

"So, what were you guys talking about?" I ask.

"We were going over security precautions. Making sure no one can break in," Ronan says.

"And I filled your *boyfriend's* in on everything. We are good to go," Asher snarks.

The word boyfriend's sounds so bitter rolling off his tongue. It instantly makes me bristle, but I don't engage, focusing on Ronan as he takes my hands into his lap. I feel Vincent make a possessive sounding grumble beneath me that has me giving him a look. He simmers down, and Ronan doesn't pay him any mind as he runs his hands up and down my legs soothingly.

"Don't worry about it, baby. We're taking care of things, okay?"

I frown at that, feeling like they are trying to push me out of the plans and keep information from me. Liam jumps to his feet, grabbing the remote for the TV before turning it on.

"Movie night?" Liam asks as he drops down onto the floor in front of me, leaning his back against the couch as he begins scrolling for a movie.

No one agrees, but then again, no one really protests, which seems to be good enough for Liam. Asher hangs back awkwardly, like he's not sure if he should stay or go. Vincent and Ronan both give him withering looks before Liam glances at me, checking in as I give him a nonchalant shrug.

"Ash, you joining us?" Liam asks.

He pauses, his eyes coming to me and only me. We stare at each other for several seconds, before he wordlessly takes up the recliner on the other side of the room. He kicks the footrest up and settles back into it, before Liam turns on a comedy movie. I'm grateful for it, because I don't think I could take anything horror or thriller. I think we have enough of that crap going on in real-life, thank you very much.

Chapter Thirteen
Vincent

The movie Liam chose is a fucking stupid one. He's the only one laughing at the bad timed one liners, and he's completely oblivious to it. My Siren entertains him occasionally when his eyes find hers to make sure she's having a good time. She slaps on a quick smile before he turns back to his show, with her fingers in his hair, drawing lazy patterns against him as he sinks further into the couch.

He's easy to fool, but she can't fool me. The way her teeth are slightly sinking into her lip, her hands twisting together subconsciously, she's nervous and scared. She's trying so hard not to let anyone see it, though.

My eyes come to Ronan, who is watching her with a pinched look of concern all his own before he looks to me. She needs a distraction, to not think about all of this for a minute, and it looks like Ronan has the same idea that I do.

I watch as his hand moves from massaging her feet to slowly working up her leg. While he does that, I cup her chin in my hand, forcing her head up to me before pressing my lips to hers. A small, surprised breath leaves her before a soft mewling sound hums in the air. Her tongue tangles with mine and plucks at my self-control like it's a game.

Gritting my teeth, I do my best to keep it together as I deepen the kiss, gripping her a little harder as my teeth come out to bite her lower lip. I pull back slightly, allowing her lip to come with me before I release it.

Her bright green eyes look up at me in a daze, before another soft gasp escapes her. This time, it's not because of me. Ronan's hand has slid under the waistline of her leggings, no doubt rubbing against her clit, before he grips the material and pulls it down to her ankles. She kicks out of it quickly, and he doesn't waste another second before he's pulling her panties to the side, burying his face in between her thighs.

"Oh my god," she moans, capturing the attention of everyone else in the room.

"Oh shit, this is way better than a movie," Liam says as he excitedly gets to his knees, turning to face us eagerly.

My eyes peer over my Siren's head, to see Asher watching us with a guarded look from the corner. He hasn't left yet, but he looks two seconds from bolting. Good, he doesn't get to see my woman like this. Piece of fucking shit.

Forcing myself to point my attention back where it belongs, my hands come down to cup her breasts as Liam jumps into action, quickly grabbing the bottom of her shirt and pulling it over her head. Her front clasp bra takes only a snap from me before her breasts spill free. My hand cups the right, flicking my thumb against her nipple, as Liam's mouth dives on the left.

Her back arches against me as I hold her tight, allowing Liam and Ronan the time to properly worship her. I watch as Ronan's head pops up, and he slaps the side of her thigh.

"Flip over, baby. Ass up."

Liam pulls away, and I release my hold on her as she does what he says. I move both of my legs onto the couch, quickly grab my rock-hard cock into my hands, running my hand up and down it a few times as she lowers herself onto her hands and knees. Slipping a hand through her silky hair, I grip it tightly before lowering her to me.

"C'mere, Siren. Let me feel that wet little mouth."

She opens up easily before her soft lips wrap around the head of my cock, slowly lowering herself inch by inch until I'm down her throat. She gags once as she stills, and I can't help but snap my hips into her. The gagging increases, before a muffled scream comes from her.

Glancing up, I see Ronan has pushed inside her, his eyes rolled into the back of his head, hands grip her bare hips. He pulls back, forcing her off my cock a few inches before thrusting again, almost sending her falling on top of me. After a few more thrusts, the three of us find a steady rhythm as we begin using my Siren. Each moan from her tells me that, little by little, we're putting a fog over this day, taking away the stress and fear for a bit. And goddamn, it feels fucking good.

I hear the jangling of Liam's pants before he stands, pierced cock in hand as he begins stroking it. Jesus. How fucking long did that shit take to heal? I'd rather get my cock tattooed than pierced. Not a bad idea, actually. It could say property of Siren down the side. I think she'd like that. It's not like I could regret it; this is the only fucking mouth I'll ever need, or desire, for the rest of my life.

From the corner of the room, I hear two feet stomp to the floor. My head lulls back as I push Siren's head down more on my cock, before I see Asher storm across the room, reaching out for the bottle of scotch before stomping his way to the stairs. Good. Glad he got the hint.

Her head pops up from me, smiling at me with a small trail of spit running down her lip before she looks to Liam, opening her mouth for him. He eagerly closes the distance, slipping his cock into her mouth.

I watch as she takes him so well, her tongue flicking against his piercings as he pulls out before pushing back in. His body shutters, with what looks like pleasure, as she does it again, but I've had enough fucking waiting. Winding my hand tighter into her hair, I yank her back to me, pushing my cock back down her throat.

"Hey, you have to share," Liam pouts, like a goddamn toddler.

I scoff at him, continuing to fuck my Siren's throat. She pulls away from me, despite my grip on her hair, offering her mouth for Liam again. Irritation flicks inside me, that I have to share her in this moment, but she comes back to me seconds later. I guess I can get over it for now.

She alternates between us evenly. Ronan picks up his pace, fucking her harder and harder until his hand comes to her clit, rubbing against it quickly before she bucks against him. Her mouth is on Liam as it drops open in pleasure, that sweet sound of her orgasm shaking the room as Ronan grunts out his own release.

He stays inside her for several seconds before she pulls away from Liam, blowing out a ragged breath as she takes me again. Liam practically hops over to the other side of the couch, shoving Ronan out of his way and out of my Siren before he's lining himself up.

Liam doesn't give her any warning or a second to breathe before he's pushing inside her. Her body tenses and her movements pause as she lets out a small whimper. He seems to hear it and takes note, slowing his hips before pulling out gently and pushing in a little deeper this time.

Slowly, her body begins to relax again, as I control the bobs of her head while Liam fucks her pussy. His eyes roll into the back of his head on a deep thrust before he grins at me, like this is some weird fucking bonding moment.

Keeping my eyes on my Siren, she looks up at me, mouth full of my cock and watery eyes. I can't help but let my other hand skim against her porcelain skin. She's so fucking perfect.

"C'mon, babygirl. I know you got another orgasm waiting for me and Vincent," Liam says, a slight clench in his jaw as he speaks.

She shakes her head 'no' as she whimpers.

"Shhh, just relax, Siren," I say, as I run my thumb against her cheek. "Relax and let us take care of you."

Those green eyes come to me, a look of trust and adoration that pierces straight through my black fucking heart as she nods. Liam and I pick up the pace together as Ronan drops down beside us, his hand going back to her clit again. She moans in response, Liam cursing as he throws his head back.

"Do it again," he groans. "She's choking the fucking life out of my cock."

Ronan obliges, forcing moans to slip from Liam and my Siren at the same time. I feel my own release begin to build, an almost numb feeling spreading across my body before my balls begin to tighten.

"One more time," Liam practically begs, as his thrusts become jerky and uneven.

Just as requested, Ronan continues playing with her, surprising us all when he pulls his hand back and slaps against her clit. She shatters apart, taking me and Liam with her. I couldn't even tell you who came first or last. It all became one white-hot pleasure filled haze.

I blink several times to get my vision back to normal, before I look down to see a lust drunk Siren and a spent Liam. Only our ragged breathing can be heard in the room, before I pull my Siren up to sprawl on top of me. She comes easily, and I tuck her against my chest, brushing her hair behind her ear as her eyes slowly flutter closed.

Chapter Fourteen
Skyla

The next morning, I woke up in my bed beneath Vincent, with Ronan and Liam on either side of us. No one was touching, by only a few inches. If sleepovers are going to be a regular thing, I'm going to need a bigger bed.

When we all eventually got up and ready for the day, Asher was noticeably absent from the house. I'm not sure if he left last night and didn't come home, or if he left early this morning. Either way, I couldn't really care less.

Wesley came and picked me up for class, despite Liam and Vincent's insistence that they could drive me. It only took one look from Ronan to know what he was thinking. That's not a good idea.

It's become clear to us all, that Wesley is more than aware of our... situation, and so there really is no hiding it at this point. If he wants to tell Christopher or someone else at the Brethren, well, we're already dead.

One by one, each of the guys kiss me before getting into their own cars. Wesley holds the door open for me, not saying a word as I slip into the black SUV. Well, he doesn't say a word for a mile or two before he finally speaks.

"So...all of them?"

I look up to meet his eyes in the rear-view mirror.

"Yes."

He nods but doesn't say anything else for several seconds.

"They're all cool with it?"

My head tips back and forth. I'm not sure you could say Vincent is 'cool' with it; more like he's tolerating it. Same could be said for Ronan, though maybe not as extreme.

"Some more than others," I say with a shrug.

Wesley lets out a short chuckle.

"They treat you well though, right?"

I can't stop the smile that spreads across my face. I nod my head, remembering how all the guys rubbed me last night when we were tucked in bed. Each wanting their hands on me before they all woke me up, peppering kisses down my body.

"Very," I smile.

"Good," he says, his eyes staying on mine in the rear-view mirror for half a beat.

There is a heaviness in the car, something I can't quite name. Before I have a chance to overthink it though, we're at Gallows Hill, and he's putting the car in park. He gets out quickly, opening my door as I dip my head in thanks.

"Have a great day," he says with a tight, yet friendly, smile.

"You too," I say with a small smile, before heading through the courtyard.

I meet up with Liam and Maggie in class, noticing that Andrew isn't here today. That's kind of odd. He's usually always here; the guy must have perfect attendance or something.

I have a few tests that I, unfortunately, am not very prepared for. Dating three men has severely cut into my study time. Ask me if I regret how I spend my time, though.

At lunch, everyone keeps a wide berth, and I didn't even see a dirty look come from Bridgette or her friends. They keep their eyes on their plates and far away from Maggie, me and Liam.

I haven't seen Asher today. I'm honestly wondering if he even came to school today when a commotion sounds from outside. A massive group of people begin filing out of the dining hall and into the courtyard. Liam and I trade curious looks when we overhear someone say, "Oh shit, it's Asher Putnam."

Our eyes widen at the same time before we are up and out of our seats, rushing outside to see what's going on. I didn't know what to expect, but it definitely wasn't this.

Asher is beating the shit out of a guy who is a few inches shorter than him and at least forty pounds lighter. A broken bottle of scotch is at Asher's feet, and it only takes me two seconds and one stumble of his to piece this together.

He's drunk off his ass.

When Asher winds back to swing on the guy he misses, stumbling a few more feet before he rights himself, delivering a swift kick to the guy's bent over face. I jerk like the hit landed on me, as teeth go flying across the courtyard, making soft little sounds as they scatter.

"Gonna threaten mys wife!" Asher slurs, his voice amazingly loud for how sloppy it is. "Fucking kills youz!"

One more hit to the jaw and the guy falls to the ground in a heap, a drunken Asher spinning around to face the audience he has suddenly gained.

"Whose next?" he snarls, his balance only wavering slightly. "No one believes me when I say things. When I says that I'llz fucking kill anyone who threatens my wifes, they'll fucking dies!"

Vincent seems to appear out of thin air, taking a spot right beside me as Liam looks to him. Liam pushes me into Vincent, like he's passing me off, before he forces his way through the crowd.

Asher bends down, grabbing the broken scotch bottle. He lifts it up to stab the guy on the ground when Liam's hand catches his wrist, whispering something into his ear. It takes a moment, but Asher's drunken eyes land on mine, his brows furrowing before he drops the bottle.

The intact glass shatters at his feet, but he doesn't seem to care; instead, his eyes stay on mine, like he's waiting for me. Maybe it's stupid, no it's definitely stupid, but I walk towards him.

He doesn't deserve my sympathy, my kindness, and he sure as hell doesn't deserve my forgiveness. For some reason though, I find myself beside him cupping his bloodied cheek softly.

I'm unable to tell if it's Asher's blood or not, either way, it doesn't really matter.

"Let's go, Ash. Please," I ask softly.

He squeezes his eyes tight, murmuring to himself as he nods.

"Fucksing love it when youz call me that."

"Come on," I say gently, trying to pull him with me.

It doesn't take much to get him to follow. Whether that's due to his completely intoxicated state or his willingness to comply with me, I'm not sure. My hand moves from his face to his hand, squeezing it tightly as his hazy brown eyes come to mine. I give him a reassuring smile as I tug on his arm, his feet stumbling after me as I pull him away.

Liam is to his left, watching him closely and prepared to catch him if needed. It takes a little while, but we finally make our way through the crowd and down the courtyard. I give Liam a concerned glance, like I don't know where to go, before he nods to the pool hall.

Once again, Vincent comes out of nowhere. I didn't even know he was following us before he opens the door.

"Thanks," I say to him softly.

He nods at Liam, and I help Asher inside. As luck would have it, we run straight into Ronan, who immediately scans us with concern when he takes a look at his nephew.

"What happened? What's going on?"

"Asher beat the shit out of Richard Knox. I'm not sure what kind of damage control we are looking at, he's piss drunk," Liam says.

"Jesus Christ," Ronan mutters before he clutches Asher's arm, pulling him towards the pool.

Asher tries to fight him off, but Ronan snaps at him.

"Knock it off and get in the fucking locker room. NOW."

Surprisingly, Asher concedes, and we follow as Ronan all but drags Asher to the locker room. When we get there, he throws Asher against one of the walls before turning on the shower head. Ice cold water begins soaking Asher from head to toe. I jump out of the way of the backsplash as Ronan keeps the shower head on him.

Asher gasps at the cold water, attempting to wipe it from his eyes and move out of the stall. Unfortunately for him, Vincent is there, pushing him back against the wall as Ronan continues to hose him down. Liam comes to stand beside me, a hot cup of what smells like black coffee in his hand, before Ronan finally stops the water, allowing Asher to slide down the wall and sit on the floor.

He sits there for several seconds, just staring at the water trailing down the drain before his bloodshot eyes look up at us. My mouth is pinched in concern, though I hate myself for having any level of concern for him, if I'm honest.

Liam offers Asher the cup of coffee, and he pushes it away before I speak.

"Please," I ask softly.

Those brown eyes snap up to mine, holding my gaze for several seconds before he nods. He grabs the cup from Liam's outstretched hand, taking small sips of it. It only takes a minute or so before Asher is on his hands and knees, retching the contents of his stomach onto the floor.

Ronan quickly moves to get a trash can, shoving it under his face as Asher heaves and groans repeatedly. When he has nothing left to throw up, he rests his head against the side of the can. I watch him with pity, unsure of what to say or do as Ronan, Liam, and Vincent begin talking amongst themselves.

At least an hour goes by with the same recycled pattern. Asher drinks more coffee and then pukes before attempting more coffee and puking some more. Finally, he begins to appear at least a little more sober. His clothes are sopping wet, but his hair is already starting to dry and there is more focus to his gaze when he looks up at me.

My phone rings in my hand, and I frown when I see Wesley's name across it.

"Hello?"

"I'm here to pick you up," he says, the typical friendly tone in his voice noticeably absent.

I glance at the clock before shaking my head.

"I still have a few more hours before I'm done for the day."

"No, I was sent to pick you and Asher up...by Christopher," he says, his name sounding just as foreboding on Wesley's tongue as it feels to my ears.

"Now?" I ask, cringing when I look to see Ronan trying to help Asher into fresh clothes.

"Now."

Chapter Fifteen
Asher

I stare straight ahead, doing my best to clear the blurred vision from my eyes. This literally couldn't have come at a worse time. Well, not true. I could have been summoned two hours ago. Now, that would have been interesting.

After Skyla hung up the phone, I towel dried my hair as best as I could. Ronan found me an extra pair of jeans and a button-down to slip on. We are practically the same height, but it doesn't hide the fact that these clothes are most definitely not tailor-made for me.

Something tells me though, that if he is summoning both Skyla and I in the middle of the day, clothes will be the last thing on his mind. Glancing over to the seat beside me, I watch Skyla's knee bounce nervously as her hands twist together in her lap. For a second, I reach my hand out. To do what, I'm not sure. It's not like I can offer her any comfort, nor would she accept any even if I could.

Blowing out a rough breath, I throw my head against the headrest and close my eyes.

Why does everything have to be so fucking hard when it comes to her?

I haven't missed the looks of concern Wesley has been giving Skyla since he picked us up. He thinks he's discreet, and maybe he is. But when you've been watching someone as close as I watch Skyla, you don't miss a thing.

When we pull through the gates and up to the main house, it feels as though a lead ball drops in my stomach. I do my best to hide my unease, putting on a mask that I've perfected over the years.

I'm out of the car as soon as Wesley parks, making my way to Skyla's side to find him already there. He offers a hand to help her out of the car, and she takes it. When her feet are on the ground, she gives him a small smile that he returns, though that look of concern never leaves his gaze. Neither does his hand.

My eyes flick down to where they are still holding on to each other before he speaks.

"I'm going to wait here. I'll be ready to take you home whenever you're able."

"Me too, right, Wes?" I say, with more of a sneer than a teasing smile.

His eyes come to mine as he nods.

"Of course. Both of you."

"Thank you," Skyla says, squeezing his hand once before she drops it.

I step up beside her, offering her my arm, and surprisingly, she takes it. No complaints. That's progress, right? Or maybe it's just self-awareness of the image we must display to my father. Either way.

We begin making our way up the steps when I lower my voice.

"How do you think your boyfriends will feel about you adding another one to the roster?"

Her head whips over to me, brows furrowed.

"Asher, you and I are not—"

I scoff, cutting her off. "No, I meant Wesley."

"Wesley?" she echoes.

"He's into you, and based on the look in your eyes, you really don't hate him."

She shrugs, her voice lowering as we get to the front door.

"There are a lot worse people to spend hateful energy on," she says, her eyes intent on me in a way that makes my chest ache.

Though, I'd never admit it to anyone.

The door opens before us, one of my father's waitstaff stepping back with a bow before we weave our way through the doorway. We don't make it far before we pause in the foyer to see Henry and my father staring down at us with scowls that send a chill down my spine.

Fuck.

"Hello, Father," I say carefully. "Henry."

Neither one of them acknowledges my greeting, and I blink hard as if that was going to chase away the slight buzz I still have. I feel myself sway on my feet for a second, but I right myself quickly.

"Are you fucking drunk?" my father spits.

"No," I defend.

I was drunk, technically. I'm at least halfway sober now.

"Oh?" he laughs. "So, now you lie to me. My boy, I don't know what has happened to you, but you are the biggest disappointment that has ever walked this god forsaken earth."

His words don't phase me; they can't penetrate the thick armor I've spent years building for myself.

"What mess have you made today, Asher?" he asks, my name sounding like acid on his tongue.

I keep silent, knowing it was rhetorical. He crosses the distance between us, opening his hand and slapping me across the face. A soft gasp of shock escapes Skyla, and I keep my head turned so that I don't have to see her fear or pity.

"Answer me!" my father roars.

"Richard Knox was threatening to hurt my wife," I grit through clenched teeth. "He was very publicly talking about how he would take a turn at her, before burying her in the cemetery where she belongs."

My father and Henry share a look. It isn't in concern for Skyla's well-being. They don't give a fuck about her. What they don't like is that a member's son, not even a legacy, is making threats to the Brethren's princess before she's even been able to bear an heir.

"And what did you do?" my father asks.

I pause for a moment before deciding it's best to be honest; he'll know soon enough.

"I beat the living shit out of him in the middle of the courtyard."

Another hit comes to the other side of my face; this time, it's a fist. I stumble a few steps before I feel small hands reach for my arm, steadying me. I want to tell her not to touch me, not to paint a target on her back as well, but my father is already laying into me before I can try.

"You do not handle private matters publicly! Do you see me doling your punishment in front of the masses? No! Private matters deserve private settings. When you lose control, you make us look weak!" he spits.

I feel his hand dig into the back of my hair as he forces me to look at him.

"Do you know how embarrassed I was to get a phone call from Brenton? He was bitching and shouting about his little cunt's hand for over an hour."

"She hurt Skyla," I answer.

My father's eyes turn to her, a lethal look in them.

"It seems all of your misbehavior lately has revolved around this girl. Did I make a mistake in selecting her? Because she seems to be turning you into a mannerless animal."

"No," I snap, forcing his eyes back to me. "It's nothing to do with her. I just can't stand the thought of people disobeying me, going after my property," I say, the words heavy on my tongue as I spin the lie easily.

My father laughs, shaking his head before he gestures behind me. He forces me to sit backwards in a chair, my chest plastered to the back of it, before Henry comes around with rope, tying my hands together around the chair.

Oh god.

"You really thought I was going to buy that bullshit?" he says on a dying chuckle.

I whip my head over my shoulder to see a butler hand my father a long black whip. One that I've only seen once, one that I will never forget. I earned myself three lashes when I was six, because I accidently interrupted a Brethren meeting while Liam and I were playing hide and go seek.

"How many?" I ask, gritting my teeth together.

"However many it takes to break down your disobedience," he says before I feel two hands on me, tearing the back of my shirt open.

"No!" Skyla screams before the first lash.

My back bows as much as humanely possible, pain contorting my face. Another lash comes before another, and a sobbed cry chokes out into the room. My head turns to the noise to see Henry grappling with his daughter, his hand over her mouth and arm banded around her waist as he holds her back. Those wide, bright green eyes are watching me in horror, and for a moment, I hold on to the comfort of them before the next lash cuts against new skin.

Chapter Sixteen
Skyla

Each lash against Asher's skin leaves a new welt, and with one more crack in the same spot, the skin splits open, blood slowly running down his back from each mark. I leaped for him after the first crack of the whip, earning a punch to the stomach from my father before he covered my screams and held me back.

I tried to turn away, but he didn't allow it, whispering that this is my doing, that I'm responsible. I'm not sure if he actually thinks that or just wants me to suffer with the guilt. Regardless, each lash does feel like my fault, and the fight in Asher's eyes leaves with each one.

Christopher is in a rage, I don't think he could stop even if he wanted to. His eyes are black as night, an evil sneer donning his face. Honestly, it looks like he's enjoying it. Asher's moans and shouts become quieter as the sheer pain no doubt begins to consume him.

Nasty gashes, welts, and cuts blending together litter his back. I know that he won't be able to handle much more. In a move that I can only describe as stupid bravery, I stomp on my father's foot as hard as I can. His hold on me weakens as he howls in pain, and I'm able to break free before I bolt towards Asher.

Just as Christopher is reeling back his arm for another lash, I practically jump on top of Asher. My legs hook around his as my chest presses against his bloody back. I wrap my arms around his torso, holding on as I feel the first sharp snap of the whip.

An agonizing scream rips out of me as Asher's defeated body seems to be reinvigorated.

"Skyla! No! Get off! Run!" he shouts as the whip comes down on me again.

Another pained scream echoes through the house, but my hold on Asher tightens, intent on not letting go. Again and again, the white-hot burn from the whip tears at my flesh. Nonstop, Asher is practically sobbing, begging me to get off him, to protect myself. I can't, though. I can't stand by and watch him be tortured any longer.

I feel Asher shake the chair from side to side like he's trying to shake me off, but with his hands tied, and me wrapped around him, he doesn't have much range of motion.

"Please, Princess! Please get off. Please," he cries as my moans of pain rattle the walls. "I'm sorry, Princess. I'm so fucking sorry! S-so sorry,"

"It's o-okay," I say, my words morphing into a scream.

"Disobedient little fucks!" Christopher snarls before a final lash cracks across my back. This one is easily the most painful, and my vision actually spots for a moment, everything turning bright white as my body attempts to process this sort of pain.

Without another word, two pairs of footsteps are heard exiting the room before heading deeper into the house. I don't know how long I stay there; my body sluggish and unmoving. It feels as though my head has been submerged under water, and I don't know how to resurface.

A faint sound registers in my ears, and I try to focus on it as best as I can, but it's proving to be more challenging than I had hoped.

"Skyla!" a muffled voice shouts.

"Princess!" It bellows again.

"Baby, sweetheart, fucking PLEASE!" Asher's voice screams, finally shaking me out of my haze.

Slowly, the pure pain radiating from my back and arms shakes me, and I can't stop the cry that escapes me.

"Oh god!" I groan the pain just from a simple breath making me wish death would just come already.

"Princess, please get off me. Please," Asher begs, his words tight and choked like he's been crying.

"Gotta protect," I moan as my words break off into a sob.

"There is no one to protect me from, Princess. They're gone. We're safe. Please get off, untie me so I can get us out of here. Please!"

It takes everything in me to let him go. I don't know how I held onto him through all of that. Adrenaline, maybe. Slowly, I'm able to unwind my arms, but I'm not able to stop myself from slumping to the ground. At first, I land on my back. The pain in my back amplifies, and I quickly roll to my side.

"Ahhh!" I shout as my blurry eyes look up to see Asher frantically watching me.

"Princess, please! Please, please, please! Just untie me, untie me, and I'll make everything better, I promise."

I nod numbly, dragging myself across the floor to his tied hands. My hands are shaking so hard it's almost impossible for me to undo these knots. They keep slipping just as I almost have it, frustration and fear taking over. Sloppily, I'm able to loosen the rope enough before Asher's hands bust them apart.

His arms stretch out, a groan escaping him as his back flexes before he drops to the ground beside me. He lays there for a moment, seemingly breathless, before his hands begin frantically brushing my hair away from my face as he holds on to me.

"Princess, talk to me!"

"It hurts," I whimper, causing a crestfallen look to come over his face.

"I know, Princess, I know. I'm gonna get us out of here. I don't want to carry you and hurt you more than you already are. Can you walk?"

Shaking my head, I feel tears begin to pour down my face.

"Hey, hey, hey," he says, his thumbs quickly swiping the tears away. "Yes, you can. You're so brave. I need you to be strong for me, just a little longer, and then we can fall apart together, okay? Can you be my brave girl?"

Something in me thumps at that. I don't know if it's my heart or what, but I find myself slowly nodding my head. Asher blows out a breath in what seems like relief, pressing a long kiss to my forehead before pushing himself to his feet. The look on his face is agonizing, like it's the most painful thing he's ever endured, and I'm not ready to feel the same.

"C'mon, Princess. Together. Come on, brave girl," he says as he reaches out his hands.

I slip my own into his palms, and I'm grateful he does most of the work in pulling me up. I screech as my back straightens out when I'm on my feet, but Asher doesn't allow me time to wallow in my pain. Instead, he's practically pulling my arm out of its socket as we race out the front door as fast as our bodies will allow.

I feel the hand he's not holding wave desperately before a car door opens and shuts. Heavy feet pound against the pavement before I look up to see that familiar pair of dark blue eyes looking at us in horror. Wesley rushes over to us, his eyes running over me from top to bottom.

"What the fuck happened?"

"Just drive. Get us the fuck out of here!" Asher snaps, as Wesley reaches to pick me up.

Asher grabs his arm quickly, stopping him on a dime.

"Don't touch her back!"

Wesley looks behind me, his eyes so wide they look as if they were going to pop out of his head before a thunderous look takes over his face. He turns on his heel sharply, opening the back door for us.

"Get in the fucking car," he says, his eyes trained on the house behind us.

Asher doesn't waste any time hurrying us in, though I wish he would. He slides in all the way, groaning as his back touches the seat before he pulls me in.

"On your stomach, Princess."

I do so happily, feeling the only semblance of relief I've been able to experience yet. And when I say relief, I mean it isn't hurting more by the second for once.

"Ronan," I hear Wesley say into his phone. "Get the others and get back to the house. It's bad."

"Liam," Asher says into his phone. "Get a doctor and have them meet us at our house. It's Skyla."

I look up to see Asher watching me with a worried look, his eyes watery and red. So, I guess I wasn't wrong about him crying. Though, it definitely wasn't from the pain like my tears. His were from me getting hurt, from him unable to do anything but listen to my screams and terror.

I think Asher and Wesley both talk on the phone some more, but all I can focus on is the way Asher's hand runs through my hair, soothing me into a desperately needed sleep.

Chapter Seventeen
Skyla

A door is thrown open, startling me awake, which I'm extremely unhappy about because, holy fucking shit, I forgot how much pain I was in for a moment. I groan in agony as a comforting voice, that isn't all that comforting, shouts into the car.

"What the fuck happened!" Ronan snarls, as his hands come to my legs.

Before Asher can respond, I turn my head to see Vincent push his way into the doorway. His eyes roam my body, memorizing each lash mark before a fury like I've never seen passes over him. He takes several steps away, his body vibrating with anger, before he digs his hands into his hair and screams.

"FUCKKKKK!"

I watch him pick up rocks that are more like boulders, throwing them anywhere and everywhere, windows smash, fountains, even his car. He doesn't seem to care though; he's on a warpath. As much as I want to comfort him, I can't do much of anything but survive right now.

Liam pops his head in next, a devastated look on his face as he takes in my injuries. I watch him slowly sink to his knees, his head shaking numbly.

"Babygirl," he whispers.

I try to give him a smile; at least it feels like one. Then again, I'm sure it looks more like a grimace.

"Everyone get the fuck back," Wesley says as he shoves Ronan and Liam to the side, crouching down to pick me up.

"I'm gonna try to be as careful as possible, okay?" he says.

I nod, clinging to Asher's hand as Wesley scoops his arms under my stomach and chest, doing his best not to touch my back as he lifts me. Ronan is right there, stabilizing my legs so that my back doesn't bend. I feel my body being pulled away from Asher as he watches me with a heavy look.

Unexplained panic rises in me at being separated from Asher, and I buck against their hold.

"No! Stop! Asher!"

He sees my panic and quickly climbs out of the car, impressively so, considering his injuries have to be worse than mine.

"I'm here, Princess. I'm here," he says as he reaches down and holds my hand again, intertwining our fingers before giving it a gentle squeeze. It's like that single squeeze calmed every nerve and smothered the flames of my anxiety.

Blowing out a soft breath, I nod, as the guys around us share confused looks before continuing to carry me inside. I feel a set of eyes on me and look to see Vincent watching us closely, his eyes flicking between me and my hand, that links me with Asher.

As disappointing as it is, Vincent doesn't come to me. Instead, he stays outside, fuming.

"The doctor is upstairs, babygirl. She will get you all patched up," Liam says as he walks beside us, gently moving a piece of my hair out of my face.

"Asher first, his are worse."

"No," they all say at once, before Asher speaks.

"I'm fine, Princess. Really, you are priority. Please," he says, enough emotion choking his voice to have me looking up at him.

So much pain and devastation is playing in those brown eyes. There are too many words unspoken between the two of us in this moment, and I don't have the energy to find them.

The stairs suck. I watch as Asher takes his time with each step, not falling too far behind that he isn't near me, but his jaw is clenched so tight I'm worried it's about to break. When we make it to the top, I breathe out a sigh of relief before we file into my bedroom.

I feel the guys slowly lower me to the plush mattress before they step back. Well, they all try to. I refuse to let go of Asher's hand, digging my nails into his in an attempt to keep my hold on him.

"Just let her take care of you," Asher says, as he gestures to the doctor in the corner sifting through her bags.

I shake my head, not allowing him to pull away.

"S-stay, please," I beg, a single tear falling down the side of my face.

"Ash, why don't you lay down beside her. You need some help too," Liam says.

Asher turns to look at him, hesitating for a moment before he nods. He pulls out of my grasp, and just like that, anxiety flares inside my chest. My head whips around so I can track his movements as he walks to the other side of the bed. This feeling is overwhelming, suffocating and it doesn't stop until I feel Asher's body sink beside mine before grabbing my hand.

I turn my head to face him, relief washing through me as his thumb rubs soft circles against the back of my hand. We are both laying on our stomachs, our torn flesh on full display, and when the doctor begins cleaning my back, I can't help but scream.

The sound of several footsteps slip out the door as I groan, doing my best to bite back the pain. Asher scoots closer to me, tilting his head as he beckons me closer.

"Scream, Princess. It's okay. Let the pain out."

I lean into him, burying my head against his neck as I scream while the doctor works quickly. She apologizes profusely, and Asher keeps telling her it's fine, to make it fast. I'm somewhere between reality and a hazy middle area. I'm not sure which I prefer in this moment, so I do my best to float in between both.

I don't know how long we lie there for. It feels like hours, but maybe it's just minutes. Eventually, the searing pain stops, and bandages start being applied to my back. It's still uncomfortable, but after Asher begged the doctor to give me a shot of morphine, things feel a little fuzzy now.

Asher was next; he hardly made a sound as she cleaned his back. He just closed his eyes and gritted his teeth together. Until I reached my hand up to his face, gently running my fingers through his hair. His eyes flew open at that, and they stayed on me the entire time, like I was his life raft out of this hell we were trapped in. Like I was his only saving grace.

Eventually, the doctor leaves, and I watch as Asher pushes up to rest on his side. He squints and grimaces a few times before lifting his left arm silently, an open invitation that I take without hesitation.

Sliding on my stomach, I curl into his hold. I don't feel a thing as he wraps his arm around me, taking care not to touch my back. With the morphine officially setting in though, I'm not sure I could feel it even if he did.

We sit there for several seconds, just basking in each other's comfort before he speaks.

"Why did you do it? Why did you get involved?"

I don't look up at him Instead, I keep my eyes on his chest.

"I don't know," I mumble.

"Princess," he chastises.

"I don't know," I defend.

He's silent for several seconds before I feel his forefinger hook beneath my chin, tilting my face up to his. Those brown eyes are drenched in sadness, his three golden flecks practically drowning behind the shimmering sheen.

"Tell me."

I look between his expressive eyes and his full lips. Lips that are only inches from my own. I don't know why I did it. Logically, it was the stupidest thing I could have done, and I have a feeling the physical result of my stupidity is only the beginning. If I could go back in time though, I'd do it again.

"It hurt," I say, my eyes flicking across his face. "It hurt to see you like that, to see you defenseless, in pain, alone."

More emotion than I ever thought Asher Putnam was capable of passes across his face.

"Not as much as it hurt me knowing you were bearing the brunt of a punishment meant for me. Not as much as me knowing that you were in pain, bleeding.... because of me," he says, with a rough swallow.

"You didn't hit me, Asher. You are not the enemy here."

"Then what am I, princess? What am I, to you?"

I open my mouth to respond, all words seeming to fade away and rendering me speechless. He doesn't let it go, though, his face inches towards mine.

"What am I?" he asks again.

Still, I don't answer. He leans in a little more, so close our lips accidentally bump against one another for a second before he speaks again. He draws out his words slowly, so his lips drag against mine.

"What. Am. I?"

"Mine," I whisper shakily, fearing what this is, what it means, and the impending rejection I'll feel, again.

"That's right, princess," he says, his words like a whispered prayer. "I'm all fucking yours."

My heart flips in my chest, but I don't have time to process it before his lips are on mine. Butterflies race through me, and the feeling of coming home washes over me. His lips move gently against mine, his tongue softly teasing my own as he deepens the kiss. He pulls away from the kiss, peppering my face with gentle, loving kisses as he begins speaking.

"I'm so sorry this happened," he whispers. "I promise I'll never let it happen again. I can't live through seeing you like that ever again."

He pulls away for a moment, looking into my eyes.

"You're everything to me, Skyla. Fucking everything."

His promises and declarations of adoration pluck at the buried hurt inside caused by none other than the man himself. I shouldn't be so stupid as to forgive him, just like that, and I'm not. All I know is that I need him, and right now, he needs me too.

A few hours go by before a knock comes from the door. Slowly, Ronan, Liam, and Vincent file into the room. Each pausing when they see Asher and I wrapped up together. I turn my head, so I'm fully facing them, but am still on my stomach as I look at them.

I'm not sure what I expect them to say or how they should react, but I definitely wasn't expecting this.

"Oh, for fucks sake! You've got to be shitting me!" Vincent practically snarls.

"Vincent," Ronan says with a shake of his head.

His gray eyes fly over to Ronan before he shakes his head.

"No! Fuck this. This is all his fucking fault. Why are we even allowing him to be in the same room as her, let alone fucking touching her!"

"It's not his fault," I say. "It was mine. He was getting whipped, and I jumped on top of him. He didn't force me. He didn't ask me. I did it. It was my decision."

The gray in his eyes turns to granite as he grits his jaw and shakes his head.

"Please don't tell me you forgive him. Do you remember what that piece of shit did to you?" Vincent snarls, like Asher isn't in the room. Or maybe he just doesn't care.

"I remember but..." I trail off, turning to catch Asher's impassive gaze. Or at least, he's trying to appear impassive. I know him better than that by now, though.

"Things change," I say as I turn to face Vincent again. He looks seconds away from detonating as I continue. "I love you, and I know you might not like it, but I...I need him. I want him around, and I'm sorry if that upsets you."

I feel Asher's arm that's around me tighten softly, like a hidden message just for the two of us. Vincent continues staring at me, not moving or speaking as Liam takes up the spotlight.

"So, are you two together now or?"

"No," I say while Asher says, "Yes."

The guys stare at me for several seconds before Ronan speaks.

"It's been a long day; let's not dig into this. We have food for you guys, and I need to go run an errand. I'll be back," he says.

Something is off about Ronan's demeanor; it's rigid and unyielding. I watch as his hand twitches near his hip, but his posture remains motionless. He's wearing a pair of dress pants and a polo shirt with the school's crest on it, so it's pretty impossible to miss the bulge of a gun on his hip beneath his shirt.

"Where are you going?" I ask.

He pauses, blinking slowly.

"Out."

"Where are you going, Ronan?" I repeat.

He grinds his teeth together, working his jaw from side to side before he speaks.

"I'm going to take care of my brother. He will never hurt you again."

My eyes widen as panic floods me.

"You can't! He could kill you!"

"Not if I kill him first. I'm fine, baby. Rest, I'll be back," he says as he moves forward, pressing a kiss to my forehead.

I scramble for his arm, digging my hands into it as I hold onto him for dear life.

"No! Please, Ronan. Please, don't do this. I can't lose you. It's not worth it!" I spiral, slowly descending into a suffocating panic attack.

My chest heaves, desperate for a breath I can't catch as the room begins to spin. I won't survive if I lose him. I won't survive if I lose any of them. Oh my god. He can't go. He can't.

"Hey! Hey, hey, hey," Ronan says, dropping to his knees as he puts his face in front of my own. "I need to, baby. I can't let him have the chance to hurt you again. If I have to see you like this again, I...I'm the one who can't."

"Think, Ronan," Asher chimes in. "My father's security team would have you gunned down before you could even reach for your gun."

"Your father has security too?" I ask over my shoulder.

"Of course."

"I've never seen them before?"

"That's the point, Princess," he says before turning back to his uncle. "No one wants him dead more than me, but...this is not how we do it," he says, as he gestures towards Ronan's weapon.

Ronan's jaw works from side to side, knowing we are right.

"I can't just sit here. I have to do something," he says.

"Stay with me?" I ask softly, causing his eyes to drop to mine and soften.

He watches me for several seconds, and for a moment, I think he is going to deny me. Then, he blows out a shaky breath, setting his gun on the bedside table as he nods.

"Always."

Chapter Eighteen
Liam

It's been almost two weeks since Skyla and Asher were beat to shit by Christopher. I've never felt a pain like that until that moment, watching the love of your life and your best friend so broken, so hurt. Knowing exactly who did it and also knowing that there isn't a fucking thing you can do? Yeah, that shit sucks.

I've also never seen Ronan so out of control. While Skyla and Asher were getting cleaned up by the doctor, we were all downstairs, trying to give them space and escape Skyla's screams. Each one had me cringing, and around the thirtieth time, Ronan sprung to his feet and went to his car. When he came back, he was loading a gun with a look on his face that promised retribution.

My attempts at getting him to calm down were futile, and if the doctor hadn't come down the stairs to inform us about their injuries, I think he would have left right then. Being reminded of his girl upstairs, injured and in pain, made him pause, at least for a little. Though, I know why he really stuck around. He wanted to see her one more time, in case he didn't make it back. Which he wouldn't have. Asher is right on that one.

I feel my hands begin to shake as Ronan drives. We still have another four hours ahead of us, but I don't think this feeling will fade in that amount of time. This is so fucking stupid. My family handles a pharmaceutical empire. Why the fuck do I have to prove to be a capable mercenary? Who am I going to be faced with killing? Reps? Doctors? My accountant?

My eyes dart over to see Ronan watching me with a pinched look. I know what he's thinking. He doesn't think I have it in me, that I'm not gonna hack it. Honestly, I'm kinda with him. The last...job, if that's what you want to call it, fucked me up. I haven't slept right in weeks, and the way I puked my fucking guts out right after...yeah, I'm definitely not like Vincent, or even Asher.

Vincent's also gone today doing whatever the fuck he does. Obviously, he doesn't share details with us, and if Ronan knows, he doesn't let on.

With all three of us out of town, that just leaves Skyla and Asher home together. Neither went to classes for the first week after that day at Putnam Manor. They honestly barely left Skyla's room. They stayed wrapped around each other like their very own trauma-bond shawl.

I think I'm the only one, apart from Skyla, that's happy about them being...whatever they have been lately. I saw how much he was hurting, and I knew it would only get worse. Did he do some fucked up shit? Absolutely. Did he do it for the right reasons? Debatable. Does he love her, though? Absofuckinglutly. Anyone who says otherwise has to be blind, an idiot, or Vincent Griggs.

One day, I heard Vincent and Skyla get into a screaming match over it. Ronan, Asher, and I were making dinner, and not one of us moved to investigate. Their relationship is very unique, and we've found it's best to let them hash out their shit on their own.

When they eventually came downstairs, Skyla took the seat at the table beside Asher, not sparing Vincent a second glance as she rested her hand on top of Asher's on the table. We all watched Vincent carefully, waiting for him to explode. Surprisingly, he didn't. I mean, he did stare at Asher like he wanted to incinerate him, but he didn't try to shoot him, so I'd call that acceptance.

I'm anxious to get back home, not just because this isn't where I want to be. I also want to get back home because I've been fantasizing about a hot threesome ever since Asher and Skyla made up, or got together, or whatever you want to call it. My beautiful girl getting fucked by me and my best friend? Sign me the fuck up.

"What are you grinning at?" Ronan asks, shaking me out of my thoughts.

I don't realize I'm smirking until he says something, and I quickly drop it before looking to him.

"Nothing."

He shakes his head. "You need to get your head into this, Liam. Christopher is worried about you. You and I both know that is never a good thing."

"I've got it. It's fine. We're gonna get there in four hours. I'm going to put this ski mask on," I say, as I lift it up to prove a point. "I'm going to walk inside the house with this gun," I say, as I wave the gun that's been sitting at my feet. "And then I'm going to shoot him in the head."

"Yeah?" Ronan asks dubiously. "And what will you do if the security alarm goes off? If someone is sleeping next to him? Are you ready to kill them too?"

I falter at that. It's one thing to kill some sleazy dude in his forties that the Brethren put a mark on. It's another entirely to kill an innocent stranger who slept with the wrong man.

"That," he says, pointing his finger at me. "That is what I'm talking about. Whatever you're thinking about, lock it down. You have to do this. If they tell you to eliminate everyone in that house, you do it without hesitation."

"Ronan—"

"No," he snaps. "This is serious, Liam. You could be taken out yourself if you're proven invaluable."

"Well, why the fuck do I even have to prove myself! I'm not going to be an eliminator, what's the fucking problem?"

He blows out a rough breath as he shakes his head.

"The problem is, Christopher gave you a task, and you do it. Period."

I sit with that for a second, not liking the way it twists my stomach.

"Is that what he told you? When you had to kill her?"

Ronan's entire body freezes, his head turning to look at me slowly.

"What?"

I stare at him, unyielding.

"C'mon, Ronan. I know you've heard the rumors, and it wouldn't surprise me if they were true. I just...was it worth it? Killing the woman you love for your brother's favor?"

He's silent for a long time. So long, I assume the topic is dropped. He only speaks through clenched teeth minutes later, his body practically trembling.

"It's complicated."

I scoff at that. "Yeah, everything in this fucked up world is complicated."

Pulling out my phone, I begin typing a message to Skyla. Anything to distract me from what's to come. I'll do this fucking job. I'll put on the show of a fucking lifetime, and then hopefully it'll be enough to get me out of the spotlight. I feel bad for whoever Christopher's attention lands on next, though.

Chapter Nineteen
Skyla

It's Saturday, and with everyone gone for the weekend, it's just Asher with me at the house. I smile when a text comes in from Liam; as I tap out my reply, Asher comes into the kitchen. Looking up from my bowl of cereal at the kitchen island, I smile softly at him.

He smiles back, striding towards me before dropping a kiss to the crown of my forehead. Butterflies erupt inside me at the simple gesture. I still haven't gotten used to this side of Asher. It feels different...yet perfect, all at the same time. Like he was the missing piece to the puzzle.

"I see you've already got yourself a nutritious breakfast," he says, as he moves to the coffee.

"Breakfast of champions," I tease, as I lift my spoon full of cinnamon toast crunch into the air.

Asher smirks as he pours his cup of coffee, facing the bay window that overlooks the backyard as he speaks.

"Well, I think we definitely need to get you a better option for dinner tonight."

"Dinner? I'm already dreaming about lunch."

I laugh because, honestly, it's true. Anyone who isn't looking forward to their next meal as soon as they have their current one...well, they clearly have a healthier relationship with food than I do.

He turns, facing me with that same smile as he nods.

"Lunch too, but I was thinking we could go grab dinner somewhere. Just the two of us."

I go to respond when I pause, noticing how rigid his posture is, how careful his breathing is. He looks nervous, downright petrified. A grin spreads across my face before I can help it, as I cock my head to the side teasingly.

"Asher Putnam, are you trying to ask me out on a date?"

He huffs, running a hand through his hair like he does when he's nervous before he shrugs.

"Well, you're my girl, aren't you?"

I raise an eyebrow in question.

"I don't know, am I?"

He sets down his cup, closing the distance between us before his hand comes to cup my jawline. Lifting my face up to meet his, I feel his lips press against mine in a deep but firm kiss before he pulls away.

"Definitely."

"Well, alrighty then," I say with a breathless smile.

"Dinner? Seven?" he confirms.

"You act like we aren't going to hang out at the house all day together anyways," I laugh.

The smile that takes over his face is breathtaking as he nods and presses another kiss to my lips, softer this time and, unfortunately, faster.

"Fair enough."

We spent the day hanging out at the house. It's been a miserably rainy New England day, so a cozy day inside felt incredible. I spoke on the phone with Aunt Steph for a little while, and she caught me up on her new boyfriend. I may have omitted the whole Asher thing, the ceremony, and having four boyfriend's thing. Oh, and the living off-campus thing. She's so worried about me, and I don't want her to have more reason to because between Christopher, the stalker, and god knows who else...there feels like plenty to worry about.

She told me that she was thinking about coming out for a visit soon, and I practically jumped all over her, begging her to. I miss her so much; I'd give practically anything just to hug her.

After I got off the phone with her, Asher told me he made us dinner reservations and to dress nice for it. I can't lie, I'm excited to have a night with just the two of us. But the whole fancy dinner and getting all dressed up thing just isn't really what I'm up for. It feels too...formal, too forced. I think we've already been through way too much to go through awkward small talk over a basket of eighteen-dollar bread.

Regardless, I slip on a red bodycon dress with my black heels and give myself some big curls before shaking them out. A scar on my back catches my eye in the mirror, and I pause before turning more to face it. A pang of sadness runs through me as I look at the fresh, angry scars against my skin. Why is it that marks like this take so long to heal? Or I guess look better. You never truly heal from a scar. Not from the experience of getting it or the mark itself. Is it weird that, in a twisted way, those lashes bring me a sort of comfort? A sort of reminder.

It's a reminder of what happened that night, between Asher and I. It's a reminder that I got a small peek inside what was no doubt a common occurrence in Asher's childhood. A reminder of how blessed I was to be able to grow up with Aunt Steph instead of my father. It's a reminder of how much hurt is possible in this world, in our world, unless you have the right people by your side.

Shaking myself out of my morose mood, I pair my dress with a bold red lip and soft eye makeup before grabbing my clutch.

When I step out of my room, I'm surprised to see Asher standing by the door, fiddling with the cuff of his sport jacket before he turns to look at me. It's one of those classic Cinderella moments. The ones you see in the movies as a little girl and desperately hope that one day you'll get to experience.

His entire body freezes, his mouth parts, and his eyes take me in. I do my best to glide down the stairs as gracefully as I'm able to, while holding his eye contact. Before I get to the bottom, he moves, meeting me there and offering a hand to help me down. I smile at him, still having to look up at him a bit, even in heels.

"Hi," I say softly.

"Hi," he says, blinking a few times before a small grin that melts me flashes across his face. "You ready?"

I nod as he lowers our hands, intertwining our fingers as he opens the front door and walks me out. We walk down the front steps and over to the side of the driveway, where Asher parks a few of his cars. The garage has two inside, but he still has another four that are parked outside. I think he has a little bit of a car fetish and an unlimited credit limit problem.

Walking over to a car that is always covered, he releases my hand before unclipping the cover. I tilt my head curiously before he pulls it back, revealing a beautiful car. I couldn't tell you what it is, only that it looks fast and classic.

"1968 Dodge Charger," Asher smirks at me as he bundles up the cover and tosses it to the side.

"It's beautiful. Is it worth a lot?" I ask as he walks around to get my door.

"A good amount, but it doesn't compare to some of my others."

My brows furrow. "Why is this one covered and not the others then?"

"It was my mom's."

I'm taken by surprise. Asher never talks about his mom; no one does, really. I can't imagine the hell that poor woman went through being married to Christopher. Even if it was only for a day, that's a day too long, in my opinion.

Asher helps me inside the car, before shutting the door and coming around the other side. I look around at the black leather interior, the scent of it, and something clean mixing in the car. It's absolutely gorgeous and clearly means a lot to him.

The drive to the restaurant goes by fast. Soon, we're being swept away to a fancy table in the back, with a hundred-dollar bottle of champagne and an expansive menu laid out before us. Asher keeps fidgeting in his seat, glancing up at me as I read through the menu.

"You okay?" I ask with a small smile.

"Yeah. Do you like it?"

"The restaurant?" I ask.

He nods.

"Well, yeah. It's beautiful. Are you nervous?" I tease, as I set my menu down.

Asher scoffs. "Me? Nervous? Never. Do you know how many women I've been with? This isn't my first rodeo, princess."

I nod at that, doing my best to fight my smile.

"And tell me, how many of those women did you take to a romantic dinner date?"

His self-assured playboy attitude slips right off, revealing the nervous man behind it that I actually respect.

"You do like it?" he asks, his voice a little softer this time, like he's unsure of himself.

I reach across the table, covering my hand with his as I nod.

"I really do, thank you."

When he exhales, it looks as if a weight lifts from his shoulders.

"Of course."

The waiter comes up to us, and we both decide on the beef welling-ton. Only to be absolutely shocked when the portions on each of our plates is no larger than a silver dollar. Genuinely, if they are going to give you mice-sized servings, shouldn't they put it on a plate that isn't twelve inches in diameter?

Asher and I share a look of disappointment before we crack up laughing. The waiter looks at us uneasily before Asher shakes his head and stands up. He fishes into his pocket, dropping several hundred dollar bills onto the table before offering me his hand.

"Let's get the fuck out of here."

I nod happily, as we practically make a break for it. Though, I don't know why we're rushing, it's not like we didn't pay. Regardless, I'm caught up in the fun of it. It feels as if I'm living out a fantasy, running away from every stuffy and underserved meal I ever had with my father. I'm sure Asher has a feeling akin to that as well.

The gesture was so sweet and would have likely made any other woman swoon. A fancy restaurant, being wined and dined by Asher Putnam, surely is on any woman in Salem's bucket list. Unfortunately for me, the shine of the hundred-dollar plates and million-dollar egos in that restaurant is something I've never had a desired taste for.

When the valet brings us Asher's car, he shakes his head as he rests it against his seat before looking at me.

"I'm sorry," he says, his smile fading. "I don't even know why I tried to take you to a place like that. I'm sure you hate them as much as I do."

I shrug. "It's fine. I was happy there."

"Not as happy as you could be, and I should have known that. I was nervous. I didn't know how to impress you or show you that this..." he trails off, gesturing between us. "I want it to work. I want you, and I want you happy."

My small smile transforms into what feels like a megawatt grin, as I lean over and press my lips to his. When I pull away his eyes look dazed, his body language relaxed.

"I'm happy, right here, with you."

"Good," he says, almost like a whisper to himself. "Now, how about we go somewhere that will actually feed us?"

I laugh and nod my agreement as Asher puts the car in drive, heading for the other side of town.

Two bacon cheeseburgers, two chocolate milkshakes, and one large chili cheese fry later, Asher and I are sitting in his car, having a greasy food feast. I asked him at least half a dozen times if he was sure he wanted to eat in his most prized possession, but he said that it was okay. Still, I'm taking each bite with the utmost care.

A comfortable silence settles over us with the soft sound of a song playing through the speakers. My eyes light up as I make eye contact with Asher and see a small grin on his face. Not wasting a second, I crank the volume almost all the way to the max before I begin belting the song.

"Just a small town girllll! Living in a lonely worlddddd!"

Asher smiles and shakes his head as I continue, egging him on to join me. Unfortunately, he leaves me hanging. I roll my eyes as I continue singing the classic. How can you not love this song?! It gets to the chorus, and I hold my hands out for him as I wiggle my fingers, practically begging him to join. He continues shaking his head before I pick up my shake, using it as a microphone as I sing into it before shoving it in Asher's face.

He looks down at it unimpressed before he takes me by surprise, belting the next line.

"Don't stop believin'!"

"Hold on to the feelin'," I sing with a smile.

"Streetlights, peopleeeeeeeee!"

We both fall apart into a fit of laughter as I set the milkshake down, and Asher reaches over for me, lifting me into his lap. My body is crammed against the steering wheel before he scoots the seat back, giving me a little more room. I feel his hand reach behind me and turn down the music to its original volume.

"God, I fucking love you," he laughs before his body freezes.

I still, staring down at him with surprised eyes. He doesn't try to cover or take it back. Doesn't fumble for his words. Instead, he stays silent, watching me carefully.

"You do?" I ask on a whisper.

He rolls his lips together before his grasp on my hips tighten.

"Yeah, princess. I do. I know I don't deserve to. I don't even deserve to fucking touch you," he says as his fingers flex. "But I've loved you for longer than I wanted to, longer than I should have, probably."

He pauses, looking up at the ceiling as he winces.

"When you said it to me that night...when the first time I heard those words come from your mouth was in that moment, and I knew what I had to do next to protect us, to protect you." Asher swallows roughly and shakes his head before his eyes come to mine.

"I think about that night, every minute of the day. I'm so sorry, Princess. So fucking sorry."

My heart twinges for him, and I lift my hand to cup his face, loving how he immediately sinks into my touch, like he's been craving it his whole life.

"I know. Hindsight, I probably shouldn't have said anything. That was dumb of me. If I could go back, I—"

"Wouldn't change a thing," Asher finishes. "Hearing you say that, seeing the truth in your eyes, it shook something lose in me. It brought me to my knees. That was the instant that I truly accepted that I loved you, so fucking much."

I don't let him speak anymore. Instead, I close the distance between us, covering his mouth with mine. His hands dig into my hips, dragging me closer as his tongue slides against my own. There is nothing soft or romantic about this kiss. Instead, it's carnal, passionate, a desperate need for us to be as close to one another as possible.

My hips begin grinding against his lap, forcing a whimper out of me when I feel Asher's hard cock against my clit. My dress has raised above my hips, only the fabric of my panties and Asher's dress pants in our way. I reach my hand for his zipper when one of his hands grabs my wrist, stopping me.

"No, princess. Not like this, I won't fuck this up twice. You deserve more than a quick fuck in the car. I want to take my time with you."

"Take your time later. I want you, Asher. Now, here, just like this. We have our whole lives to have long, passionate lovemaking," I say, the realization of my words hitting me suddenly. I stumble with my next words for a few seconds, before I speak again. "Uhm, right?"

His eyes darken with lust and something a little more tender.

"Yes, princess. Our entire lives, I'm yours."

He releases my hand, and I quickly unzip his pants, reaching inside and gasping when I realize he isn't wearing any boxers. A sly grin spreads across his ridiculously handsome face as I pull his cock out of his pants.

Obviously, the one and only time I saw Asher's cock, I was a little too...preoccupied to truly admire it, but my god, it might be the prettiest penis I've ever seen. Is that possible? For a penis to be pretty? If so, the award goes to Asher.

"It's all yours, princess. Whatever you want with it," he says, with a low chuckle as he settles back into his seat.

My eyes come to his as I raise up on my knees, lining myself up over him before slowly settling down. I hold my panties to the side as I do, and I can't help but gasp as his cock begins sliding inside me inch by inch. Sex has been getting less painful, but it's still not exactly the most comfortable thing at first.

Lifting my head to look to the roof of the car, I close my eyes when I'm fully seated against him, his cock twitching inside me as a pleasured groan falls from his lips.

"Eyes on me, princess. Let me see those pretty green gems."

I force myself to look down at him, the feeling of his hand skating against my bare thigh forcing a wake of goosebumps to race up my body.

"Asher," I whimper softly.

"Yeah, princess. Use me. I'm yours."

Something flutters inside me at his words, and I lift myself off him almost completely before lowering back down. My rhythm soon picks up, and Asher's hold on me tightens. Any pain that was there quickly slips away, only leaving pleasure and want.

"You look so beautiful like this, Skyla. Just for me. So fucking perfect," he says through clenched teeth.

I lean towards him, forcing my clit to grind against him as I do and causing a moan to tear through me. My thrusts are nearly frantic as Asher meets me with each one. I feel the car shaking, squeaking with each thrust in the busy parking lot.

"Ash, someone is going to see," I whimper.

"I'll gouge their fucking eyes out if they do," he snarls, as his thrusts become punishing. "You're mine, Skyla. My girl, my princess, my wife. You're lucky I share you with the others, but I'll never allow another soul to see you like this again; that's a fucking promise."

My chuckle at his words morph into a groan as his cock rubs against my g-spot just right.

"More like you're lucky they are willing to share me with you.

Vincent still wants you dead," I tease, though the closer I get to my orgasm, the less I care about what we're talking about.

Something akin to a growl sounds through Asher's chest at that, his hand coming up to my neck and squeezing on the sides roughly. I can still breathe easily, but I feel my pulse begin to thunder at the restriction of blood flow.

"All that matters is that you want me. That's all that fucking matters, you hear me?"

I nod my head as much as his hold allows, my eyes shuttering closed as I circle my hips, desperate for just a little more friction.

"Say it," Asher grits out.

"I'm yours, Ash. I'm so completely yours. I want you all the time, forever," I whimper, just as my orgasm slams into me like a freight train.

I hear him curse under his breath, his hips snapping into me several times before letting out a guttural roar. His cock throbs and jerks inside me, as I feel the warmth of his cum flood me.

Slowly, our movements become less steady until they stop altogether. I feel Asher release my neck, pushing my hair out of my face before running his thumb against my cheek tenderly.

"Fuck, I love you," he says, reverence heavy in his tone.

I smile into his touch, a fluttering feeling in my chest.

"I love you too."

Chapter Twenty
Skyla

Vincent got home last night from his job. That's what he calls it, at least. To be honest, I don't ask, and he sure as hell doesn't tell me. All I know is that what he does for the Brethren is violent, and he doesn't like to talk about it. I have an equal amount of curiosity as I do the desire to remain ignorant.

All the guys have essentially moved into the house at this point, and though Asher and I were snuggling in each other's arms last night, that didn't stop Vincent from slipping into bed behind me.

When I woke up, Asher was noticeably absent, and Vincent was already awake, running his fingers through my hair.

"Good morning, Siren."

I smile at him softly, wiping the sleep from my eyes.

"Good morning. How long have you been awake?"

"Not long," he answers, as his tattooed hand tangles with my blonde strands. "Did you have a good night?" he asks, his voice tighter than before.

"I did, how about you?"

"Coming home to you made it worth it," he says, before pressing a kiss to my shoulder.

Smiling, I roll over so that I'm facing him, those silver eyes looking at me as if I hold all the secrets to the universe.

"What?" I laugh.

"Hm?"

"You're staring at me very intently. What's going on in that beautiful mind of yours?" I ask as my fingers play with his hair, pushing it back so I can see him.

"You're just perfect like this, sleepy and comfortable. Safe in my arms."

"And no one else around?" I guess.

"Exactly," he hmphs, as he buries his face into my neck.

We're both quiet for a few seconds before he speaks again.

"I'm beginning to suspect that you'll never choose. That given the choice, you wouldn't."

I swallow, as I think over his words.

"You're right, I don't think I could."

Vincent nods like he expected that but doesn't say anything more.

"How does that make you feel?" I edge.

He releases a rough breath, before he pulls his head away from my neck to look at me.

"I fucking hate it."

I can't help but laugh at him; the man is like a pouty toddler.

"But sharing you is better than not having you at all, I suppose."

"You sure about that?" I ask, semi-teasing, but also kind of hoping he will drop this idea that I'll just run away with him one day.

His eyes flick back and forth between my own as he speaks.

"I'm getting used to it. It's not in my nature to compromise; you have to give me some grace here."

A chuckle escapes me as I nod, pressing a soft kiss to his lips.

"I know, and I know how unfair it is of me to ask you to be okay with it all. If you came to me and said that you had fallen in love with another woman. That you wanted me to share you with her, I'd—"

"Never be put in that position," Vincent finishes. "Ever. All I see is you; all I breathe is you. You rule my entire world. I have no doubt you'll rule my afterlife as well. Everything, forever, is you, Siren."

My heart skips a beat, literally. His words are so raw, so perfect, that it affects my current heart rhythm. Before I can even attempt to formulate a response, I feel his lips dust against my forehead and then again to my nose before moving to my lips. Our mouths move together effortlessly, like they were always meant to. Everything with Vincent is so easy, so intrinsic, like we are one soul divided in two.

I feel his hands glide up and down my sides, slipping beneath the hem of my tank top. His hand cups one of my breasts, thumb flicking against my nipple in a way that has me gasping into his mouth.

The door opens to my left, and I break away from Vincent to see Liam in a black t-shirt and a pair of jeans. His eyes land on us, practically lighting up when he understands what he's just walked in on.

"Don't stop on my account, pretend I'm not even here," Liam says, as he kicks his shoes off and grips the back of his shirt, pulling it over his head and tossing it to the ground.

"I always do," Vincent snarks before one of his hands grasps my chin, forcing my eyes back on him before he's back to kissing me.

I hear the sound of Liam's jeans hit the floor, before the bed besides me dips. A hand slides around my throat, pulling me towards him. He smiles down at me, his green eyes looking a little dimmer than normal, but that bright smile is all I can focus on.

"Hi, babygirl. I missed you."

"I missed you, too," I say before his mouth is on mine.

His hands roam across my body, and I notice Vincent pull away. Before I can ask him where he's going though, I feel my sleep shorts slip off my legs and Vincent's hands spreading my thighs apart. I moan into Liam's mouth as I feel Vincent's tongue run through me before circling my clit.

Liam pulls away, smirking as Vincent hooks my thighs over his shoulders.

"Yeah, eat that pussy, Vinny. Look at you being such a good boy," Liam praises teasingly.

Vincent's eyes snap up to Liam, irritation heavy in them before he ignores him, doubling his efforts while slipping a finger inside me. I gasp at the feeling when two more figures appear in the doorway, plates of food in their hands as they still.

Ronan and Asher stare at us for several seconds, me practically naked, Liam fully naked, and Vincent between my thighs. Surprisingly, Ronan doesn't hesitate. He sets the plates on the ground and crosses the room, shoving Liam's shoulder so hard he falls to the ground.

"Hey!" he grouses, as Ronan cups the back of my neck and smashes his lips to mine.

"I've missed you, so fucking much," he grumbles before moving to my neck.

"I missed you too," I gasp as Vincent's tongue flicks against my clit, his fingers massaging my g-spot.

I reach my hand out for Ronan's pants, fumbling with the belt before he quickly undoes it with one hand. My hand wraps around his cock through his boxers before I pull it out. I feel his hand come behind my head before guiding me to it.

His cock slides into my mouth, pushing until I gag around it and he groans. Again, I feel Vincent shift as he pulls his fingers and mouth away from me. I whimper at the loss, but it's short-lived, before I feel the head of his cock pushing inside me.

Moaning around Ronan's cock, my eyes swing over to Vincent as best I can as he grips my hips. In the next moment, Liam is by my side, somehow just to the side of Ronan before his mouth closes around my nipple. Asher comes to my other side, repeating the action to my other breast, and instantly, I'm in heaven.

Since Asher and I have become...official, I guess, we haven't all had sex. This is the first time we are all together, and something feels incredibly perfect about it. Ronan and Vincent's thrusts seem to fall into a similar rhythm as Asher and Liam lavish me with kisses, their tongues twirling around my nipples while Asher begins nipping at me.

I'm no longer in control of my body as the overstimulation becomes too much. I don't even realize that I'm coming until it's too late. My body shakes, and my muffled screams rumble against Ronan's cock as my pussy throbs around Vincent.

I feel Vincent tense first as he follows, shortly before Ronan does as well, his warm cum coating my tongue as he fucks it further down my throat. I swallow him down quickly, before I look to see Liam and Asher stroking their cocks while sucking on my tits. I go to ask them if they are going to switch places with Vincent and Ronan, but before I can, they both pull away from my tits. They lean over me, both covering my stomach and chest with their cum. Holy shit. Talk about a brother bond.

They both collapse against the bed, and all that can be heard in the room is heavy breathing. Eventually, Ronan and Vincent both pull out of me as Liam stands and moves to the bathroom. He grabs a warm washcloth and begins cleaning up the mess they left behind.

When I'm all cleaned up, Asher helps me get dressed before settling me back into bed. Ronan brings over a plate of eggs, pancakes, and bacon before sitting beside me. Liam and Vincent grab their own plates, as well as Asher's, before they take a seat at the foot of the bed. We all eat with very little words exchanged, the post orgasm high still heavily weighted over us all.

Jesus, I wouldn't mind that kind of a wake-up call every morning from now on.

The next day, we all had different things to do. Ronan had to go help some of the other legacies, Vincent had to go report on his latest job, and Liam had to have lunch with his parents. Maggie ended up calling me, asking if I wanted to go to the mall to which I obviously accepted. Since Asher and I were out of school for a few weeks and with Thanksgiving break next week, we haven't gotten to see each other much lately.

Asher is currently driving us back from the mall, the back of his Range Rover absolutely filled to the brim with bags. My father is good for one thing— that handy black card.

For a moment, Asher tried to pay for my things, until I reminded him that I wanted my father to see the outrageous credit card bill. That after everything he was a part of, the least he could do was buy me a few new outfits. Or ten, whatever.

I watch as he drives with one hand, his other intertwined with mine, resting on the center console as I turn in my seat to face Maggie. She watches us with a sly grin before speaking.

"I like you guys together. You're a hot couple."

Asher scoffs, but doesn't say anything as I roll my eyes at her.

"Thanks, Mags. That's what we were going for."

She shrugs and laughs. Well, I don't know what the requirements to enter your harem are! Judging by the current members, I'd guess it's one of the base-level requirements."

"The current members?" I ask with my brows raised and a shake of my head.

"Yeah. Hey, how do those members 'members' compare?"

"Jesus Christ," Asher grumbles under his breath.

"What?" Maggie defends.

"Aren't you supposed to be a lesbian?" Asher asks.

"Just because I like pussy doesn't mean I can't admire a fine penis. I'm queer, not blind."

I can't help but laugh. There is no way in hell I'm discussing my boyfriends' penises with her, especially not in front of one of them.

"That's why you guys were gone for those two weeks, huh? A little delayed honeymoon? Some good ole post-wedding boning?"

Asher and I tense at her words, not responding as I turn to face forward in the seat. I glance at Asher to see his shoulders are tight, his grip on the steering wheel practically punishing. I continue holding his hand with my right one as I reach over with my left, rubbing soft circles against his back in a spot where I know several scars reside.

They are healing well, but both of our backs will never be the same. Even with plastic surgery, it will always look...off. I'd still do it again if given the choice. I'd jump in front of a million whips for Asher, and I know he'd do the same for me, probably tenfold.

Maggie is smart enough to realize she's struck a nerve and none of us speak for the rest of the ride back to our house. When we park, we move Maggie's bags to her car before Asher and I carry all mine upstairs.

"So, have you guys gotten one of those ginormous Alaskan kings yet? Or a custom-made bed that goes from like wall to wall?" Maggie asks, as she trudges up the stairs behind us.

"No, why?" I laugh.

"Well, I'm just saying, five people in one bed sounds like a space issue. I'd want to be able to spread out during group playtime."

Asher's nose wrinkles at that. "Can you not call it that."

"Fine, group fuck-sesh time. Better?" Maggie amends.

Asher rolls his eyes at her, giving me a look that screams, 'are you sure you want to be friends with her?'. I smile and nod, wordlessly answering that even though I love him, I love Maggie too. She will not be going anywhere.

When we get to my room, I push the door open, moving over to the armchair in the corner. and dumping my bags onto it. I turn to take the bags from Asher when I pause. He's still in the doorway, body frozen in place as he stares at my bed. My eyes follow his before a cold chill sets in. Oh my god.

The mattress has been sliced open, literally. A jagged cut through the material leading down to a sunken knife. That's not the only thing on the bed, though. Beneath the knife is a picture; technically, the picture is stabbed through. Slowly, I take a few steps forward, my hands shaking as I get a better look at it. My stomach rolls the instant I do, and I immediately regret my choice.

It's from yesterday, all five of us tangled up on the bed together. The image captured is a private moment, one drenched in passion and love, feelings that are easily conveyed through the photograph. The most chilling part, though? The angle is obviously taken from my closet.

My eyes look up to see Asher already staring in that direction, before he dumps my bags on the floor and begins ripping through my closet. Piece by piece, my clothes, shoes, and bags are thrown to the ground as Asher hastily searches for a camera. When he doesn't find what he's looking for, he punches a hole in the wall, grabbing the broken sheetrock and ripping it apart as he searches deeper.

I don't realize that my entire body is shaking until Maggie is beside me, wrapping her arms around me in an attempt to stabilize me.

"Are you okay?" she asks softly.

Asher's head whips in my direction, eyes wild and panicked.

"D-did you find anything?" I ask.

He shakes his head.

"S-sso that means, he was there? Taking the pictures real time, as we were...."

My skin crawls at the thought, goosebumps scattering across my body. There was no letter this time, no note. The intention far too clear, though.

Chapter Twenty One
Skyla

Asher immediately called the calvary in. In a matter of an hour, all four of them plus Wesley were here, prior responsibilities abandoned. They all started screaming at each other, Ronan actually putting hands on Asher when Wesley pulled him away. Ronan blames Asher because he assured everyone the house is well equipped with security, and it is, at least I thought it was.

Liam hasn't left my side; some part of him knowing that I need him. While Vincent, Asher, Ronan, and Wesley have some kind of blame-game pissing match. Maggie slipped out quietly when the chaos began, can't blame her. I wouldn't want to be here either.

"How you doing, babygirl?" Liam asks, with a squeeze against my thigh.

I look over to him numbly, he's hard to see through my watery eyes.

"I'm scared," I say, though my voice lacks any real emotion. I sound more like a robot than anything.

He frowns, wrapping his arm around my shoulders tightly, as he kisses the side of my head.

"I know. We all are. Why do you think they are tearing each other's heads off? They all are scared for you, even Wesley. I think he has a little crush on you," Liam teases, in a way that tells me he's trying to get a reaction out of me. It doesn't work, though.

Wesley looks over to us like he heard Liam before those concerned blue eyes land on me. He doesn't come closer, and he doesn't say anything, but there are so many emotions playing across his face it damn near hits me square in the chest.

Turning back to the guys, his demeanor changes, and one word has everyone quieting.

"Enough!"

Everyone in the room stares at him, and he takes his time collecting his thoughts before he speaks again.

"It doesn't matter whose fault it is or how the guy got in. What matters is we prevent it from happening again. Ronan and I will sweep this place top to bottom, installing new security measures that will turn this place into an extravagant bunker. Anyone who wants to help is welcome."

Without another word, he stalks off to his car, Asher and Vincent hot on his heels as Ronan hangs back. He comes over to me, sitting beside me on the couch as he cups my knee.

"What can I do, baby?"

I shake my head. "I just want to feel safe. I'm tired of this. Every time we start to let our guard down, he shows back up again. He's getting more violent. What if he tries to hurt me or one of you or—"

"He won't get the opportunity. He's been relatively quiet because he hasn't had the same access that he did to you at school. I don't know how he managed to get inside this time, but I can promise you it was a mistake that will not be repeated."

I nod.

"This is what Wesley specializes in; there is no one with better access to tech apart from maybe the Hutchinson's."

"That's good," I say, doing my best to sound enthusiastic but knowing that it all just sounds flat.

Ronan fakes a smile as he nods. "It is. We're gonna keep you safe, baby. Okay?"

I nod again, and he gives me another smile that looks a lot less convincing than before as he stands up, following Wesley and the guys. Liam squeezes me once, forcing me to look at him.

"Will you eat something for me? If I have something delivered or I make something?"

My stomach revolts at the idea of food, but I can tell this is his way of trying to help. He knows that there is nothing he can actually do to put me at ease, but he's trying. So, I lie. I give him my most convincing smile that I can muster and nod.

He practically leaps to his feet with relief as he pulls out his phone.

"What are you in the mood for? Pizza? Burgers? Thai? Indian?"

I shrug. "Variety?"

We do have six people at the house currently, wouldn't hurt to have a little bit of everything. Liam nods as his fingers begin flying across the screen. Unfortunately, my phone begins ringing and when I look down to see who it is, I know I have to answer.

Steph and I planned a call the other night and I missed it. She tried to call me again shortly after we found the bed upstairs, so I obviously missed that one. She's just going to worry if I don't answer.

Maybe she should.

Begrudgingly I answer the phone, doing my best to sound as normal as possible.

"Hey!"

"What's wrong?" Steph counters.

Well, I tried.

"Nothing, sorry I missed you. I was shopping with Maggie."

"Uh huh, and why does your voice sound like that?" she asks.

"Like what?"

"Like you're one second away from crying."

I could play this a hundred different ways, but I figure the safest and easiest is to blame my father.

"Just got in a fight with dad about school stuff. I'm fine."

"What's his problem? You're doing great in all your classes."

"I don't know," I say, with a heavy sigh that isn't all that forced.

Aunt Steph lets out an irritated grumble.

"I'm sorry, sweetheart. How is that asshole fiancé of yours? Still the worst?"

My eyes come to Asher's, a small smile spreading across his face when he looks at me.

"No, he's actually pretty great."

"What?" Steph practically gasps.

"Just a few weeks ago, you were telling me how horrible he treats you."

I shrug, staring at my nails.

"I don't know. Things have changed. We've spent some time together, gotten to know each other. He's good to me now."

She's silent for several seconds before she speaks.

"Just be careful, sweetheart. The Putnam men are...complicated."

I do my best to hold back my derisive snort. Yeah, no shit.

We stay on the phone for a little longer, catching up and promising to talk soon when Wesley walks in, installing a camera in the corner of the living room. His large arms reach above his head, the drill in one hand and camera in the other as he secures it. I can't help but admire the way the muscles of his shoulders bunch up, flexing beneath his grey t-shirt.

My eyes roam down the smooth surface, the shirt hugging him like a second skin as it wraps around his tapered waistline before stopping where his jeans pick up. His ass is full and round, not in an over-the-top way, but in a way that he should definitely be getting some endorsement deals because, my god, that is a biteable ass.

He must feel my eyes on him, or maybe I said that out loud because he turns around, eyes locking onto mine before smirking. Clearly caught ogling, I watch as his eyes begin roaming over me from head to toe before settling back on my face. Wesley shakes his head, looking back to the wall in a way that has me curious.

I stand to my feet as I cock my head to the side.

"What?"

He doesn't turn around, just shakes his head.

"Nothing."

Furrowing my brows, I cross the room coming to stand beside him. He towers over me, but that doesn't stop me from forcing him to make eye contact with me.

"Tell me."

He blows out a short breath before looking down at me. His blue eyes are sharp, more intense than usual, for sure. I watch as his shoulders square off, like he's standing a little taller.

"I was thinking that you shouldn't look at me like that."

A pang of embarrassment runs through me as I shake my head.

"I wasn't looking at you like anything."

He raises a disbelieving eyebrow but doesn't say anything.

"I wasn't!" I defend.

Wesley just continues to stare at me before shaking his head.

"Whatever you say, little one."

He gets back to what he was doing, and for some reason, my mouth moves before my brain can tell it to shut the hell up.

"Why? For argument's sake, why shouldn't I be looking at you?"

"You can look at me," Wesley answers, before his eyes drop down to mine. He takes a half a step closer, until our chests brush against each other as he angles his head down to me.

"But if I catch you looking at me like you want to know what I taste like again, I will satisfy that curiosity without an ounce of hesitation."

His bold words take me surprise, but then again, so do my own when I reply.

"How?"

A sexy smirk lifts his mouth as his thumb reaches up, running over my lips. He does it slowly but with enough pressure that he's able to pull my lower lip down.

"By stuffing this pretty little mouth with my cock," he says simply, releasing my lip with his final word.

My eyes widen as all the air in the room is suddenly sucked straight out. I can't breathe, or maybe I'm breathing too much. The tension is so fucking thick I'm practically suffocating, but fuck me, I can't find it in me to move from my spot.

"I don't think the guys would like that very much," I defend weakly.

"Probably not, but I think you would."

Holy fucking shit. He has never been flirty with me like this. We don't banter. He drives me around. We make small talk. That's it. I thought Liam was just teasing me before. Now, I have a feeling he was trying to give me a heads-up.

"You act like it wouldn't be the best day of your life," I scoff, trying desperately to get the attention off of me because what the hell is going on?

That same smirk is still in place as he nods.

"I won't deny that at all. I've spent way too much time...fantasizing," he says, his eyes running down my body before coming back up again.

"About what?" I practically whisper.

Wesley tilts his head to the side curiously, a single brow risen in surprise, as he sets down the drill and adjusts his stance. I have no choice but to bump against the wall, and before I can move, he cages me in with his palms pressed against the wall above my head.

"You sure you want to know, little one?"

I hesitate for a moment before nodding.

His tongue pokes out, running along his lower lip as he inches his face towards mine until our noses brush against one another.

"An answer like that will cost you, you willing to pay?"

I don't speak, mainly because I don't remember how to. All I can do is intake oxygen, output carbon dioxide, and stare into those dark blue eyes.

"What's going on?" Ronan asks, forcing me to physically jump before my head whips over to him.

Wesley drops his head like he's disappointed for a second. His mouth bumping against my neck in what I think is an accident before he stands up fully. He pushes away from the wall before bending down and picking up the drill.

"Not much, got that one hung. Gonna go throw a couple in the garage and laundry room."

Ronan's eyes narrow, but he doesn't say anything as Wesley leaves the room. As soon as he's out of sight, Ronan begins casually strolling over to me, a curious tilt to his head.

"Baby?" he asks softly.

"Yeah?" I rasp, clearing my throat as I look up to him.

"Am I going to have to stop introducing you to other men? I know I said I'd share you with as many as it took, but you know you don't have to make it a 'how many boyfriends can I collect' game, right?"

Well, if I wasn't already feeling bad about my reaction to Wesley, I feel fucking terrible now. I push away from the wall, moving to walk past him, when Ronan catches my arm easily, a chuckle escaping him as he shakes his head.

"Hey, now. Don't be like that. I'm just teasing you. What am I supposed to do when I find my girl all hot and heavy with my bond brother?"

"It wasn't like that," I say weakly.

Ronan's brows rise. "So, now we're lying to each other?"

I blow out a breath and shake my head as I look away.

"I think he's attractive. He called me out for staring too long. That was it."

"I don't know," Ronan says as his hand comes to cup my jaw, tilting it up so that I can face him. "Looked like it could have been more to me."

I shrug my shoulders, not knowing what to say, as Ronan leans towards my neck, his mouth grazing against the same spot that Wesley's did.

"What have you done to me? I've always been a jealous fucking bastard, but the idea of sharing you, it's so fucking hot."

"It is? I thought Liam was the only one into it."

He shakes his head against my neck before looking at me, his grip on me firm.

"We're all into it, baby, because it's you. You're the sexiest fucking woman on the planet, and watching you be worshipped by the others is like my own tailor fitted porn."

"I like that," I say softly. "I like that you're into it, not that you just put up with it."

Ronan shakes his head again.

"Wesley would be into it too, if that's something you ever wanted to explore."

My mouth opens, but I don't know how to respond. Thankfully, I don't have to because Liam walks in with arms filled with bags of food. I take the very graciously gifted out to move away from Ronan, helping Liam with the bags before unpacking all the food. I still feel Ronan's eyes trained on me, but I do my best to ignore it, smiling up at Liam as if everything is fine when, in fact, there is very little in my life that could be described as fine.

Chapter Twenty Two
Liam

Once the house was officially pimped out, Ronan had to get back to his brother's house, something about an update on the other legacies. I don't know how the fuck he can even be in the same room as Christopher after what he did to Skyla and Asher. I'm thankful I haven't had to, but I know the time is coming, and soon.

Vincent also had to get back to his meeting, that he literally ran out on when Asher called him in a panic. Wesley surprisingly stuck around, making up excuses of double and triple checking all the bars we installed on the outside of all the windows and doors. Though, not that surprising as his eyes tracked to Skyla's every other second, when he thought nobody was looking. Asher and I were always looking though, the whole time.

Eventually, he ran out of excuses for being here and left as well. It was just Asher, Skyla, and me. We're sitting on the couch downstairs, Skyla watching some comfort TV show while Asher and I play black-jack. He's all pissy right now because I'm banker, and he's on his last dollar bill.

He throws it down aggressively just as I flip over a king and an ace. Goddamn, beautiful. Can a pair of cards get any prettier than that?

Asher, being the sore loser he is, kicks at the table, pouring himself a drink from the scotch bottle before grumbling in his seat. I chuckle at his sour mood, pocketing all his cash before pouring myself a glass. I lift it to my mouth, tipping it back when I notice Skyla staring at me.

"What does that taste like?"

"Fire," Asher grouches.

I reach around Skyla, smacking Asher in the back of the head.

"Stop being a pouty bitch. Our girl wants to know what scotch tastes like. I think it's only polite we give her a taste."

"Oh, I don't want a glass. I was just curious."

I smirk at her.

"Who said anything about a glass, babygirl?"

Curiosity sparks in those beautiful green eyes before I sit up, facing her fully. My hand comes up to cup her cheeks, squeezing slightly.

"Open."

She does as I say, excitement flaring to life in those irises, while I lift my glass to my mouth with my other hand, taking a small sip before setting it down.

The alcohol burns, but I can't help but drag this moment out for a little longer before I spit it into her waiting mouth. Surprise flashes across her face, and she quickly swallows it down before coughing. My eyes meet Asher's over her head; his pupils dilated, face drenched in lust as I nod to him and release Skyla's cheeks.

Before she has a moment to say anything, Asher lifts the bottle to his mouth, taking a larger pull than I did before yanking her jaw to face him, spitting the contents into her mouth and down her throat. She swallows roughly before Asher smashes his lips to hers, his tongue clearly chasing the taste down. My cock immediately hardens at the sight. Goddamnit, I wish I would have done that.

They are so lust drunk they practically fall into my lap, the back of Skyla's head inches from my cock as Asher covers her body with his. I watch in rapt fascination as they devour each other in front of me. I run my fingers through Skyla's hair, before dragging my fingertips down her cheek and over her chest. Her eyes open, making eye contact with me as she pulls away from Asher.

He breathes heavily like he just came up for air as she sits up, arching her neck to meet my mouth as I close the distance between us.

Her pillowy lips are like heaven against mine, soft and smooth. My tongue strokes against hers as my hand cups the front of her throat when I feel her body being tugged away from me.

Asher, the greedy little fucker, literally drags her out of my lap, yanks down her leggings, and begins eating her pussy. I'd be pissed off if I didn't love where this is going. Skyla moans at the feeling, before wrapping her legs around Asher's neck like a goddamn succubus ready to consume him whole. I don't think he'd be all that mad about it, considering the hot as fuck groans coming from him as well.

I pull my cock out of my pants, spitting into my hand before dragging it up and down my length as I watch them. Skyla's hands dig into Asher's hair, her hips lifting to grind against his face as I slowly pick up my pace. Asher's hand slips between her thigh, a finger or two slipping inside her if her gasp is anything to go off of.

My cock jerks in reaction, and I groan as my hand moves faster. Asher's eyes fly open, coming directly to me as they do. I won't even pretend that when my cock jerks again, it has nothing to do with Asher's eyes on me. Sure, he's my best friend and he's very obviously straight, but it doesn't mean I don't find him attractive. In fact, he's hot as fuck, and having him watch me stroke my cock while he's eating my girl's pussy, yeah, I'm fucking turned on.

He pulls away from Skyla, his hand coming down and slapping her clit. She arches her back, a whimper escaping her as he speaks.

"Get up there and suck Liam's cock for him, princess."

Skyla does as he says, quickly flipping over onto her stomach and crawling up to me. I spread my legs as wide as I can, giving her the room she needs before her mouth sucks me down her throat. My mouth parts, and I feel my head hit the armrest of the couch as I groan.

Fuck. Yes.

She takes it slow at first, bobbing her head up and down. She's getting so fucking good. She hardly ever gags these days, and she's really learned to open up her throat. I don't know who taught her that one, but goddamn, I owe him a blowjob just for that.

My hand trails over her perfect face before weaving through her golden hair. I spin the silky strands around my fist several times until I have a nice hold on her. Looking up, I watch as Asher grabs her hips, forcing her up onto her knees before he lines his cock up to her, pushing inside with a guttural groan that makes my cock jerk down Skyla's throat.

Goddamnit. I don't think I've ever noticed how sexy his moans are.

Skyla moans around my cock; she's thrown off for a moment before her and Asher fall into a nice rhythm. Meanwhile, I lay back like a fucking king as I have my beautiful girl suck my cock like a pro.

My head is thrown back against the couch, eyes lazily watching Skyla take me, her tongue twirling around each piercing before going down again when Asher catches my eye. He's watching her intently, his thrusts becoming more and more aggressive. I watch as his knuckles practically turn white from his grip on her hips as he savagely fucks her.

It seems to be too much for her as she pulls away from me for a second, gasping deep breaths. I'm so fucking close to coming, but I know she needs a second. Apparently, Asher doesn't agree, though. He reaches down, gripping the back of her neck before lifting her over to me.

"No breaks. Be a good girl and suck the cum out of him," he says through clenched teeth.

Asher doesn't release his hold on her. Instead, he uses his grip to practically fuck my cock with her face. He shoves her down over and over again, his thrusts becoming erratic as he continues staring at the slobbery mess that Skyla's leaving all over my cock.

I know it doesn't mean anything to him, but having him take control like this, forcing her head down onto me like this, him practically feral to make sure she makes both of us come...it's my fucking undoing.

Tightening my grip on her hair, I feel Asher push her down once more, hard, my cock pushing down her throat as my cum spills down her.

"Yeah, good girl. Drink, princess. Don't you fucking waste a goddamn drop," Asher groans, before his eyes roll into the back of his head, and he cums.

Several low moans tear through his chest as Skyla follows him, moaning and screaming her release with her mouth still full of my cock.

After several seconds, Asher opens his eyes, shaking his head as he looks down at me. Our eyes lock for several seconds, but neither of us speak. Things I shouldn't be thinking, shouldn't be wondering, pop into my head, but before I can truly explore them, his eyes look down at Skyla.

He releases his hold on her, rolling onto his back, his hard cock still holding strong as he takes deep, labored breaths. Of course, I'm going to stare at it, at least for a second; who wouldn't? God, he's got a pretty fucking cock.

"You okay?" Skyla asks me breathlessly from my lap.

My eyes snap down to hers, a smirk on my face.

"I'm on cloud fucking nine right now, babygirl. What about you?"

"Same," she smiles.

"Motion carried," Asher snarks on a labored breath, before pushing to his feet, stuffing his cock back into his pants, and moving to the kitchen.

Fuck. Ronan and Vincent should leave the house more often.

Chapter Twenty Three
Skyla

The next day goes by smoothly. There is no altercations at school, no tests or papers due that I forgot about, and Vincent was even able to pull me into the closet for a quickie. It's been a great day.

That is until Asher pulls into the driveway of our house, and I see a very pissed-off looking Aunt Steph just outside the gate.

Oh shit.

"Who is that?" Asher asks.

"My aunt," I respond.

"She looks mad," he says.

I glance down at my engagement ring. I've been wearing it more often lately. Asher said he was going to get a wedding band added to it soon, since everyone knows we are essentially married anyways. Slipping the ring off my hand, I put it in my purse. I don't miss the way Asher frowns as he watches me do so, but he doesn't say anything.

"Oh, she is," I say, before I open my door and slide out of the car.

"Hey! What are you doing here?" I ask as I walk towards her.

"Skyla Ann, what the fuck is going on here!" she seethes.

First and middle name, I'm in for it.

"Where exactly? Like here, at school, or just in general?" I ask, causing smoke to practically billow out of her ears.

"Since *when* did you move off campus? Since *when* did you move in here? Why the fuck did the front office tell me that you moved in with your *husband?*" she snaps, shooting a glare at Asher, who chose now to exit the car.

"Is this the little shit?" she practically snarls, storming her way up to us.

"I'm Asher Putnam. Skyla has told me a lot about—"

His words are cut off with a sharp slap. His head snaps to the side as I push Steph away.

"That's for how you treated my niece, you little fucker! You're just like your father, all of you are the same!"

Asher doesn't respond, and to my surprise, he doesn't get mad either. He just stands there stoically and lets Steph get out all her rage.

"That's enough. I get that you're mad, but take it up with me," I say, as I stand in front of Asher protectively.

She looks at me as if I've grown two heads, before she blinks rapidly.

"How could you not tell me? How could you not invite me to the wedding?" she asks, emotion choking her as she looks away harshly.

"We haven't had a wedding yet, technically."

"Then how are you married?" she asks, her eyes narrowing before they widen. "No...sweetheart. You...you didn't. They didn't..."

I wordlessly nod. Clearly she already knows what happened, though I'm not sure how. It's obvious the knowledge of the ritual is very sacred.

Her hand scrambles for mine, pulling my branded palm to her face before unshed tears fill her eyes. She pulls me into her, hugging me tightly to her chest in a way that feels like coming home. I wrap my arms around her tightly, a relief like I didn't know I needed wrapping around me. We stand there for I don't even know how long, but it's not long enough. Mad at me or not, I've missed her so much.

When we pull apart, she quickly wipes away her tears before brushing a few of my own away.

"Well, are you going to show me around this mansion or what?" she asks with a sad smile.

"Yeah, come on," I say, as I loop my arm through hers and walk her to the front door. Asher jogs in front of us, unlocking the metal bar door that now sits outside our wooden door before placing his finger on the biometric scanner, as well as scanning his eye through a retina scanner. Once all of that is done, he inserts a key, unlocking the deadbolt.

I glance at Steph to see her watching Asher with a worried furrow to her brow. As soon as the door opens though, the frown slips away as her eyes begin eating up the space. Asher politely bows out, allowing Steph and I time to visit, as I give her a tour through the house. I tell her about when Asher and I first came here, it was empty, and he had it set up exactly as I envisioned it.

We didn't get into the details of the ceremony, or what has occurred since, and I'm grateful for that. I don't think I could handle it right now.

Eventually, we make our way downstairs to the kitchen, where she decides she's going to cook us dinner.

"Oh, that's okay. We usually get takeout," I say.

"All the more reason," she says, as she steps into the pantry.

I hear the front door open and shut, two pairs of footsteps sounding through the house. My wide eyes come to Asher, who curses under his breath.

Shit.

"Babygirl! We brought food! I hope you're hungry. Vincent made me order double everything because he's a creep and tracks your cycle. Says you're about to start your period any day now, and it wouldn't hurt to have some of your favorites around the house."

Liam and Vincent walk into the kitchen; Vincent carrying two large bags of groceries while Liam is carrying three bags of what smells like Chinese. My stomach growls in appreciation, but when Liam leans down to kiss me, I know we won't be eating anytime soon.

Steph pops out of the pantry, cocking her head to the side as she stares at Liam before moving to Vincent and then to me.

"Sky...who are these...boys?"

I lick my lips, not finding the words to describe our situation. Well, best to just rip off the band-aid.

"My boyfriends," I answer simply.

Steph doesn't react; her face is frozen as she stares at me, almost waiting for me to elaborate. When I don't, her eyes swing back and forth between everyone in the room.

"All of them?"

"Technically, I'm her husband, and they are the boyfriends," Asher adds unhelpfully.

I make that known with the irritated look I shoot him.

"No," Aunt Steph says.

We all glance at each other before I tilt my head.

"What?"

"No. Break up with them, right now."

When no one reacts to that, she slams her hand against the island, startling me as she shouts.

"Break up with them, right fucking now! I will not watch you make the same mistakes she did, suffer the same fate. No, no, no! Break up with them!"

"Hey now," Liam says with raised hands. "Let's just take a breath. No need to shout."

She turns on him like a cornered animal, practically gnashing her teeth at him.

"There is every reason to shout! Do you have any idea what the Brethren will do to her if they find out? She's making a mockery out of a match! Do you know how fast Christopher will have her throat slit! He will send the nearest eliminator and—"

"That would be me," Vincent answers coolly, taking several steps forward until he is toe to toe with her.

I feel him wedge himself between us, like he's trying to protect me. He can't see it, but she'd never hurt me. She's just terrified for me, and honestly, rightfully so.

"And I can assure you, I'd suffer a thousand deaths before I allow any harm to come to her," he continues.

Steph's jaw is tight, as she shakes her head and throws her hands up.

"This cannot be happening! Not again, you can't ask me to live through this again, Sky. I can't!" she snaps frantically.

"Live through what? Who are you talking about?" I ask, pausing for a moment as I guess. "Mom?"

She looks away from me roughly, shaking her head as she mutters something to herself that I can't quite make out. Of course, what better timing would there be for Ronan to make his grand entrance? When his footsteps sound through the house, Steph's accusing eyes fly to mine before Ronan crests the corner. When she does, her mouth drops.

"Ronan?"

His eyebrows raise in surprise as he looks at her.

"Stephanie, It's been a while."

She stares at him before her head turns to me, that look of shock morphing to judgment as she shakes her head. A bitter laugh escapes her, as she tosses her hands out at her sides.

"Please, please, for the love of god, tell me you are not sleeping with my niece."

Ronan stands a little taller but doesn't speak, causing Steph to shout once more.

"What the fuck, Skyla! Oh my god. It's bad enough you're cheating on Christopher's son, but you're doing so with his BROTHER! Let me guess, you both are legacies as well?" she asks Liam and Vincent.

They nod as she runs her hands through her hair.

"She's not cheating on me," Asher clarifies. "She's in a relationship with all of us."

"That doesn't matter to the Brethren, and you know it! What happens when it's time to produce your heir, hm? How will you know which one knocks her up?"

"It wouldn't matter. Any child she has will be mine, biologically so or not, doesn't matter to me," Asher says confidently, crossing his arms across his chest.

My heart swells at his words, my dumb, lovestruck brain running wild with images of me having a baby, all these wonderful men by my side every step of the way and loving that baby unconditionally. Is that too much to ask? Probably, actually, definitely. Still, it's one hell of a fantasy.

"You'll all be married off. What, you're gonna cheat on your wives? Get them on board with this? Put Skyla at even more risk?" Steph guffaws.

"We haven't gotten that far," Liam interjects. "We're taking things step by step."

"Oh," she says sarcastically. "Well, when that goes to shit, what the fuck do you think is going to happen to my niece? If you truly cared about her, you'd stay the hell away from her, you especially," she says, pointing to Ronan.

He doesn't seem phased as he lets her rage and shout. When she has no choice but to take a breath, he speaks.

"Stephanie, I understand this is a shock to you and I know that you're concerned for Skyla's safety. We all are. It's all any of us ever think about. She is our number one priority. You can trust us."

"You and I both know trust is not something to be had in Salem," she snaps back.

"How do you guys know each other exactly?" Liam asks.

Steph rolls her eyes at him.

"Before I moved to London with Skyla, I was just as a part of this world as you all are. Born and raised in Salem, graduated from Gallows Hill. Watched as my sister became a pawn in this fucked up quest for power before she was ripped away from us."

"What do you mean?" I ask, noting that's the third time she's brought up my mom in some way. "What happened to Mom, Steph?"

She looks at me, shaking her head from side to side.

"I can't."

"Yes, you can. I'm right here. Please," I beg.

She shakes her head faster, a choked sob ripping through her chest.

"I can't, Sky. I can't. If I tell, they kill me. If I tell, they kill you. I can't, I'm sorry. I can't, can't," she says, as she breaks off into a fit of sobs.

I move towards her, wrapping my arms around her as she cries into my neck. I hush her softly, sending worried eyes to the guys who all watch us with varying looks.

"C'mon. Let's get you upstairs," I say, as I begin walking her towards the staircase.

To my surprise, she doesn't fight me and when I open one of the spare rooms, she lays down almost immediately. I lie beside her, running my hand in circles on her back like she always did for me as a child. Eventually, her sobs quiet, soon replaced with soft snores.

She clearly needs the rest. I'm sure jetlag alone has her turned around, then the emotional distress of finding out everything that she has in the last three hours. So many questions are fluttering through my mind, though. So many new puzzle pieces suddenly thrown onto the board, I don't know what the fuck to do with them.

Chapter Twenty Four
Ronan

We decided to stay downstairs while Skyla consoled Stephanie. I haven't seen her since I was probably fifteen. I remember her leaving Salem, vaguely. I was too caught up in my own shit to pay too much attention to it all, but I remember enough. I remember how hardened she became after Giselle's death. She became the black sheep of the Brethren overnight, and she was fine with that. I'm sure Henry was glad to be rid of his daughter and his late wife's sister all in one swoop.

I knew Skyla not telling her about all of us was going to cause problems, but I also knew that the right time hadn't come up yet. There was no secure way to have that kind of conversation an ocean away. Every panicked fear she spewed is something I've thought about a dozen times over. I'm sure the same can be said for all the guys.

She doesn't know us, though. She knew me as a young kid, always in my brother's shadow. She probably never met Asher, Liam, or Vincent. Maybe once or twice, but from my memory, Skyla was everything to her. Nothing else mattered.

At least an hour goes by, and we spend it in silence. Liam fucks around on his phone, Asher wipes down the kitchen only to start over again, and Vincent sits at the kitchen table, playing with his knife. Eventually, Skyla makes her way into the kitchen, alone.

"How is she?" I ask.

"Sleeping," she says with a shrug.

I open my arms up for her, and she comes to me easily, burying her face in my chest as she lets out a deep breath. I press a kiss to the top of her head as she murmurs against me.

"She was so mad. I've never seen her so mad at me."

I nod. "You gotta look at it from her perspective, baby. She's scared for you. You mean everything to her, and she's just trying to protect you."

"Want to watch some trash TV and eat some garbage food?" Liam offers, with a sympathetic smile that has Skyla letting out a choked laugh.

She nods softly, and I release her. Liam holds out his hand, wrapping it around hers as he walks her out to the living room, where he turns on a show. Vincent follows them, grabbing her favorite blanket from the basket in the corner, before laying it over her legs and lifting her feet to tuck the blanket beneath them as she leans on Liam's shoulder.

Vincent takes the other seat beside her, intertwining their fingers together, as Skyla stares mindlessly at the TV. I look to see Asher watching her with a pinched look of concern before his eyes come to mine. I know what he's thinking; it's the same thing I am. What does Stephanie know about Giselle? Clearly more than she's ever let on to Skyla before. She made it sound like she had a similar arrangement. A similar relationship?

That can't be, though. I would have heard about it. The rumors, the scandal, it would have been all anyone spoke about. Then again, I was sixteen when she died. I suppose it's possible there were things going on that I wasn't privy to yet.

Eventually, Skyla passes out on Liam's shoulder. Both him and Vincent remain still as statues, too worried about waking her up to move. Asher and I dig into some of the food Liam brought home, when soft footsteps come down the stairs. A sleep-mussed Stephanie steps into the kitchen, her eyes instantly seeking out Skyla's.

I point to where she's sleeping on the couch, and relief fills her eyes as she nods.

Wordlessly, Asher dishes her up a plate of food, pushing it towards her in offer. She glances down at it for a moment, before she nods her thanks and takes a seat. We all sit there, eating in silence, before she speaks in a low tone.

"I'm sorry I flipped out. I shouldn't have reacted like that."

I shrug. "It was understandable. You were caught off guard."

She shakes her head, grimacing.

"I hate it here. This town, this world, I...I hate that she's here, that she's in it. I knew it was inevitable, obviously, but...I love her so much," she says, through watery eyes. "I practically raised her. She will always be my sister's baby, but she's my baby too, you know?"

I reach out my hand, resting it on hers as I nod empathetically.

"Absolutely. I know she loves you with everything she has. You only want what's best for her."

Stephanie nods. "So, please. Do the right thing."

I grimace at that, shaking my head before looking up at her.

"That's a choice only she can make, Stephanie. I'm all in. If Skyla wants me, I'm here."

"You could be killed too, you get that?" she asks.

My eyes move to Skyla's sleeping form, her chest slowly rising and falling as she's squished between the two guys. I nod.

"And you're okay with that?" she asks.

"I've accepted it as a possibility. I think we all have. She's worth it."

Asher nods his agreement, forcing Stephanie to frown. She stares into her Lo Mein, silent for several seconds before speaking again.

"Then you'll keep her safe. With your dying breath, you swear?"

"Of course," I vow, never meaning anything more.

"All of you?" she questions Asher, before looking to Liam and Vincent.

They both have their heads turned enough to look at us, all three of them nodding in unison.

"Well, what can I say to that, I guess?" she shrugs helplessly.

"Maybe an 'I'm sorry' to Skyla when she wakes up?" Asher offers like an ass.

Stephanie scoffs but surprisingly smirks.

"She definitely wasn't exaggerating about you being an asshole."

"No, she definitely wasn't," Asher agrees, before taking a big bite of his chicken.

I shake my head at him, and Stephanie actually chuckles before we go back to eating in silence.

When Skyla woke up, Stephanie practically tackled her, hugging her tight and apologizing profusely. They spoke for a while on the couch, a conversation we all pretended not to listen to, though we were all most definitely eavesdropping.

Skyla asked Stephanie about her mom again, about what she was going on about, but unfortunately, she clammed up yet again. She said she would tell her anything she wanted to know, except that. I can tell by the look in Asher's eyes, he's already thinking about what kind of resources he can utilize to look into this. I know because I'm doing the same.

I already texted Wesley and gave him some very rough information to go off. At first, he questioned me, but as soon as I clarified it was for Skyla, he was more than willing. My oldest friend has it bad for her. Though I'm fairly certain she feels something for him, I can't quite tell if it's on the same level as what she feels for us. I teased her about it yesterday, but there are worse men out there, by a long shot. He's one of the best men I know, and between my brother, this stalker, and *them*, it wouldn't be the worst thing in the world to have extra eyes on Skyla.

"How long are you staying for?" Skyla asks her.

Stephanie grimaces. "Don't hate me. I leave tomorrow."

Skyla frowns. "Really? I thought when you'd come to visit, you'd stay a while."

A sad smile touches her mouth as Stephanie pulls her in for another hug.

"I know, I'm sorry. I just can't handle being...here. It's already messing with me," she says as she shakes her head.

"Take me with you?" Skyla teases sadly.

"You know you'd be in my luggage if I thought we could get away with it. I love you so much, you know that, right?"

"Of course I do."

"Good, I reminded your boyfriends of that, and I think they understand if any of them hurt you, they'll have me to deal with."

All eyes come to Asher, and he looks at everyone before throwing his hands in the air.

"Why the fuck is everyone looking at me?"

Skyla and Stephanie laugh as Vincent answers.

"Well, you do have a nasty track record."

"Fuck you. At least mine isn't littered with dead bodies," Asher snarks back.

"All you're doing is reminding yourself that I'm extremely skilled in making underserving people disappear."

"Are they always like this?" Stephanie whispers to Skyla.

She nods. "Always."

Chapter Twenty Five
Vincent

True to her word, Stephanie left the next day. It's rare that someone can make it out of Salem with no strings attached. She obviously knows that and is running like hell in case they try to rescind that allowance. It pisses me the fuck off, that she would leave because of her own cowardice, when her niece is very much not okay.

You can't convince me that she doesn't know more is going on with Skyla. Despite her not outright bringing up the stalker, the way she spooks at the slightest sound or creeps around every corner like she's waiting for someone to get her is obvious. If her aunt can't see that, she's either a fucking idiot or a selfish bitch.

In the following days, we all kept our regular routines– to class and back here. Asher has been driving her to and from, rendering that little gutter snake Wesley useless. I don't like how he watches my Siren, how he lusts after her. It makes me want to carve his fucking eyes out.

Liam and Ronan have great excuses for being seen at the house often, Asher actually likes them. Not that I think anyone is watching the house too closely these days. According to Ronan, his brother's interest with Skyla and Asher has waned as he focused in on what the other legacies can bring to the table.

Still, never hurts to be too cautious. I always park my car down the block and take alternating routes to get in the house just in case anyone does catch on. Though, after Wesley's security overhaul, even I can admit that has proved to be more challenging.

When I approach the house, I notice that the garage door is open. Asher's Maserati, that he drove this morning, is parked and empty. And the goddamn moron forgot to close the garage door. I'm gonna kill him.

I sprint across the driveway, ducking into the garage before hitting the button to close it. Kicking the door open, I storm through the house, finding him and Skyla laughing on the couch. I slip behind him, wrapping my arm around his throat and securing him in a headlock.

"Vincent! What the hell!" Skyla shouts, as Asher begins wailing on my arms, his oxygen quickly fading.

"Let him go! He can't breathe!" she screams.

"Good," I grit, as my eyes lock on his. "He left the garage door open! He put your life in danger, *again*. He's wasted too many chances. He's a liability."

Asher's face begins to turn blue, and Skyla's screams are more frantic when two sets of hands pull on my shoulders, ripping me away from Asher. I hear him choke and gag for breath as Skyla soothingly rubs his back, shooting me a furious look.

I attempt to shrug Liam and Ronan off me, but they hold on tighter, pushing me against the wall as Skyla stands to confront me.

"I was supposed to shut the garage door. He asked me to do it since he had groceries in his hands, and I said sure. I must have forgotten. I'm sorry."

"Sorry isn't good enough, Siren! Don't you see how dangerous this man could be? Not just with what he could do, but what he knows? Asher swears he is capable of protecting you, he should be double and triple checking that he can actually back that statement up."

Skyla opens her mouth to argue when Asher nods.

"You're right. I should have made sure. That was on me."

"Fuck yes, it was!" I seethe, still not able to let go of this anger inside me.

I feel my entire body trembling, hate and anger boiling through my veins as I close my eyes, taking in shaky breaths and blowing them out. Nothing works, though. Nothing ever works.

Skyla frowns, looking at me seriously as she crosses the room, stopping just a few inches shy of me. Hesitantly, I watch as she carefully lifts her hands, cupping my face gently as she speaks.

"What's wrong, baby?"

I feel my racing pulse slow just a bit. My blinding anger is pushed to the side for a moment as I stare at my beautiful siren.

"I'm trying to protect you."

"I know, you always are, and you do it so well. Why are you *this* angry, though?"

I don't know how to respond, so I don't. Instead, I lift my hands up to her wrists, carefully pulling them away from me before I head out the back door. Liam and Ronan finally let me go, and I slam the door shut behind me as I stomp off into their backyard.

Pulling a cigarette from my pocket, I light the end before tossing my lighter into my jeans, taking a long drag of that sweet nicotine as I stare off into the distance. Drag by drag, my cigarette slowly shrinks until I'm dropping the butt on the ground, stomping it out before tossing it into the trash can out here.

The door cracks open and I don't have to turn to know who it is.

"Are you okay?" she asks.

"Yeah," I answer stiffly.

"Liar," she says, coming around to meet my eyes.

She smiles at me softly, but I don't match it. Instead, I hold my arm out in offering, and she instantly takes the invitation, burrowing herself into my side as the chill of the November air ripples through her.

"You should go inside," I say.

"Only if you come with me."

I shake my head.

"Because of Asher? It was a mistake, Vincent. I know you two don't get along, but he feels bad, so do I. I should have just shut the door. It was simple enough. I don't know why I didn't. You should be upset with me, not him."

I look down at her and shake my head.

"I could never be upset with you, Siren. It's not your responsibility to keep yourself safe; it's ours."

"Doesn't that seem a little backwards to you?" she teases.

"No."

Her smile flattens, and she nods, staring off in the same direction that I am.

"Well, what's the plan? Are we just going to move out here? I gotta say I wish I would have packed a jacket or something."

Wordlessly, I slip off my leather jacket and wrap it around her shoulders before zipping it to her chin. She smiles up at me softly.

"I was kidding."

Shrugging my shoulders, I slip my hands into my pockets. I need to get the fuck away from here, at least for the night, preferably longer. I know that if I even see Asher's goddamn face, I'm sure to beat it to a pulp, and as much pleasure as it would bring me, I know how much pain it would bring my siren. So, I refrain. Like always.

"Wanna go somewhere with me for the weekend?" I ask.

"Just the two of us?" she questions.

I nod before turning to face her.

"Where?"

"In the hills, near where I took you to that spring."

"When would we leave?" she asks, as she crosses her arms.

"Now."

"Like right now?" she asks. "It's a little cold for a bike ride, don't you think?"

"I drove my car today. What do you say?"

She rolls her lips together in thought before she nods.

"Okay, let me go grab some clothes."

"I'll meet you outside the gate," I say, gesturing to the front gate of the house.

Skyla nods as she slips back inside, handing me my jacket before shutting the door. I slip it on, inhaling her sweet perfume that is already lingering against the cool leather. My steps quickly cross the yard, slipping through a shortcut in the trees that drops me right out to my car. I hop inside and fire up the car, before popping off the plates just in case. I'm not sure if anyone would think to follow us, but I'm always acting on the side of caution.

Once that's done, I drive the block to their house, pausing just outside the gate.

My car has the darkest tint on the market, so no one can see in, only out. It makes jobs that much easier, or in cases like this, where I am taking my girlfriend away to without anyone knowing who she is getting in the car with.

She steps out the front door, kissing Asher as she does, before making her way down the driveway and to the gate. It swings open before she can reach it, and Ronan nods at her from the doorway. She gives a grateful wave before slipping into the passenger seat. I already turned on the heated seats, and I have the heater on full blast for her.

I watch as she practically melts into her seat, tossing her tote bag into the back.

"Where are we going?" she asks.

"You'll see."

The sun is beginning to set when we pull up the long wooded driveway. I haven't been here in years; hardly even thought about it, really. I'm not sure why it was the first place that popped in my head that I wanted to take her, though.

I look out at the simple two-story log cabin. It's nothing compared to what many of the Elder's possess. My parents loved it though, so did I.

"Whose cabin is this?" Skyla asks as I undo my seatbelt.

"My family's," I say, as I push open my door and come around to get hers.

I grab her bag from the back, before lacing our fingers together and walking her up the front steps. My keys feel heavier than normal as I fish them out of my pocket and insert the key into the deadbolt. It turns with ease, an eerie creek echoing through the cold house as the door swings open.

The smell of wood and must instantly permeates my nose, and

though some may not like it, it feels like home to me. Flicking on the light, the entire place glows at once. I'm glad I didn't have the power cut here.

Shrugging off my jacket, I toss it onto the couch before moving to the fireplace.

"Make yourself at home. I'll start a fire."

"You can start a fire?" she asks with raised eyebrows. "Like out of two rocks or something?"

"I can, though sticks are easier to get things going. Tonight, I figured I'd settle with a lighter, though," I say as I pull my lighter out of my pocket, lining up some of the old kindling before lighting it.

"Hmm, too bad. It would have been hot to see you start it with your bare hands– all tough and rugged. Like a mountain man," she says, with a teasing smirk.

I scoff and shake my head, fighting back a small smile as I grab one of the pre-split logs, setting one on for now so I don't smother it. After a minute, I add another two, and the fire takes off from there, intense heat immediately radiating from the fireplace as I stand up.

Skyla's eyes are roaming around the room, all the way up to the vaulted ceilings and the loft on the second floor. The kitchen is open but it's not huge. Everything is just the way I remember– simple, minimalistic, perfect.

"How long has it been since you've been here?"

"About seven years," I answer, before I move towards her, resting my hands on her hips as I look down at her.

She frowns. "Why so long?"

I shrug. "Didn't feel like coming back without them."

"Your parents?" she guesses.

I nod but don't speak. We've never discussed the death of my parents. Mainly because there isn't much to tell. One day they were here; the next, they weren't.

"What were they like?" Skyla asks.

I think about that for a moment, mulling over my words.

"Cold, disconnected."

That seems to upset her, and I don't like that, so I grapple to come up with some of the good.

"I used to get really bad growing pains as a kid, and my mom would sit up with me all night. She'd rub my legs until I fell asleep almost every night for years. My dad taught me how to fight; he told me to always stand up for myself and those I care about. To never allow anyone to take what I don't readily give. He taught me how to shoot, how to work with knives, basic grappling, and MMA for hand-to-hand combat."

Skyla watches me with rapt attention, like she's absorbing every ounce of information I'm willing to give her.

"Were you all happy?"

I pause on this for a bit before I nod.

"I think so."

I appreciate that she doesn't question me more on that. Unfortunately, she was saving her breath for a heavier question.

"How did they die?"

My eyes come to her, those bright green orbs looking up at me, entrancing me, pulling the secrets out of the deep recesses of my mind against my will. Whatever she wants to know, I'll tell her. Anything she wants, it's hers. I'd cut out my own fucking heart and lay it at her feet, if that's what she asked of me.

"They were eliminators like me," I say, before rolling my lips together, stretching this out as long as I can. "They worked as a team. It's not uncommon, most prefer it, actually. One day, they were given orders, to take down a manufacturing plant with all the workers inside, and they didn't get out in time...boom. Gone."

My siren's eyes are widened with horror as she looks at me, as if she was waiting for me to say more. There isn't more to say, though. We are all born, and we all die; we never know what job will be our last or if we'll choke on a fucking bagel on a Tuesday morning. It's fucked, but there is no changing it.

"Vincent," she says, her voice rasping as she shakes her head. "I'm so sorry. You were what? Fifteen?"

"Fourteen," I correct.

She shakes her head like her heart is broken. I'm surprised it upsets her so much. She lost her mother when she was three. At least I have memories of my parents; she hardly has anything of hers, and Henry Parris is about the furthest thing from a father. He doesn't even count. Then again, I guess she had Stephanie.

"Who did you stay with after that? You didn't live on your own, right?"

He shakes his head.

"I moved in with my bond brother."

"You had a bond brother? I mean, it makes sense. I had wondered if there was a reason you didn't have one, but...where is he?"

"Dead," I say curtly.

Fuck. I haven't spoke about him in over two years. I still think about him nearly every day. He was my brother in every sense of the word, in every way that counted. It's fucked up, but his death haunts me more than my parents ever will. It's also the reason I will never trust or forgive Asher Putnam.

Skyla opens her mouth, closing it before opening and closing it again. My face must be easily readable. That is a subject I don't want to go into. Not right now, not ever.

"What was his name?" she asks softly.

My heart tugs at the timid tone beneath her words, and I force myself to soften, just a little, as I answer her this.

"Nathaniel Ingersoll."

She nods, before tilting her head to the side.

"Was his father in the room that night? I don't think I've heard the name before."

I shake my head. "His dad had a heart attack when we were seventeen. His mom died giving birth to him. Nate was the only true heir. With him gone, the Ingersol bloodline nearly went extinct. A mysterious cousin appeared practically from thin air and claimed the seat at the table. There was a lot of controversy over it. Many, including your father, questioning the validity of his heritage."

Her lips roll together. "I'm sure Christopher didn't love that."

"He wasn't the head of the Brethren back then; it was his dad, Luther Putnam."

"Asher's grandfather?"

I nod.

"God, how do you keep it all straight? All the families and legacies and stories."

"It was all we learned from birth. Like a religion poured down our throat from infancy, injected into our veins through adolescence, and beat into our brains as adults. We live and breathe our history."

She's quiet for a moment, before she lifts her hand to cup my face like she did earlier today.

"I'm sorry."

Two simple words, two words that really mean nothing. They don't take anything away. They don't make anything better. They don't heal all, and yet, coming from her, those two words mean fucking everything.

I squeeze her hips in thanks, and she pulls me down to her. I go easily, drawn to her like a sailor pulled into the sea. This is why she's my siren. She could lure me right to my death, and I would go, happily, willingly, spending eternity submerged in water, forever embalmed by her side.

My hands move down her legs as our mouths melt against one another. I take my time, adoring every inch of her before I grip the back of her knees and lift her into the air. She comes easily, wrapping her legs around my back as I pepper her neck with kisses and move into the living room, laying her down on the couch in front of the fire.

Her skin glows in the orange-tinted light, those pouty lips and needy eyes begging for me. Who am I to ever deny her a thing? Piece by piece, I shed every article of clothing between the two of us until there is nothing left but me and her.

I do my best to push away the dark thoughts flittering through my mind. Too much of the past has been dug up tonight– too many feelings, too much hurt. I struggle to push it away, focusing on my siren as my hands roughly knead her breasts, my teeth leaving a scattering of bite marks along her naked body.

"Vincent!" she gasps, when I bite her inner thigh so hard a tiny bit of blood emerges.

My eyes come to hers as she looks at the mark. The blood pricks to the top, dotting the teeth marks in a way that should be considered art. I stare at it in awe, her blood more beautiful than I ever thought it could be. I feel a darker side of me set in, one that I rarely give into, especially not with my siren. She's too perfect for my desires, too pure for my unsatiated appetite.

When I tear my eyes away, I see her watching me curiously.

"You like to see me bleed?"

I run my tongue along my lower lip, a small taste of that metallic flavor blooming across my tongue.

"Only when I'm the one to cause it."

"Show me," she says, catching me by surprise.

I look at her in question, and she nods.

"Show me. I can see it in your eyes. You want something, I'm not sure what, but if I can give it to you...I-I want to."

I shake my head roughly, closing my eyes as I break eye contact. She doesn't know what she's saying.

"Show me, Vincent. I want to satisfy your every desire, your every curiosity."

"You do," I say, my head snapping up to face her.

"I don't," she responds, too observant for her own good. "Not yet."

I feel my breathing become labored, my chest rising and falling as I grapple with the end of my control. It slips through my fingers, and in the next moment, my face is buried against her thigh. My tongue laps at the bite mark, a sick part of me craving the taste of her. I reach for my discarded jeans, flick out my blade, and glance up at her for permission.

Fear dilates her eyes as she nods and fuck me, it only makes me want it more. I press the tip of the blade to her other side, watching in awe as blood follows in a perfect line. Her body tenses, and I hear her muffled, pained groan.

A release like I've never felt before washes through me, something more satisfying than any kill. It's something pure, totally surrendered for my taking. My fingers smear against the blood before I line my cock up to her, shoving myself inside.

To my surprise, she's absolutely drenched, my cock easily sliding in and out of her as I lift her bleeding thigh. Looking down at it, my cock throbs as I fuck her deeper, pressing the blade against the skin just above it, giving her perfect thigh a matching cut.

"Ow," she grumbles softly.

My eyes swing to hers.

"Does that hurt, Siren?"

"It's fine. I love what it's doing to you," she moans as she reaches down, rubbing her clit with her hand.

"Yeah?" I grit through clenched teeth. "Like what it's doing to me? Like that it's turning me into a fucking savage?" I practically snarl, as my thrusts become choppy and erratic.

My hand is wet, and I look down to see it soaking with blood. Fuck, I shouldn't have cut her that deep. Holding it up, I stare at my crimson covered palm, a wave of ecstasy rolling through me as she reaches for my wrist.

I let her take it, watching in fascination as she guides it up and over to her chest, pushing it firmly just over her heart. I rest my weight between the couch and her chest as I abandon the knife, holding onto her like I'll float away and suffocate in my demons if I don't.

"Vincent," she whimpers. "Oh my god! Vincent, Vincent, Vincent!" she screams as I slam into her g-spot, her pulsating pussy squeezing the cum out of me as I fall over the edge.

We moan and grind against each other, practically shaking the walls of this cabin before we quiet, my thrusts stilling all together.

Slowly, I pull my hand away from her chest, watching in awe, as a perfect red handprint covers part of her breast just over her heart. My eyes come up to find hers half-lidded and satiated. She gives me a small smile, and I can't find myself to return it. Mainly because I'm rendered motionless, speechless. I'm in awe.

She just gave me a gift. One I didn't know I needed, didn't know I craved from her. And for her to have given it to me so willingly, so happily, so trusting....in this moment, more than any of the others all combined, I know with every fiber in my being that this woman was made for me. I will be by her side in this life, the next, and until the end of time. Where she goes, I go. Where she stays, I stay. Where she falls, I will be there with open arms, waiting, every goddamn time.

Chapter Twenty Six
Asher

I went fucking batshit the entire time that Skyla was gone with Vincent. I didn't like him just taking her like that, not even telling us where he was going. The guy has made way too many off-handed comments about having her for himself. He's also mentally unstable as fuck. I wouldn't be surprised if he murder-suicided them, just so no one else could have her but him.

When they walked into the house late Sunday night, relief literally washed over me. I practically yanked her out of his arms and threw her over my shoulder before carrying her to my room. We haven't been staying in her room lately. Firstly, because we got rid of her bed, for obvious reasons. Secondly, she says she doesn't really feel comfortable in there anymore, and I completely get it.

Now, it's Monday night, Ronan and Wesley are up to something back at Ronan's house, Vincent is off on another job, and Liam, Skyla, and I are watching a movie in my room. Skyla's head is resting on my chest while her body is draped over Liam's lap.

It's clear that Liam hasn't been paying attention to the movie for the last ten minutes or so, instead choosing to play with the hemline of Skyla's sleep shorts. She keeps playfully pushing him away, and the little shit seems to love it, continuing to smirk as he tries his shot again and again.

Memories of the last time we had the house to just the three of us aren't lost on me, in fact, it's almost all I've been thinking about. We've obviously all shared Skyla before, a lot, but that was the first time it was just Liam and I and goddamn...it was fucking hot.

Watching her suck his cock was such a unique but erotic experience; my cock jerks in my sweats just thinking about it. Not knowing what comes over me, I cup the front of Skyla's throat, tipping her head back as I bend over and kiss her upside down. My tongue runs along hers before I tear away from her, speaking loud enough for Liam to hear.

"Why don't you be a good girl and put Liam out of his misery? Go suck his cock, princess."

She blinks up at me, nodding softly, as Liam practically bounces with excitement. He rips off his basketball shorts, chucking them to the side before he begins stroking his ridiculously pierced cock. Seriously, I don't know how he did one, let alone eight of them. I can't deny that it looks pretty fucking cool, though.

Skyla and Liam switch spots so he is more in the center of the bed before she crawls between his legs, lowering her mouth over his head. He throws his head back and groans, burying his fingers into her hair as he slowly starts guiding her movements.

The movie immediately forgotten, I turn my head to watch them. As Skyla pulls her mouth up, each glint of Liam's piercings shine from her saliva, before she lowers back down, hiding them down her throat once more.

My hand begins slowly rubbing my cock through my sweats, already throbbing in anticipation. Filthy ideas run rampant in my mind, and I speak them before I can think better of it. Liam's eyes are squeezed tight, Skyla's mouth more than full as I muse out loud.

"I wonder if she's ready. What do you think, brother?"

Liam's eyes pop open at that, practically sparkling as he looks down at her before back up to me.

"You think?" he asks.

I shrug. "That's up to her, I suppose."

"What?" she asks, as she pulls her mouth away from Liam breathlessly.

"Do you think you could take us both? Together?" I ask.

She frowns and nods.

"Well, yeah. I've done it before."

Liam and I share matching smirks as we shake our heads.

"No, babygirl," Liam says. "He means, do you think you could take two cocks at once. One in your pussy and one in your ass."

Her eyes widen, and she swallows roughly.

"Oh...I-I don't know. We've only done a little assplay. I can try?" she offers.

I shake my head, cupping her chin as I look at her.

"We aren't pressuring you, princess. Only if you want it. We're more than happy with any kind of attention you're willing to give us, right, Liam?"

"Mhmm!" he cheers happily.

She seems to think it over for a moment before she nods.

"I want to try."

Hunger burns inside me at her words, and I nod to Liam.

"C'mere, babygirl," he says, as he lifts her up by her hips, pulling her oversized sleep shirt off as I grab her panties, pulling them down her thighs before tossing them to the side.

With our beautiful girl, naked and bare for us, Liam easily sets her onto his lap.

"There you go," he groans, as she sinks down onto him.

I reach over into my bedside table, grabbing a bottle of lube, before sliding off the bed and making my way up behind her. Liam takes it slow at first, his thrusts even and measured while Skyla lifts up and down on him. Setting the lube to the side, I push down on her back, forcing her to poke her ass out a little more for me.

"Beautiful," I murmur, watching in awe at her perfect asshole, as Liam's cock stretches her pussy.

I run my tongue through her, getting dangerously close to Liam's cock before doing it again and again. She moans as I rest my hands on her ass cheeks, eating her ass while my best friend fucks her. Goddamnit, I can already feel my cock leaking pre-cum.

I feel Skyla relax little by little as I grab the lube and apply a small amount on my finger. Slowly, I push inside, listening to her gasp turn into a moan, as Liam's thrusts come almost to a halt.

"There you go, princess. Look at you. Just relax and focus how good it feels."

She lets out a shuttering breath as she nods.

"I-it feels pretty good."

I smirk. "Just pretty good? We can do better than that."

Applying a little more lube, I slide another finger in, pumping them in and out of her as her asshole tenses around me.

"Oh fuck!" she groans, something sounding like a mix of pleasure and pain.

"Fuck," Liam grits out.

"You good?" I ask.

"Yeah, she's just so goddamn tight right now," he says through clenched teeth.

Grinning at that, I take my time with her, working her slowly, until I hear nothing but pleasured moans fall from those beautiful lips. When she relaxes and thrusts back into my touch, I know it's time.

Carefully, I withdraw my fingers, loving the disappointed whimper that comes from her. I grab the bottle of lube and absolutely coat my cock, shoving my sweats to the floor before lining myself up to her.

"Big breath in, princess," I say.

She does as I say beautifully.

"Big breath out."

When she blows a breath out, I push in. I'm a little rougher than I want to be, but I know that if I'm not, she could push me out and make it more painful in general. The feeling is so goddamn tight, though. I've never felt anything like it. Not even her virgin cunt felt like this. Liam pulls out slightly, pushing back in, and I feel the ripple of several of his piercings, pulling a moan out of me.

"Fuck dude!" I snap, as I fight back another moan.

"What?" Liam pants.

"I can feel your fucking piercings through her," I say, as I look down at him over her shoulder.

A smug grin crosses his face.

"You're welcome," he says, as he arches his back, causing Skyla and I to both groan in unison.

Together, we all find a rhythm. Skyla whimpers softly at first, but when Liam starts playing with her clit those sounds fade away, only leaving behind begging and want in her voice.

"Oh god! I'm so full! Holy shit. It hurts and it's amazing. Oh god," she shouts.

"You like being stuffed full of cock like a dirty girl?" I ask.

She nods her head helplessly, seemingly unable to speak as I pick up my pace. My cock rubs against Liam's through her, and I'd never admit it, but I fucking love it. I've never felt anything like it, and I know that I don't want this moment to end, fucking ever.

His eyes are on mine, lust-drunk and hazed, as his hand continues rubbing Skyla's clit. Those eyes, though? Those soft, pale green eyes? They never leave mine.

A challenging look crosses his face, as he gives a short and hard thrust through Skyla that hits right against my tip. I grit my teeth, not wanting to show how that affects me before I do the same in return. He doesn't seem to have the same willpower though, or isn't ashamed of it. He lets out a sharp moan that is like something out of a porno.

Kinda hot, honestly.

Something in me likes getting the upper hand. I do it again and again, pulling moan after moan out of both him and Skyla. I feel like a fucking king, a god, doling out pleasure with the barest amount of effort.

When his eyes come to mine again, something changes. I don't know if it's the air in the room or too much pleasure wrapped up in one moment, but I feel it in the pit of my stomach. I swallow roughly as I attempt to look away from him, focusing on the beautiful view of Skyla bent over for me. Possessing a mind of their own though, my eyes track back to Liam's waiting gaze.

I watch as he sinks his straight teeth into his lip, and it makes my cock jerk inside Skyla. She turns her head to look at me, her eyes moving from both of us before she whispers to me.

"Kiss him."

"What?" I snap, ripping my eyes away from Liam.

"Kiss him, please. I want to watch you."

I scoff, sparing a look at Liam, who is staring at me with that same challenging gaze.

"You're barking up the wrong tree, babygirl," Liam says after a moment.

She pouts, her ass thrusting against me as she whines.

"For me? Please," she begs the two of us.

Liam shakes his head.

"You'd have a better chance of getting Vincent to kiss me than Asher, babygirl."

I don't like that. Something in me really doesn't fucking like that, and before I know what I'm doing, I lean over Skyla, wrapping my hand around Liam's throat and crush my lips to his.

For a moment, neither of us move. Not our hips, not our mouths. Nothing. I think he's in shock, or maybe it's me. All I know, is that when his lips close around my bottom lip, I lose myself in this moment. Our thrusts pick up, lips brushing against each other, and I feel Skyla pulsate around me.

"Oh my god! Oh my god!"

She screams out her release, and I have no choice but to follow along with her. Liam is right there with us, letting out a strangled whimper into my mouth. I feel his cock jerk inside her, so I know he can feel mine as well.

Savagely, I rip my mouth away from his, still holding a firm grip on his throat as he looks up at me and I pull every last drop of cum I can out of me. When I'm finished, I carefully pull out of Skyla, finally releasing Liam's neck before I stand up and move to the bathroom. I start up the shower, jumping in before the water is even hot as I rest my head against the cool tile.

What the fuck just happened.

Chapter Twenty Seven
Liam

When I woke up this morning, it was from Skyla sneaking out of bed and into the shower. I blinked my eyes open in time to watch her perfect naked ass slink off to the bathroom before the water turned on.

I looked to my left to see Asher on his side, facing me, still in a deep sleep. Fuck me, last night was definitely a night that I'll never forget. I'm sure it's one none of us will. I can't lie that since the other day on the couch, I'd been noticing Asher a little more, outside of the normal obvious thought that he's attractive. I found myself watching him talk, the way his Adam's apple bobbed when he swallowed roughly, or how he'd run his fingers through his hair when he was frustrated.

My fingers flex at my side, before I reach my hand up gently, pushing a little bit of his hair back. Shit, his hair is so soft. It's not nearly as long as mine, but mine is wavy and kind of frizzy. His is so smooth.

Like his mouth.

Was I goading him last night? Absolutely. Did I think he was actually going to kiss me? Fuck no. I was just enjoying the banter, while having his cock rub against mine through Skyla. Everything was great, then he had to go and make it perfect. His lips on mine, even unmoving, was my undoing. I don't think I've ever cum that hard in my life. And though I know the chances of something like that happening again are slim to absolutely never, it won't stop it from becoming one of my top five highlight reels of all time.

The tip of my fingers graze against his head a little too much, forcing his eyes to flutter open. They immediately land on me, and I still, waiting for his reaction. It takes him a moment for his mind to wake up, and as I suspected, he freaks.

Scrambling away from me like I'm diseased, he sits up, scooting as far away from me as possible as he looks down at me.

"What the fuck! Were you watching me sleep?" he snaps.

"Calm down," I draw out with an eye roll, doing my best to push down the disappointment inside me.

"No, Liam! You can't just run your fingers through someone's hair while their sleeping!" he says, before burying his own fingers into his hair, shaking his head.

"Look," he says, as he faces me. "I'm not gay, okay? I don't like guys, and I know last night happened, but I—"

"Bro, stop," I say, cutting him off as I sit up to face him.

His eyes are wild; he looks as if he's ready to bolt out this room, down the stairs, and through the front door. I can't deny that it kinda hurts. He's allowed to not be into it but he doesn't have to make me feel like I'm contagious. He's never treated me differently for my sexuality, so I know this is just a freakout in reflection from last night.

"You need to chill," I say. "Last night, was whatever. I know you're not gay. You love Skyla, you're into women. I know, man. I'm not gonna fucking take advantage of you," I say, with a sarcastic laugh and a shake of my head.

Asher's brows furrow as he watches me, but he doesn't speak.

"You did it for Skyla, you wanted to make her happy, and guess what? It worked. She came so hard she made us both nut, immediately," I say with a teasing smile, satisfied when I see his posture relax slightly. "We don't have to talk about it, and just tell Skyla you don't want to be put into that position again. It doesn't have to be anything more than that, okay?"

Asher continues breathing heavily, but he remains silent. I can practically see the million and one things running through his head as he stares at me. I go to offer him more reassurances, that last night didn't strip him of his manhood or whatever crazy shit he's thinking, when he speaks through a throaty rasp.

"I'm not gay."

God, I really hate labels. People get so hung up on them, they are so limiting. I don't say anything, though. Nodding my understanding as he scoots a half a foot closer, blowing out a heavy breath.

"I love Skyla," he says, his eyes dropping to my mouth as he moves even closer.

My chest tightens, and my stomach flips, but I don't dare move a muscle, unsure of where he's going with this.

"I know. I love her, too. She's my everything," I say carefully.

"Mine too," he says, moving until our thighs brush against each other.

Asher put on sweats after he got out of the shower last night, but I'm still naked, and my hardening cock is way too aware of how close he is to me right now.

I watch as his eyes flicker back and forth between mine and my mouth, the tension so suffocating I can hardly breathe. Shit, I think I officially have a thing for my best friend. If he wasn't having such an extreme bi-panic a few moments ago, based on the way he's looking at me, I'd say he has a thing for me, too. Then again, I'd bet my life that's want that is muddling his normally deep brown eyes.

Slowly, his hand comes to my throat, similar to how it did last night, and my cock jerks under the sheets at the reminder. He doesn't move his face closer at first, his eyes raking over me before his fingers squeeze the sides of my throat. My eyes flutter shut, unable to stop them for a moment as the welcomed grip overtakes me.

When my eyes open again, he's inching towards me. I want nothing more in this moment than to bury my hand into his hair and pull him the rest of the way, but I know he needs to come to me. He needs to want this. He needs to be in control.

So, I let him, happily. I wait with bated breath, that gorgeous fucking mouth inches from mine as indecision leaves his eyes, and he closes them. The first touch of his lips against mine does something to me. It sends a flipping in my stomach that is euphoric. I don't move my lips, allowing him to test his boundaries.

I feel his grip on my throat tighten as his tongue slips into my mouth, stroking against my own. Pleasure rolls through me, as I gently begin kissing him back. We sit there for a few minutes, softly kissing each other, enjoying the feel of our bodies pressed against each other when I lift my hand to cup his face.

He jerks, his eyes flying open at the same time mine do. He doesn't pull away, though. Our tongues are still wrapped around each other, eyes locked. We pause for no more than two seconds before Asher closes his eyes again, the kiss turning more heated and aggressive.

Sinking his teeth into my lower lip, he bites hard, forcing a soft moan to escape me. What sounds like a groan echoes from his chest as he does it again, the hand not on my throat beginning to trail down my body. I feel him angle towards me, pressing his body flush against mine when our cocks rub against one another.

Asher moans, his sweats pushing against me once more. Goddamnit, why does that feel so fucking good. This isn't my first rodeo. I sleep with men almost as regularly as women, at least I did before Skyla. I don't usually get so overly excited with some over-the-pants rubbing. Is it over-the-pants rubbing though, if my cock is out and it's my supposedly straight best friend grinding his cock against mine?

He now has one hand on my throat and the other on my hip, squeezing like he's ready to break me in two. Fuck, I wish he would.

I make a risky move when I twirl my tongue around his, sucking on it as he moans. I reach my hand out, trailing over his abs before my fingers slip beneath his waistband. He gasps roughly, but my fingers don't make it more than an inch or two before the bathroom door is opening and Asher is leaping away.

Looking up at Skyla, she watches us with surprised eyes as Asher sits hunched over the bed, storming out of the room without a second wasted. I watch him go, a small part of me hurting at his hot and cold attitude, before I turn to Skyla and shrug. She gives me a sad smile before crawling on top of me. She lays there for several minutes just holding me and it feels amazing. I guess she's not mad that she found us making out. I didn't expect she would be since she kind of initiated this whole thing. Only problem now is, I don't know how I'm ever going to be expected to forget it.

Chapter Twenty Eight
Skyla

Liam and I lay there for several minutes before he kisses the top of my head and moves to stand up. I let him go as he heads to the shower, shutting the door behind him. I don't know what I was expecting today to entail, but it definitely wasn't that. Not that I'm complaining. Have I manifested my boyfriends becoming boyfriends?

Probably not, if Asher's reaction is anything to go off. Deciding to get dressed and go in search of him, I slip on a cozy green sweater and a pair of jeans before padding my way down the stairs. In the kitchen, I find Asher making coffee, his hands gripping the countertop tightly.

Frowning to myself, I step up behind him, wrapping my arms around his waist as I rest my head against his back. I feel his hand cover my arm as he stands up straighter before turning to face me.

When he does, so many emotions are playing across his face that I'm not sure which ones to focus on first. So, instead of trying to guess, I go for the old-school method of communication.

"Are you okay?"

"I'm fine," he snaps quickly. "Are we okay, though?"

I tilt my head in confusion.

"Why wouldn't we be?"

"I just figured maybe you'd be upset about...you know."

He turns his head to look anywhere but at me, and I lift my hand to force his eyes to meet my own.

"Babe, I'm not mad. Not even a little. I practically begged for it last night," I laugh. "It was hot to walk in on; I only wish you wouldn't have ran away."

He pushes out of my hold, shaking his head as he laps the kitchen.

"I don't know what I was thinking. I'm probably still drunk or something."

I frown at that.

"We didn't drink last night."

Asher pauses, his hand running through his hair as he shrugs.

"Whatever. Don't worry, princess. I can promise that shit will never happen again," he says as he comes back over to me, grabbing a cup for his coffee.

"But it can if you want it to, that's what I'm saying. I have no problem with it, at all. Trust me," I say, with a short laugh.

Asher shakes his head tersely, and my smile falls as I nod. Clearly, he doesn't want to talk, and I'm not going to force him. So, I reach into my pocket and shoot a text to Wesley asking if he's free to give me a ride to the university. He responds almost immediately, telling me that he's on his way.

Liam appears in the next moment, wet hair from the shower and fresh clothes from his stash in my room. He sends Asher a hesitant look, to which he doesn't even meet his eyes before Liam gives me a tight smile and a kiss to the forehead.

Asher finishes his coffee, setting the cup down and rinsing it out before storming out of the room.

"Wesley is picking me up," I say, so he doesn't wonder why I'm gone when he gets out of the shower.

He pauses, and I expect him to say something. To argue, to forbid it or even just acknowledge that I spoke. Instead, he just keeps moving, acting as if he never heard me.

"I'm sorry," Liam says. "I think that's my fault," he says, as he nods in the direction Asher disappeared.

I shake my head. "Whatever is going on in his head is a him problem. You're golden," I say, as I lean up and press a kiss to his lips.

He accepts the peck happily, wrapping his arms around me when I get a text from Wesley.

Wesley: Here.

Pulling away from Liam, I smile as I grab my bag off the table.

"So is that how it is, babygirl? One of your boyfriends act up, so you call in a new recruit?"

I roll my eyes and, surprisingly, Liam laughs. It's a sweet sound that warms my chest and tells me that he will be just fine, eventually.

Waving goodbye to Liam, I step out the front door and see Wesley, standing outside my open door, with a cup of what I know to be apple cider in his hand.

"Good morning," he smiles, his body wrapped in a white dress shirt that is tucked into a pair of black dress pants.

"Morning. Were you really just hanging out this morning wearing that?" I laugh.

He looks down at himself with pinched brows.

"What's wrong with it?"

I shake my head.

"Nothing, nothing. It's just a little formal for seven in the morning."

"I dress to impress," he says, with a wink that has me rolling my eyes but laughing at the same time.

Taking the drink from him, I thank him before sliding into the seat. He shuts the door behind me as he climbs into the driver's seat and loops around the driveway.

"So, what did Asher do?" Wesley asks.

"Nothing," I answer. "Why?"

He shrugs.

"If he did nothing, I'm sure he'd be the one driving you to school. I'm like the backup guy these days. So, if I'm driving, he must have done something."

"You're not the backup guy," I defend.

"Hey, it doesn't bother me. I get paid either way."

"Who's paying you?" I ask, with my head tilted.

"The Brethren."

"And who is authorizing it?" I rephrase.

He grins at me through the rear-view mirror.

"Ronan."

I nod. That makes more sense.

"So, what did he do?" Wesley pushes again.

"Why do you care? Why are you so interested?" I huff.

That same grin spreads across his face as we come to a red light.

"Just seeing if my odds are increasing."

"Your odds?"

His head nods.

"Odds of what?" I ask, though, by that flirty look in his eye, I suspect I know the answer.

"Another time, little one. Now, it's time for school," he says, somehow miraculously pulling up to the school.

I blink as I glance around. How did we get here so fast? Or was I just really not paying attention?

Wesley gets out, grabbing my door for me. I sling my bag over my shoulder and slide out of the car, looking up at his gorgeous face.

"Thank you," I say.

"Absolutely. Anytime, Miss Parris," he says, though he usually only does that to piss Asher off. There is something sensual about the way the words roll off his tongue, though. I force myself to look away from him, before nodding my appreciation and heading down the courtyard.

I glance at the stone building beside me, the wrought iron gate like a safe haven for once. It's not like Wesley is necessarily something to run away from, but there is something about him that feels a lot like danger.

"Hey, babe!" Maggie greets.

I practically startle at her greeting before looking over to her.

"Shit, you scared me."

"Uh, sorry?" she laughs. "Everything okay?"

"Yeah, crazy morning," I nod, as we head to the class.

"Oh really? Give me all the horny details," she says, with a waggle of her eyebrows.

I laugh at her, shaking my head as we step into a sea of students on their way to class.

Chapter Twenty Nine
Skyla

Ronan: **Come to my office during lunch**

Glancing down at the text, I smile as I split off from Liam and Maggie. I haven't had lunch with Ronan in a while. Honestly, with how busy he's been lately, I feel like I haven't seen him at all. He said that it's always like this as the school year progresses. More legacies begin coming of age, I'm assuming, to be officially inducted into the Brethren, and Ronan is like their guide, I suppose.

Considering all the...events that have been occurring lately, it's been a while since I've been able to swim, which feels practically criminal. Not meaning to, I can feel myself pick up my pace as I step into the pool building, opening the door to the pool and moving down the walkway to Ronan's office. Knocking on the door, I hear his gruff, 'come in', before I push inside.

He's sitting at his desk, eyes on his computer, when they swing over to me. He looks a little stressed, his eyes hazy and eyebrows pinched. That look falls away in seconds, though. I watch as he leans back into his chair, smiling at me as his eyes roam over me.

"Shut the door," he smiles.

Closing the door behind me, I lock it and smile at him as I cross the room. He turns in his chair to face me and I waste no time crawling into his lap, straddling him as I wrap my arms around his shoulders.

"Hi," I smile.

"Hi, baby," he grins, as his hands come to rest on my ass.

"How are you?"

His smile falters for a moment before he nods.

"Good."

I give him a doubtful look but remain silent, watching as his expression falls until he's frowning. His thumbs rub soothing circles against my ass.

"I have to have dinner tonight with Annie Williams, at my brother's house."

Frowning at that, I pull away a bit as I look down at him.

"The desk slut?"

"Desk slut?" he questions, a hint of amusement in his eyes.

"Yeah, that's what I've been referring to her as in my head."

Ronan lets out a short chuckle as he nods.

"That's the one."

"Why do you have to have dinner with her at Christopher's?"

He rolls his lips together, he looks down at his lap for a second before looking back up at me. The look in his eyes alone is like a gut punch.

"To talk about the engagement."

Nope, I lied. The look in his eyes was nothing. His words? That was the true gut punch. Pushing out of his grasp, I stand, looking at him in shock before I shake my head.

"So, what? That's just it? You're going to marry her?"

He stays silent, staring at me like a fucking idiot. I smack my hand against his desk in anger.

"Answer me!"

"What do you want me to say, Skyla?" he huffs. "What choice do I have? Should I tell my brother I can't because I'm in love with his daughter-in-law? Should I tell her that there is no way I could ever truly love her, because she will always pale in comparison to the one woman I'll never be able to fully have?"

His words feel like a slap to the face. I take a step back, then another, heading for the door. I get it unlocked and cracked open before it's slammed shut. Ronan's hand is on the door above my head, while the other is on the doorknob.

"Stop," he grouses, before blowing out a long breath. "I'm sorry. I...I don't know what the fuck to do. I've got Christopher and the Williams family breathing down my fucking neck. There is some piece of shit out there, stalking the woman I love and I...I feel so goddamn out of control. I'm never out of control. I always have a plan, always have a solution."

I do my best to fight the quiver in my voice, but with the hot, scratchy feeling taking over my throat, I don't have much choice.

"So...what? We're just...over?" I choke out, as I stare at the wooden door.

"No!" he snaps, before spinning me until I'm facing him.

His body closes in on me, pressing me against the door as he shakes his head.

"No, baby. We aren't over. We will never be over. I'll figure something out. I just...I gotta play the part occasionally, for now."

I stare up into his clear blue eyes, the ones that are begging me to understand. I can't help but shake my head, though.

"Is that what happened to your last fiancé?"

He tenses at that, his face remaining blank.

"What?"

"I've heard Asher and Liam talk before, off-handedly, about how you were engaged after you graduated from Gallows Hill."

Ronan blinks at me, looking down at me solemnly.

"Every man is arranged to be married post-graduation."

"I know," I say. "I just was waiting for you to tell me the story."

"What story?"

I scoff, rolling my eyes.

"The story where you had a fiancé and now you don't?"

He's quiet for several seconds as if he were trying to gather his thoughts before he speaks.

"Her name was Madison Williams."

My mouth parts at that. "As in..."

"Annie's older sister, yes," he finishes.

"So, you were engaged to her sister and now you're expected to marry Annie? What, as a replacement?"

Ronan shrugs.

"Well, what does Madison have to say about this?"

His eyes stay on mine, a darkness coming over them.

"Nothing. She died when we were twenty-two."

"What?" I ask hollowly. "What the fuck is it with all the women in the Brethren dying?"

"What do you mean?" he asks.

"I mean, Madison, my mother, your mother, Asher's mother, Vincent's mother. Everyone's mom, sister or aunt is dead. Why?"

Ronan mulls over his answer for a while, his mouth opening and then closing before he finally spits something out.

"Women are...the Brethren don't hold women in high value. They are seen as bargaining chips, incubators for heirs and then...nothing. Madison tried to run away, she wanted me to come too. She wanted out of the Brethren, away from our families, on our own."

I frown. "Did you want that?"

He hesitates before nodding.

"I had my bags packed and car waiting for her outside her house. We were going to run to Canada, then get on a plane to Prague. I don't know, she said that's where she wanted to go and I..."

"You were in love with her," I guess.

He nods. "As in love as I was capable of being at the time. I was a lot different man than I am now. I've grown, learned a lot. The most important thing that I've learned though, is that there is no escape."

His words are heavy and ominous, like a dark black sludge seeping into me.

"What happened?" I ask.

"Her dad found out about our plans, at least the part about her running. I heard a gunshot in the house and by the time I got to the door, Annie was there, covered in her sister's blood, sobbing," he says, a shiver running through him that he tries to conceal.

Lifting my hand, I cup the side of his face.

"Ronan...I'm so sorry."

He leans into my hold and gives me a sympathetic smile.

"It was a long time ago, baby. I've coped, moved on. The next morning, I asked my father if I could pursue swimming as a distraction; miraculously, he allowed it. He clearly didn't know I had the same intentions as Madison, otherwise he would have killed me, not let me go off to compete in the Olympics," he laughs bitterly.

"Still, you loved her. That's not something you just forget," I say.

His hand lifts to cup my face, his thumb brushing against my lips.

"The way I loved her was so different. I loved spending time with her. She was beautiful and kind, but our love for each other was very surface-level, very familiar. We were told we would end up together for years. It wasn't as much a choice as it was an inevitability. The love I have for you, though...." He breaks off with a shake of his head.

"I love you wholly, completely. I love you even when I know it's the worst possible thing for both of us. I love you so much it fucking hurts to be away from you, and when I have you in my arms again," he says, gripping my face a little tighter, "it's like I can breathe for the first time. You're like coming up for air, baby. You're just...everything to me."

"Ronan," I whisper, my heart thundering in my chest.

"I think there are different types of love that you experience. There is that familial love, for your parents and siblings. There is the friendship love, when you would do anything for your best friends. There is your first love, when you think it couldn't possibly get any better, that it couldn't be anything more intense than what you have. And then you meet them."

"Who?"

"Your true love. The one that calls out to your soul, the one that makes every day worth living. You meet the person that compliments you, in every way possible. The one that shapes you into the best version of yourself and calls you on your shit when you aren't living up to your potential. That's what you are for me, baby. That's what I know we are. What we have is forever and I'll never give you up. I'll fix this, I'll solve it. Just don't give up on me while I do."

A soft huff comes from me as I shake my head.

"You big dumb idiot, like that's even a choice."

A half smile touches his face as sincerity drenches his features. He leans forward, pressing his lips to mine when my phone buzzes in my pocket. I ignore it, instead winding my arms around Ronan's shoulders. The buzzing thankfully stops before starting up again. I let it ring through again before it starts up for a third time. Ronan grumbles, pulling away from me before grabbing my phone out of my pocket.

He practically snarls as he hits a button, holding the phone up to his face.

"What?" he snarls.

Liam's wide smile comes through the phone, the picture of him driving his car fully displayed.

"Is that any way to answer my girlfriend's phone?" he teases.

"What the fuck do you want?" Ronan grumbles.

"I'm getting you two lunch because I'm obviously the best boyfriend you've ever had," he grins cheekily.

"Thank you, Liam," I say, forcing Ronan to angle the phone to me.

He smiles. "Anything for you, babygirl. Any requests?"

"Whatever is fine. We were in the middle of something," Ronan answers.

Liam's eyes that were on the road are now back to the phone, a mischievous look to them.

"Oh, really? Don't stop on my account," he says, with a waggle of his brows.

I chuckle and Ronan scoffs as Liam's smile shifts. Concern morphing his face.

"Fuck," he says.

"What?" I ask.

His eyes become more panicked as his body begins moving.

"Fuck, fuck, fuck. I don't have brakes!" he shouts.

"What?" Ronan asks. "Get off the gas. Downshift."

"I'm trying!" he snaps. "Oh fuck!" he shouts.

That's all we hear before a horn blares and a sickening crunch sounds through the speaker. The picture goes black, but the sound is still there for several seconds. Metal on metal, tires screeching and Liam's screams echoing through before the call is lost completely.

My entire body is instantly frozen, my veins cold as ice as I look at Ronan in horror. He stares down at me for a moment before grabbing his keys and opening the door. I feel his hand wrap around my arm as he begins running, dragging me with him. I don't really register it, though. I try to keep up, forcing my legs to cooperate, but they feel sluggish and numb, like they don't belong to me.

Oh my god. Oh my god. This isn't real. This can't be real.

Chapter Thirty

Liam

That distinct sterile smell, that always seems to turn my stomach, fills my nose. A faint beeping sounds in the background as I attempt to open my eyes.

"Oh my god! He's awake!" I hear Skyla say, her sweet voice going straight to my chest, forcing my heart to beat a little faster.

"Liam! Liam! Can you hear me?" she practically shouts.

Voice of an angel aside, she could turn it down a bit.

It takes a few tries but I'm finally able to pry my eyes open. When I do, at first, all I see is Skyla. She's inches away from my face, black streaks tracked down her cheeks, her eyes red and swollen. Concern instantly fills me.

"What's wrong, babygirl?" I rasp, my throat drier than a fucking desert.

She laughs hollowly as it breaks off into a sob. Skyla rests her head on my chest, sobbing her eyes out as my eyes fully adjust to the room. I'm in a hospital room, I'm in the bed and Asher, Ronan and Vincent are here as well.

Looking past Skyla, I see one of my legs has rods going through it, keeping it straight. It's fucking nasty to look at. Everything else looks fine, but when I lift my hand and touch my head, I realize it's wrapped in a bandage.

"What the fuck happened to me?" I ask.

Skyla pulls away from me, sniffing back tears as she looks down at me.

"You were in an accident. You lost your brakes, and you went into an intersection. You're lucky to be alive," she says, her voice cracking at the end.

I reach out for her hand, cupping it in mine as I squeeze.

"I'm okay, babygirl. Look at me? Picture of health!" I try to smile.

Asher scoffs. "Yeah, except for the leg that's broken in three places, two fractured ribs, a concussion and your ear that was damn near sliced off."

My head turns to look at Skyla.

"Yeah, except all that."

She lets out a pitiful chuckle as I look back to Asher.

"My *ear*?"

He nods. "They were able to reattach it, but it got all fucked up."

"My car?" I ask, way more concerned about that than a fucking ear right now.

Ronan shakes his head. I feel my body deflate, and my ribs scream in pain at the exhale I let out. Ah, that must be those pesky fractured ribs Asher was talking about.

"We will get you a new one. It's just a car," Skyla says. "When we pulled up...I thought you were..." she trails off, fresh tears spilling over her cheeks.

"Hey, hey, hey. I'm fine. I'm here," I say. "C'mere."

I attempt to scoot over, but the whole leg being screwed together makes that a little hard. Skyla settles for sitting on the side of the bed as I wrap my arm around her.

"What happened?" Vincent asks, direct and un-personable as ever.

I wrack my brain to try to think of the last moments I can remember.

"I was driving to get food for Skyla," I say with a frown. "I facetimed her and Ronan answered. I was about to watch them have sex—"

"No, you weren't," Ronan interrupts.

"Hush," I say, as I continue thinking. "I was coming up to a light and I hit my brakes, but there was nothing."

"What do you mean, there was nothing?" Vincent asks.

"I mean, I pushed the pedal, and nothing happened. It went straight to the floor."

"Did you change your brake pads recently? Not bleed them properly?" Vincent asks.

I roll my eyes at him. "I'm a car guy. You really think I don't know how to bleed my brakes?"

He doesn't answer, just continues staring at me.

"But no," I continue. "I haven't changed them in a few months."

Vincent, Ronan and Asher all share a look that puts me on edge. They don't say anything for several seconds, but it doesn't take a genius to guess what they are thinking.

"They were cut, weren't they?"

"What?" Skyla gasps, clearly out of the loop. "Who would do that?"

We all look to her, and she covers her mouth in horror.

"No," she says, with a shake of her head. "He's not capable of this... right?"

"He's been leaving pictures of us with our eyes crossed out, Asher being hung by a rope. He broke into the house and stabbed your bed, Siren. I think it's safe to say we don't know what the fuck he's capable of," Vincent says.

The room is heavy with silence for several seconds as we all grapple with the situation.

"What parking lot did you park in today?" Ronan asks.

"South, why?"

He nods, typing on his phone. "I'm gonna have Wesley pull the footage. See if we can tell who clipped your brakes during class."

Fuck. That's a good point. They definitely worked when I got to the university this morning. I look over to see Skyla staring off, a haunted look on her face. I squeeze her hand and her eyes meet mine, but they are a pale comparison to her normally vivid eyes.

I can see it all over her face. She feels responsible somehow, which is ridiculous. It's not her fault that she's so goddamn perfect she's caught the attention of some freak. No one is to blame, except the son of a bitch who cut my brakes. I'm not fucking scared, not even a little bit. I'm goddamn pissed. I can see it on all the other guys' faces as well. They look ready to burn the world down and I know it's not for my benefit. It's to make sure that his next target isn't her.

I spent another two days in the hospital before they finally let me go. I've got a cast from my foot up and over my knee, which makes my range of motion practically nonexistent. Scooting my ass as far out of the car as possible, Skyla lines up my crutches for me. I grab them, thankfully, lifting myself up to stand without putting any weight on my left leg. Thank god I'm so incredibly chiseled, otherwise this would be impossible.

I made that joke to Skyla several times. Still haven't gotten her to laugh.

She's been right by my side the entire time, yet distant. I can't really describe it; I just feel it. She's pulling away from me, from all of us really. I don't know what the fuck to do to stop it.

When I get to the bottom of the front steps, I blow out a breath in preparation before I take them one at a time. Asher is walking behind me, ready to catch me if I fall. My hero.

He's the other person who has been hovering nonstop. I appreciate his concern, but it puts me on edge more than anything. Could I have died? Easily. Did I? No, thankfully, so I don't need all the fuss. Not sure why I'm not soaking it up more. Normally, I'd kill for the attention. My mother even came to the hospital one day, thankfully while Skyla and the guys were gone. She spent twenty minutes where her entire attention was on me, which, trust me, after twenty-one years that's probably the longest I've ever held her attention.

It all feels cheap under the guise of looking after the injured dude, though. I just want things to go back to normal, and I want to figure out who the fuck this piece of shit stalker is so that Vincent can kill him. I'd say so I can kill him, but we all know Vincent will be much more efficient and bloody about it, this guy deserves for it to hurt. He fucking made me destroy my baby. It'll take buckets of money and countless hours to get a new car to the same place she was. Even then, it won't be the same. Oh, and obviously, the whole almost killing me and tormenting the woman I love thing.

Unfortunately, Wesley wasn't able to pull the footage from the south building. Conveniently, the cameras were down for routine maintenance that had been scheduled for months. It's either extremely lucky timing, or they knew about it and planned their move perfectly. I'll say one thing about this motherfucker, he sure is patient.

When I finally make it to the top of the stairs, I feel like I just did a decathlon. My chest is heaving, my forehead is dotted with sweat and my arms are shaking. I hate to break it to them, but there is no way in fuck I'm making it upstairs to any of the bedrooms.

"C'mon," Asher says, as he claps my shoulder and begins leading us into the living room.

I crutch my way through the foyer and when I round the corner, my eyebrows raise. The couch has been moved and in place is one of the beds from upstairs. I turn my head to look at Asher and Skyla as she points to Asher.

He shrugs and stuffs his hands in his pockets.

"It's not a big deal. Just figured those stairs would be a bitch. Also, figured you wouldn't want to be away from Skyla and stay at the dorm so... yeah."

"Thank you, man. I appreciate it," I say, as I make my way over to the edge of the bed, sitting down and leaning my crutches against the frame. Yeah, it's an entire bed, headboard and all.

Skyla comes to lay beside me, and I raise my arm for her to come closer, only wincing for a moment when she brushes against my ribs. Asher lingers for a moment before he comes and lays on the other side of her, handing me the remote. I click on the first thing I see and relax into bed, my eyes slowly drifting closed.

Chapter Thirty One
Skyla

As soon as Liam falls asleep and Asher is immersed in the show, I pull my phone out of my pocket, sending a text to Maggie.

Me: Ready.

Her reply takes a moment before it comes through.

Maggie: Are you sure about this?

My eyes flick over to a sleeping Liam and a distracted Asher. Unfortunately, I just don't have a choice.

Me: Yes.

Maggie: Okay. On my way.

Nodding to myself, I pocket my phone before turning to Asher.

"I'm going to head over to Maggie's for a bit."

He frowns, his eyes coming to Liam.

"He'll want you here when he wakes up."

I nod, forcing a small smile.

"I just need a little bit of...air, you know?"

Asher watches me carefully, hesitancy all over his face.

"Okay. Wesley picking you up?"

"Already on his way," I lie, almost seamlessly.

He nods, leaning in and pressing his lips against mine. I can't help but draw the kiss out for a few more seconds. Goodbyes are always so hard, especially hard when you don't want to say it, but you know it's the only way.

When I pull back, Asher looks at me with a little confusion before he smiles.

"Love you."

Dagger meet heart. Swallowing back the building tears, I smile.

"I love you too."

And I do. I mean it. I love him. I love them all. That's why I have to go.

Climbing over Asher, I crawl out of bed before heading to the foyer. Casually looking over my shoulder I notice that Asher isn't watching me, his attention back on the TV. Good.

I crack the closet door open, grabbing the backpack that I stashed there this morning before I slip out of the front door. It's starting to rain but my jacket is inside the bag. So, I duck my head and make a run for it. Once I'm through the front gate, I see Maggie's red car on the other side of the road.

She pops the trunk and I throw my bag in before running to the passenger seat.

"Go, go, go," I say, twisting in my seat to see if Asher has followed me outside.

Thankfully, the coast is clear.

"Jesus, this isn't a bank robbery, Sky," Maggie says, with a shake of her head.

I shake my head but don't respond as she drives in the direction of the docks. My knee bounces anxiously, as I look from side to side, like someone will pop out at any moment.

"You know you can still change your mind, right? No one knows what you're planning. If you don't go through with it, no harm done?" Maggie offers with a weak smile.

"I can't, Maggie. That guy is still out there. We don't even have a clue who it could be. The only thing we do know is that he has enough information to have us all murdered by the Brethren, that is, if he doesn't do it himself. He almost killed Liam!"

"I know, I know," Maggie says, raising a hand in a pacifying way.

"I'm just saying...there has to be a better option than this. If you can make it out of Massachusetts before the guys find you, and that's a big if, Christopher will no doubt assign every eliminator to you. You'll be dead by breakfast."

"Starting to feel like I'll be dead either way," I say numbly, as I stare out the window.

It's true. Especially from what Ronan told me, the Brethren doesn't do well with defectors. At this point, I can stick around, watch as everyone I love is killed at the hands of some psychopath, or I can run away as fast as I can and inevitably die at the hands of the Brethren. Neither outcomes are great, I'm dead in both, but the guys aren't in the second. My fate is clearly sealed; they still have a chance and I'm going to do everything in my power to protect them. Even if they don't want me to.

I've been thinking about running away for a little while. The idea would come to me, and I'd banish it as fast as it came. Then Liam had his accident...though it obviously wasn't an accident. Everything changed that day.

Ronan and I ended up coming up on the accident as Liam was being pried out of the car unconscious, his leg bent at an unnatural angle, blood pouring down his face from his ear. I thought he was dead. I collapsed in the middle of the road, sobbing my eyes out as I watched a piece of my heart be loaded up into an ambulance and driven away.

It took everything in me to stand up and get back in the car so that we could follow him. I stared at the mangled remnants of his car for several seconds, remembering vividly how it looked prior. How it felt to ride in it by his side.

When we got to the hospital, they gave Ronan an update on his condition immediately and though they said he was stable, I didn't believe them. No matter how much reassurance I was given, I thought for sure that he was about to be taken from me. That's when it really sank in for me, I had to give them up if I didn't want them taken away. They were never supposed to be mine to keep. My selfish need to have them all has now put a target on all of their backs, the only responsible thing I can think to do is to run like hell, and hope the psycho chases me.

Maggie pulls into a parking lot beside the docks. I pull up the ticket I bought last night for a seven-day cruise. It'll take me to Canada where I'll then fly out to a random destination. I haven't even chosen where I'm going to go. It's best that way. I don't know how far or powerful the Brethren's reach is. My guess, is far and strong. Is it a bulletproof plan? Absolutely not, but it was the best I could come up with this quickly.

Turning in her seat, Maggie reaches for my hand.

"Are you *sure* sure?"

I squeeze hers with a sad nod. Tears gather in her eyes as she pulls me in for a hug, holding me for several seconds as she speaks.

"I'll hold them off for as long as I can. When does the ship leave?" she asks.

"It says six o'clock, so that's in two hours," I say, as I glance at my ticket before my eyes move to my phone, the drafted text message in the group chat just waiting to be sent.

She nods. "I'll go back to campus. I'm sure they'll come there first."

Blowing out a heavy breath, I push open the car door as Maggie pops the trunk. She doesn't get out and I don't blame her. The less people who see her, the better. She could already be putting herself at risk just by helping me.

Walking back over to the front, she rolls down her window.

"I love you," she says.

"I love you too, Mags. I'd say I would check in but..."

"I know," she says, a tear dropping down her cheek.

"Stay safe," I say as I squeeze her arm through the window before standing upright and heading towards the ship.

My phone feels heavy in my hand as I look down at the waiting message, re-reading the words I've had saved for days. I know when I send it they will undoubtedly go crazy trying to find me. It's too late for any of that, though. So, I hit send and throw my phone into the ocean before handing the employee my ticket. They look at me strangely but scan it before nodding.

An ache settles inside my chest, one that I have no doubt will stay with me for the rest of my life, however long or short that may be.

Chapter Thirty Two
Vincent

Closing the door behind me, I carry the two bags of take-out in my fingers as I come into the living room. A huge bed is in the center, Liam and Asher hanging out on it while Ronan is sitting at the kitchen island.

"Where is Skyla?" I ask.

"Out," Asher says. "Wesley took her to Maggie's."

"And you thought that was acceptable?" I ask carefully.

Asher turns around to look at me, a sneer lifting his mouth as he speaks.

"Yeah, I did. Wesley is more than capable of keeping her safe, and we all know he's just about as gone for her as we all are. He won't let anything happen to her."

"If anything does, I'll skin Wesley from head to toe," I promise, as a door shuts and footsteps sound through the house.

"Whoa, what the fuck did I do to deserve that kind of threat?" Wesley says, as he walks into the room.

Rolling my eyes, I move my head to look behind him.

"Where's Skyla?"

Wesley frowns, his eyes roaming around the house.

"Isn't she here?"

The entire room goes still, all our eyes swinging to him.

"What?" I snap sharply.

"Didn't Asher drive her home with Liam from the hospital?" Wesley asks.

Asher is to his feet, moving towards him.

"I did. Then she told me that you were picking her up to take her to Maggie's."

Wesley shakes his head. "I haven't spoken to her today."

His eyes move to Ronan, their minds working a million miles a minute when my phone buzzes in my pocket. At the same time, Ronan's buzzes against the counter as Asher and Liam's ding with a notification. We all trade a look before scrambling for our phones.

Skyla: I'm sorry. I know this is the cowards' way out, but I also knew that if I did this in person, none of you would let me go, and you have to. I can't sit by anymore, waiting for him to hurt one of you, or worse, kill you. I hope you know that my heart is breaking as I type this, but I also hope you see why I had to do this. If I lost one of you, I'd never survive. I'm protecting you, like you all have protected me. Please don't look for me, please don't come for me. I'm trying to do the right thing...let me, please.

I love you all. Forever.

As I stare at the words, an icy chill settles into my chest. I watch as Ronan lifts his phone to his ear, hanging it up with a curse and trying again. Asher and Liam's fingers are flying across the screen as they begin panicking.

"Fuck! It's going straight to voicemail," Ronan snaps, as he throws his phone against the wall, shattering the device to pieces.

"Where could she be? What is she thinking!" Liam says, as his eyes look frantically to any of us for answers.

My thumbs are already moving at lightning speed. Hacking into the city's street cameras is almost too easy these days. I keep my eyes on my phone as I move towards the front door.

"Wesley with me. Asher and Ronan, go interrogate Bartlett. If she doesn't talk, start removing body parts," I say coolly.

"We're not going to hack up her best friend," Liam scoffs.

I pause on my heel, looking over my shoulder.

"I'll hack up anyone I need to if it means we get her back."

With that, I step out of the front door, feeling a presence beside me.

"What's the game plan?" Wesley asks.

I angle my screen for him, showing the moment Skyla jumped into Bartlett's car and they took off eastbound. Wesley's eyebrows lift in surprise as he assesses me.

"You work fast."

"Have to," I say shortly, before sliding into the front seat of his car. I begin fast forwarding the footage, directing Wesley before my jaw clenches as I watch the car park. My little siren. Of course she'd go to the water.

"You got access to a boat?" I ask Wesley.

"Maybe. Why?"

I turn to face him. "Because we're gonna need it."

Forty-five minutes later, I'm slipping inside her room on the cruise ship. Wesley is in a drag boat following closely behind, waiting for us. A few words with a guy at the docks and we were given the keys to a boat.

According to the dipshits back at the house, she could have been gone anywhere between forty-five minutes to four motherfucking hours. Based on how long it took us to catch up with the boat, I'd say it was closer to four hours. Worthless piece of shits.

When we got close enough, I was able to find a spot that allowed me to climb up and onto the stern. From there, it was almost too easy. A gun to the temple can pull information rather quickly, though unfortunately, 'security' is searching for me. It's fine, we won't be long.

My eyes scan the empty room, ready to go tear the ship apart in search of her, when I hear the sound of a bath running. Grabbing the bathroom door handle, I notice that it's locked. Not for long.

Lifting my boot, I kick it open, splintering the frame apart as a completely naked Skyla screams. Her screams stop when she sees it's me, but they shouldn't because with the anger I have inside me right now, I'm ready to fucking kill her.

"Vincent, how did you—"

I cut her words off, gripping her throat tighter than I should as I push my nose against hers.

"What the fuck do you think you're doing? Huh? Running away? Taking my goddamn heart with you? Do you honestly think there is a single place in this world that you could run to that I would not find you? Land or sea, I will always find you, Siren," I spit.

Tears begin welling in her eyes as her voice rasps.

"Leave, please. I need to keep you safe. I need to—"

"No!" I snap with a sharp shake. "It's my job to keep you safe, it's your job to let me."

"What if he kills you!" she sobs, as I loosen my hold on her neck.

I lift my other hand, cupping the back of her head to hold her in place as I look straight into those green eyes.

"Then I fucking die! But as long as I'm breathing, I will not let you go."

Her watery eyes glisten, and I shake my head at her stupidity before crushing my lips to hers. She doesn't fight me, but she doesn't engage either, which pisses me the fuck off. Pulling away from her, I spin her in my arms, forcing her to bend over the bathtub.

"What are you doing?" she asks, as my hand releases her throat fully. My hand on the back of her head slides down to her neck as my free hand unzips my pants, freeing my cock.

"Reminding you of who you belong to since you've obviously forgotten," I say, as I shove myself inside her.

As soon as her mouth drops open to gasp, I shove her fucking head underwater as I begin thrusting. I only leave her there for two seconds before I rip her out, thrusting my hips as I speak into her ear.

"You think you can just leave us like that? That you can leave me?" I snarl as I shove her back under.

She takes a deep breath before her head is submerged, her body bucking and fighting against me. If she thinks she can pull this shit and not face consequences, she's fucking insane. The anger thrumming in my veins has sinister voices whispering to me. Ones that suggest if she wants to run off and get killed, I'll do it myself. I'd rather be the one to feel her life drain from my hands than let another. I know my death would come only moments later because my life doesn't exist without hers anymore. So if she dies, I die, and I've never been so tempted to end it all until this moment.

Yanking her back out of the water, I brush my lips against her dripping wet cheek, speaking against her skin.

"You can't hide from me, Siren. I'll never stop coming for you. Run away all you want. I'll take pleasure in hunting you down every time."

Skyla lets out a pitiful cry as she shakes her head.

"I have to do this," she wheezes, though I can hear the fight in her voice dying by the second.

"I've got all night. Hold your breath," I say, before shoving her underwater again.

My pace quickens and her pussy contracts, squeezing the life out of my cock. Her body begins wriggling in panic under the water, like she's out of oxygen. I hold her for several more seconds, though. I know what she's capable of. She's held her breath this long before and I know I need to ride that line if I want to break this fucking attitude.

When her movements begin to slow I pull her out of the water again, smacking the side of her cheek to force her to breathe. Watery coughs erupt from her as she pants and gasps for breath.

"Please, please. No more," she begs.

"Have you had enough? You ready to come home, Siren?" I ask, as I angle my hips, forcing a moan to fall from her lips.

"I'm scared," she cries, a broken sound that hurts something inside me.

Forcing her to look at me, I continue fucking her, my cock throbbing and her pussy pulsing as I speak.

"I know, but I'll never let him get you. I'll never let anyone touch you again. I'm a very dangerous man. Few can go against me. You're mine, Siren, and you need to act like it."

Defeat fills her eyes as she weakly nods, her back arching against me as she begins to fall over the edge. I feel my own orgasm build, the anger inside me fueling the intensity as I fill her pussy with my cum. She takes me so well, screaming and moaning her release as I fuck her mercilessly.

When we've both come down from our highs, she slumps against the tub, her head just barely resting above the water as she blows out a heavy breath. Turning her head towards me, she shakes it as she speaks.

"For a second there, I thought you were going to kill me."

Slowly I pull out of her, leaning my face down to hers as I press a featherlight kiss against her lips.

"If you ever try to leave me again, I will."

Fear dilates in her green eyes before acceptance fills them. Is she just as fucked up as me, to accept such a statement? Most definitely. Is that one of the reasons she's my goddamn soulmate? Undoubtedly.

"Get dressed and get your things together. Wesley is waiting for us," I say, as I pull away from her.

"Wesley? Why?"

"Because Ronan and Asher are interrogating Maggie."

Skyla turns to face me, her face pinched with worry.

"It's not her fault! Please don't blame her."

I don't respond, grabbing the few items she's pulled out of a duffel bag on her bed before stuffing them back inside.

"Vincent! I'm serious," she shouts, as she begins getting dressed.

Again, I ignore her, zipping up the bag as I move into the bathroom, grabbing her arm and pulling her out. She's barely able to slip on her shoes before we're at the door. She attempts to pull out of my grasp as she looks at me desperately.

"Vincent, please!"

"Enough," I snap. "I don't give a fuck about your friend. I care about getting you home safe. Now stay quiet and stick close to me...please," I add on, pressing a kiss to her forehead that thankfully has her nodding her agreement.

I grip her duffle bag in one hand, her wrist in my other as I peek out the door, looking from side to side before pulling her with me. We walk a hundred feet or so before two men in security uniforms come up to us. Shit.

"Hey! Stop!" they shout, as they begin to run towards us.

We take off running the way we came, ditching into a side door that leads to the boiler room. I push Skyla to go first, scrambling behind her before shutting the door. Conveniently, there is a latch and I engage it before we begin making our way down the ladder.

When we get to the bottom, I take Skyla's hand, weaving through the pipes before coming to an exit. I pause outside the door, looking at her.

"You trust me?"

"Of course," she says.

"Good," I nod, before pushing the door open.

Half a dozen security guards are surrounding the door, all waiting for us. I drop my hold on Skyla, handing her the bag before I take on the first guy, punching him in the throat before kicking in his kneecap. He screams, falling to the floor as the rest charge me. I take each down, one by one, before I reach out for Skyla. She runs to me and I rush her to the edge of the boat, grabbing the rope ladder and throwing it over the side.

Her terrified eyes meet mine and I nod as I take her bag, throwing it over the edge. She looks over to see it sail through the air, landing just barely in Wesley's arms. He's trying to maneuver the boat close enough to us, without getting in the way of the ship's wake.

Another security guard charges me as Skyla begins scrambling down the side of the boat. I pull out my gun, jamming the butt of it against the bridge of his nose. He howls in pain, stumbling backwards as I jump onto the ladder, following Skyla before she reaches the end.

The breeze is forcing the ladder from side to side and Wesley is trying to reach for her while steering the boat at the same time.

"C'mon, little one. I got you!" he shouts over the roaring of the ship.

She glances anxiously at the distance between them before looking up to me. I give her an encouraging nod and she leaps through the air, my heart seizing in my chest when I see she didn't jump out far enough.

Wesley miraculously scrambles to the edge of the boat, holding his hands out for hers as she slips into the ocean. His hold on her keeps her head barely above water, before he's pulling her body out and into the boat.

Once she's safe, he wraps a blanket around her before steering the boat closer. I climb the rest of the way down before springing off the ship and onto the boat. I land in a crouch and next thing I know, Wesley flips us around to head back to shore.

Skyla is shivering and I wrap my arms around her, pulling her into my lap as we sail through the water. Flashing lights are easily seen on shore from here and I share a look with Wesley as he veers off, heading for a more discreet docking position.

I'm sure the Brethren will be down our throats for this one and I have no idea how we're gonna explain it away.

Chapter Thirty Three
Ronan

I'm sitting at the table, my knee bouncing anxiously as I watch the door. Wesley called me twenty minutes ago and said that they have Skyla, that they were on their way home. They should be here by now, though.

Asher is pacing the same six feet, over and over, his eyes moving from his steps to the door– back and forth. Liam is sitting on the side of the bed, facing the entrance as we all just wait.

Finally, the door opens. Asher and I sprint towards it while Liam grabs his crutches and lifts himself to stand. When we get there, Vincent is holding a soaked and shivering Skyla. He doesn't say a word, just carries her upstairs, assumingly to get changed.

Wesley trails in behind them, shutting the door before looking at me.

"What happened?" Asher asks.

"She got on a cruise ship to Canada. I don't know what her plan was."

"How'd you get her to come with you?" I ask.

He shakes his head and holds his hands up.

"I just drove the boat. Vincent pulled some mission impossible shit getting on and off the ship. I don't know how he talked her into coming with him, but there's a fuck-ton of security guards looking for him."

Lovely. Another mess to clean up.

"Why would she do that?" Liam asks, hurt clear in his voice.

"My guess is she feels responsible for what happened to you," Wesley answers Liam.

"Well, that's fucking stupid!" Liam snaps. "She can't just flip out and leave us like that. Can't fucking smash my heart through text just because she's scared. She can't..." he trails off, his chest fuming.

Asher reaches out to clap his shoulder, but Liam jerks away from him, using his crutches to move back into the living room before getting on his bed. Leaning forward, Asher offers Wesley his hand.

"Thank you," he says, the sincerest appreciation I've ever heard come out of my nephew's mouth.

Wesley takes his hand, nodding before Asher looks up at the stairs longingly. I can tell he wants to go be with her, but I also see the hurt inside him. The same one that Liam has, but Asher refuses to show. The kind that lives inside me.

Liam's right, she can't pull this shit. Never again. I was ready to break her little friend's goddamn neck when she wouldn't tell us where she took her. She's lucky Vincent sent a vague text about finding Skyla before he went MIA, otherwise we'd probably be burying a body on Gallows Hill.

Shaking his head, Asher moves back into the living room, taking a seat on the bed next to Liam as they begin speaking quietly.

My eyes glance upstairs as the shower in her bedroom turns on.

"You going up there?" Wesley asks.

"Yeah," I say before looking to him. "You?" I test.

He scoffs, getting a little flustered at my question before shaking his head.

"Definitely not. What business would I have up there?"

"I'd say the same as me or any of these other guys. You're not subtle, brother. If it was anyone else..." I trail off with a shake of my head.

He narrows his eyes at me, like he's studying me before he speaks.

"Is this a weird way of you giving me your blessing to pursue your girlfriend?"

Running a hand through my hair I let out a heavy sigh.

"Why not? Clearly we could use all the help we can get when it comes to her."

Wesley doesn't say anything, but I don't miss the way his eyes go to the stairs, just for half a second before he shakes his head.

"I gotta get going. Tell her I'm here if she needs me."

"Oh, I'm sure you are," I call out as he turns, heading out the door with another shake of his head.

Running my hand along my jaw, I make my way towards the stairs. I push open her bedroom door, my eyes taking inventory of the empty room. Or at least it feels that way with her bed and bedframe in the trash. We need to get her a new bed. She needs her own space away from all of us. That's for another night, though. She's had plenty of space from us and now she needs to face the consequences of her actions.

When I move into the bathroom, I find Vincent gathering her wet clothes. She's in the shower alone and I'm surprised when he wordlessly nods at me, carrying her clothes out the door before shutting it behind me. Damn, look at little Griggs sharing. He's all grown up. Then again, maybe he needs some space from her too. With his temper, I can't imagine how much anger he has right now.

As quietly as I can manage, I begin undressing before slipping into the shower. Her eyes come to mine, a deep sadness mixed with regret shine in them. She gives me a small smile that quickly fades when I don't return the gesture.

"Hi," she says quietly.

I raise an eyebrow in question because fucking seriously?

"Hi?" I question. "Is that really all you have to say?"

She shakes her head.

"I'm sorry. I didn't mean to hurt you, any of you. I was just trying to do the right thing and—"

"I know baby, but what you did was not the right thing. It was foolish, impulsive and immature. We don't run off into battle on our own trying to carry the weight of the world on our shoulders. We come together to talk, strategize and plan. What you did tonight is not something I want any part of."

Her lower lip begins to quiver as a tear falls down her cheek and she nods.

"I understand," she says brokenly.

"What do you understand?"

"That I ruined everything. That you can't forgive me."

Exhaling roughly through my nostrils, I shake my head as I pull hers to me, forcing our mouths together. She's stiff at first, but melts into me with ease when I pull away roughly.

"Baby, cut that shit out right now. You know that you didn't ruin anything. As long as my heart is beating, it's yours. When it stops beating, it'll still be yours too."

Her eyes beg me that this is real, that I'm not lying or going to change my mind. Which is absurd. I could never change my mind about her, but that doesn't mean she's off the hook.

"But," I begin, "I'm fucking pissed with you. Liam is downstairs heartbroken, Asher is devastated. Vincent...fuck, I'm surprised he didn't rough you up a bit or something."

She winces. "In his own way, he kind of did."

I frown, not liking that no matter how mad he was or is.

"He hurt you?"

"No, scared me more like it."

Nodding, my hand reaches out to her, sliding down her wet, naked body. I pause on her ass, rubbing my hand in a circular motion before I pull it away and smack it against her. She gasps at the spank.

"Ow! What the fuck?"

"He may not have hurt you, but I'm going to. You tried to run away and leave me, baby. Daddy is very mad at you right now."

Her eyes look up at me with sadness, but I don't miss the excitement that also comes to the surface.

"I'm sorry, daddy. Really."

"Sorry isn't going to cut it this time, baby. Be a good girl and brace yourself on the edge," I say, as I gesture to the shower seat in here.

She does as I say, bending over as her hands splay across the wooden bench. I reach up, adjusting the shower so it's not on her head, the warm water running down her ass cheeks and legs.

"How many spanks do you think you deserve?" I ask.

"As many as you think, daddy," she responds perfectly, slipping into her submissive role like she was born for it.

"You broke so many hearts with a single text message tonight, baby. One hundred and twenty-five words, nine sentences and over four hours worried sick about you. Would a simple 'I'm sorry' be good enough for that?" I ask.

She shakes her head.

"What do you need then? What do we need to do to make sure this never happens again?"

Looking over her shoulder at me, her lips form the most beautiful sentence in the English language.

"Punish me, daddy."

Something raw and primal flares up inside me, and my hand is smacking down against her ass before I realize what's happening. She yelps in pain but doesn't ask me to stop. Again and again, I spank her bratty ass.

How fucking dare she hurt me like that. I thought I was going to throw up at first, then a sadness like I haven't felt in over a decade sank down inside me. Only this time, it felt worse because though I knew I would move on from Madison's death one way or another, the same can't be said for Skyla. She's my everything and she not only put herself in an insurmountable amount of danger, she tried to end us? Hell fucking no.

On the last smack she whimpers, a choked sob ripping out of her that catches my attention. I look down to her beet red cheek, my hand covering it gently as I begin rubbing small soothing circles over it.

"You did so well, baby," I praise softly, my hands continuing to massage her carefully.

"I'm so sorry," she says on a cry, shaking her head.

"Shhh, it's okay. I understand why you did it, I just...you can't scare me like that again, do you hear me? My heart can't take it."

Sniffling, she looks over her shoulder to me. I pull her to stand upright before I scoop her up into my arms, pressing her back against the tiled wall. Peppering kisses against her neck as I whisper affirmations into her skin.

"I love you so much, baby. Please don't ever try to leave me again," I beg.

She shakes her head, wrapping her arms around my neck.

"I won't, I promise. I just got scared."

Nodding my head, I kiss a trail up to her face before pressing my lips to hers.

"I love you," she murmurs against me.

"I love you, forever."

A softness overcomes her as she relaxes into my arms.

"Make love to me, Ronan."

Pulling back to meet her eyes, I cup the side of her face tenderly.

"My pleasure, hold on tight, baby."

Lining myself up to her, I lift her for a moment before lowering her down onto me. Her mouth opens, before a sexy as fuck moan slips out of her. I feel her hands dig into the back of my shoulders as I lift her up again, pulling her down once more.

Slowly, we find a steady rhythm while Skyla just does her best to hold on. I try to be easy with her, to cherish her the way she deserves, but I've never needed her like I do now. It's almost like if I can fuck her deep enough, we will never have to be apart again. I'll never have to worry about her running off with my heart, never have to worry about someone taking her from me or hurting her.

My hold on her tightens, my knuckles turning white as the wet sound of her back slapping against the tiled wall echoes through the bathroom.

"Fuck, baby!" I bark out. "Look at us," I say as I look down, watching as my cock slides in and out of her tight pussy. "You're taking me so well, baby. I'm so goddamn proud of you," I say, as she moans in response.

"Harder! Fuck, Ronan, right there."

Happily, I oblige, fucking her to the point that I know is teetering that pain-to-pleasure scale before one more deep thrust has her spasming around my cock. Her mouth drops open in surprise as she screams out her release, her pussy convulsing around me so tightly that I have no choice but to follow after her.

My cock jerks and throbs inside her, that much needed release rushing through me as my movements begin to slow. Looking down at her, I press a kiss to her forehead before slowly lowering her to her feet. She smiles up at me softly, sending my heart practically tripping over itself. It's so dangerous to love someone the way I love Skyla. No going back now, though.

Chapter Thirty Four
Asher

I hear the echoed shouts from Skyla all the way downstairs. I thought maybe it was her, Ronan, and Vincent up there. But Vincent came downstairs a few minutes after he carried her up, letting us know he was going back to his place for the night. He didn't give any explanation, just left.

Glancing to my left, I see Liam isn't watching the show in front of him but rather looking the ceiling above him. The area that has the room with Skyla in it.

"You okay?" I finally ask.

Liam turns to me, shrugging his shoulders.

"I'm glad she's okay, but I'm fucking pissed, dude."

I nod as he continues.

"I mean, I get where she's coming from. I get that she was trying to look out for us, but c'mon. That is not how you handle that! You don't break four people's hearts over a fucking text. You don't disappear, running off to god knows where with god knows who. She needs to trust that we will always keep her safe, that we will do our best to keep ourselves safe, and if that isn't good enough for her then—"

"Then what?" I interject. "You going to break up with her?"

Liam scoffs like the very suggestion is absurd.

"Of course not. I love her more than anything in the world, I'm just saying...I'm pissed and I think I have a right to be."

I nod, staring at my hands as I speak.

"I'm sad," I admit quietly.

"Really?"

Nodding again, I look up at him.

"I'm sad she felt she had no other choice. Sad she doesn't think we're capable of keeping her safe, keeping all of us safe. Though, I'm mostly sad because she's right to feel that way. I mean, look at you," I say with a wave of my hand.

"It was a freak thing," Liam brushed off.

"But it wasn't. It was planned, methodical. That sick fuck tried to kill you man, and I just..."

I trail off for a moment, not sure how to explain in words what I'm feeling before I shrug.

"It was scary as fuck, man. I thought we lost you for a minute."

Liam hesitates for a moment before he reaches a hand out, cupping my shoulder and squeezing empathetically. My eyes move to his, something shifting inside me that I don't know how to name, nor do I want to try. In the chaos of things, Liam and I haven't really had time to talk about...everything that went down the other day. Then again, there isn't much to say. Skyla asked us to kiss, we did, and everyone got off. Yeah, the next morning there was a little more to it, but chalk it up to curiosity. Trying to discern if it was hot in the moment because Skyla requested it, or if it was just hot period.

I'll definitely be keeping my findings to myself.

A few minutes go by before Skyla pads downstairs wearing a black silk nightgown, her hair wet and combed as she gives us small smiles. When we don't return it, her smile falls, and she gestures to the end of the bed.

"Can I sit down?"

We both nod and she does so quietly before staring at us.

"I'm sorry," she says.

"We know," Liam responds coldly.

She frowns, lowering her head as she nods.

"You're mad," she states.

"Yes, and we're sad," Liam corrects.

I look over to him. He squeezes my shoulder once more before returning his hand to his side.

"I'm sure you've gotten this lecture from the other two, but now you're gonna get it from us," he says. "You will absolutely never run off like that again. You will never pull some hero bullshit to 'save us'. You will never ever try to break up with us again because try as you might, babygirl, I can promise you won't win that fight."

Skyla's brows furrow as she tilts her head to the side.

"What do you mean?"

"He means that if you try to break up with us, we will simply decline," I finish for my friend.

"Exactly," Liam agrees.

A laugh bubbles out of Skyla as she shakes her head.

"I'm not sure that's how that works."

"Sure it is," Liam says. "It takes all parties to willingly enter the arrangement. Therefore, it should take all parties to willingly exit."

"So I just don't get a say?" she asks in mock offense.

"Pretty much," I say, causing Liam to crack a barely there smile before Skyla does the same.

"C'mere, babygirl. I need to hold you," Liam says, patting the space between us.

She crawls in between us, wiggling under the covers, before resting her head on his upper chest. I waste no time in plastering myself against her back, wrapping my arms around her waist, a sense of peace I didn't know I was desperate for settling over me as I do.

I'm not sure who is the first to fall asleep. All I know is that my eyes get heavy almost immediately and I slowly drift off with my two favorite people.

Dreading this conversation but knowing that it needs to be had, I click on that familiar contact. The phone rings for several seconds before he answers.

"What?"

"Hello, father. How are you?"

"As well as can be expected, considering one of my eliminators is currently wanted for the assault of several cruise ship staff members and the kidnapping of a passenger. You wouldn't know anything about that, would you?" he asks, his voice stony and unforgiving.

Keeping my tone even, the story I've practiced over and over again until it's polished to perfection, I put him at ease.

"Yes, that's why I'm calling. He needed to fetch her for me."

"Who?"

"Skyla. She threw a tantrum and tried to get on a cruise ship without me. Said she needed a vacation from my ego," I scoff.

My father does a matching one that tells me he's buying it so far.

"Fucking typical woman."

I grunt my agreement before continuing.

So, I sent Griggs to retrieve her."

"Why send an eliminator?" he pushes.

"With my bond brother being injured, I figured he was the only one unstable enough to do whatever it took to bring her back to me."

He makes a noise. I can't quite tell if it's in agreement or argument, but he stays quiet for several more seconds before he speaks again.

"I'll take care of it. Next time, I expect you to handle the aftermath on your own. I'm not your fucking babysitter," he says, before the call drops off.

No, you're not my babysitter, you're my fucking dad.

Pocketing my phone, I shake my head as I make my way upstairs to jump in the shower and start my day.

Chapter Thirty Five
Skyla

Asher was going to drive me, but I had to get to class early to talk with Professor Corwin about catching up on some assignments. With the time Asher and I spent out of school, I've struggled to balance the catch-up game, and I'm hoping he will cut me a little slack.

Wesley brought me my cider and my favorite lemon loaf cake. Since he picked me up, we haven't spoke much, mainly just driving in comfortable silence, that is until we round the block near the university.

"So, am I going to have to commandeer another boat and pull you out of the Atlantic Ocean today or?"

I roll my eyes, shooting him a very unimpressed look that forces him to smile.

"Ha ha, you're hilarious. You should have let me drown."

"Afraid I couldn't have let that happen, it would be a direct risk to my health," he says as he pulls up to the curb, putting the car in park.

"Why? Because the guys would break all the bones in your body if you let something happen to me?" I tease.

He scoffs. "Absolutely not. None of those guys intimidate me."

I lift an eyebrow in question. "Then how would me getting hurt be a risk to your health?"

"My heart," he says dramatically, resting his hand over his chest as he slips out of the car.

I can't help but laugh at that, still smiling when he opens the door. Instead of letting me slide out, he lowers himself, pushing his body to hang halfway into the car.

"You laugh, but it's the truth," he smiles before a seriousness takes over. "We were all very worried about you."

My smile slowly starts to drop, my eyes moving from his and down to his mouth before back to his eyes again.

"Is there...something...between us," I hedge softly, my breathing increasing slightly as I do.

Those deep blue eyes sparkle with curiosity as he tilts his head to the side, closing the distance between us as he speaks.

"Do you want there to be something between us, little one?"

I swallow, butterflies fluttering through me at the nickname. I love all the little nicknames my guys have for me. I mean, my boyfriends, obviously. Wesley most definitely not included. We couldn't be together even if that's what I would want...not that it is. It probably wouldn't hurt to have at least one male friend that I'm not in a relationship with. I can't be greedy and have every attractive man who looks my way...right? Right.

"I-I don't know," I answer honestly, hating the way my voice shakes as I do.

He nods thoughtfully before his hand lifts, running his thumb over my lower lip before pulling it down. My lip goes down until he releases it with a simple flick, my lip bouncing back into place though where he touched is still tingling.

"You let me know when you figure it out," he says, his eyes tracing over my face one more time before pulling away.

Wesley stands up, holding the door open like a proper chauffeur. Sliding out of the seat, I nod my thanks, not sticking around for any more sultry moments together. The more space that I can give us, the better.

Maggie meets me at our usual spot, pulling me in for a hug before we fall into step.

"You waited for me?" I ask.

She nods. "I was with Asher and Ronan when they got word that Vincent found you."

I grimace at that. "They weren't mean to you, were they?"

Maggie lifts her eyebrow and laughs.

"Babe, they are mean to everyone who isn't you."

Shrugging at that, I continue. "But still, they didn't...hurt you, did they?"

She shakes her head. "Though I'm not gonna lie, I thought Asher's head was going to explode while I was playing stupid. Ronan looked like he was two seconds away from stringing me up by my toes," she laughs.

I shake my head at her. "You know, normally people wouldn't find either of those things to be funny."

"Most people don't have an awesome sense of humor like me," she shrugs, as she opens the class door for me. "Besides, I know they are just protective of you. How could I be mad at them for trying to love on my bestie?"

I roll my eyes, but I can't help but smile because she's got a point. They can be overbearing as hell at times, but I can't forget for a moment how lucky I am to have all of these incredible men that are in love with me, that want to keep me safe and protected.

As we make our way up to our seats, I turn to respond when something catches my eye, forcing my attention back over to my seat.

My stomach instantly turns, my body on full alert as I stare down at the single stemmed rose. I see a small tag attached to it, fear filling me to the brim as I creep towards the flower, lifting the tag with shaky hands.

Only a little longer until we're together. Stay patient. I love you.

Maggie leans over, reading the note before cursing under her breath.

"That's not from one of the guys, is it?"

I shake my head as Liam comes into the room, stopping at the bottom of the stairs as his eyes seek mine out. When his eyes meet mine, though, he knows something is wrong. Lifting up the rose, I wave it to him as his mouth rounds and I can see him say, 'oh shit'.

He gestures for me to come to him and I do as he says, bringing the rose with me. Liam reads the tag, a pinched look crossing his face as his eyes roam around the room. There is hardly anyone here today, maybe because it's still twenty minutes before class starts. Still, it had to be someone in here, right?

Whatever Liam was looking for, he clearly comes up short before shaking his head again and gesturing for the door.

"C'mon, we're going home."

I don't bother to argue, a slimy feeling of unease settling into my bones as I look around the room accusingly. As if the stalker is about to pop out at any moment shouting 'Boo! Gotcha!'.

Liam turns in his crutches, making his way for the door as Professor Corwin steps inside, giving us a frown.

"Where are you two going?"

Liam doesn't answer, and I turn to do so when I think better of it. What am I supposed to explain? That I have had a stalker for months now, that he's becoming aggressive and is now leaving me notes and roses in class? Yeah, for some reason, I don't think that would go over well.

It only takes a few phone calls for all of the guys to meet us in the pool hall, minus Vincent, who is away doing god knows what. Ronan locks the door behind us as the guys begin reading the note,

"Do we think it's the stalker or maybe a copycat situation?" Liam throws out.

"What about the teacher? He has to unlock the class before anyone can get in," Asher points out.

"Yeah, but most of the time the teachers fuck off to the lounge as soon as they do, not even bothering to go inside," Ronan says.

Asher turns to face me.

"Think about it, princess. Think hard. Is there anyone in that class who has ever made you uncomfortable? Stared at you for too long? Taken an interest in you? Overall given bad vibes?

I shake my head, my brows furrowed as I rack my brain to think of something useful when I still. Oh, my god.

"Yes," I say, the revelation a surprise to even me.

"Who?" they all demand at once.

My eyes move from all of them as I roughly swallow.

"Andrew Hutchinson."

Understanding dons on Liam's face before he nods.

"He's always had a thing for Skyla. He sits right in front of her and usually watches her walk in and out of the room."

"Well, let's go have a little chat with him," Ronan suggests.

Asher nods. "Let's. Can someone call Wesley? Tell him he needs to get back here and get Skyla home."

"Wait, home?" I ask.

Asher nods. "As of right now, you won't be leaving the house. Period."

"But what about my schoolwork? I can't afford to fall behind, Asher."

"We'll bring your work home. It'll be fine."

"I don't know, Ash. If she doesn't want to stay home, I don't blame her," Liam says.

"I agree. She can still come to school, we just need to be more vigilant," Ronan says.

Asher throws his arms out to his sides.

"Oh, I'm sorry. I didn't realize this was a town council meeting. Let me simplify this for you all. My wife, my call. She's staying home."

"Are you really going to keep playing that card?" Liam drawls sarcastically.

"Absolutely. If any of you could, I know you would. Don't pretend otherwise."

They are all silent, proving once and for all that men are nothing but possessive cavemen.

"Clear?" Asher asks, extra douchey this time.

We all grumble, including me, before he nods his head and I pull out my phone, dialing Wesley.

"Can you come pick me up?"

Chapter Thirty Six
Vincent

Smashing the guy's hand against his desk, I grab it before sliding it through the walnut cracker I brought. One slip through, a pinch of the handle, and the bone makes a sickening crunch, followed by his muffled screams. It's hard to scream when your tongue has been cut out and your sweaty socks have been stuffed inside your mouth. You know, to help stop the bleeding. He'll thank me someday.

The task assigned to me was simple. Make sure he can never speak or write what happened to him but make it hurt. Once I go through each broken finger, I pull out his left hand, resting it on his desk as I pull out the meat cleaver from my little bag of tricks.

The man begins bucking and squirming, even going as far as to kick me. Fucking rude.

Lifting up the cleaver, I bring it down with a solid swing that sends his entire wrist and hand flopping to the side. Blood shoots out of his arm and I get a rag from my bag, making a quick tourniquet. If the Brethren wanted him dead, they would have said that.

The next hand goes easier than the other, mainly because he passes out from the shock and probably from the blood loss. It's one hell of a way to spend a morning. I'm just grateful this guy works out of his home office. Can't imagine how many people I'd have to take care of if this was an office building.

Sometimes I wonder if I'm a little too fucked up for this world. Death, blood and violence, they don't affect me like they do normal people. I've been raised with it. I remember my parents coming home as a child, seeing them dripping the blood of their targets. It's been engrained in me since birth– receive orders, follow orders, repeat. There is no room for error or self-will and for a while I was okay with that, until Nathaniel. Then things started to really come into focus.

We aren't some guardians of the Brethren, actively protecting our people from harm. We are doing the harm. We are the henchmen, the yes men. For years I was mind warped, thinking what we did was important, that it mattered. Now, I follow my orders to stay alive until a better opportunity arises, or a better escape plan.

I was so close to being ready too. My things were packed, fake death planned, and then...I saw her. Just a glimpse of her getting out of her father's car, following his security guards to the Parris Dorm and suddenly, instead of driving away in my car like planned, I stayed. I blew all of my plans of freedom to hell and followed her like a moth to a flame.

I spent the next week obsessing over every scrap of information I could pull on Skyla Parris. Despite my best efforts, I was infuriated to find that there wasn't much available. She had been hidden away perfectly. The exquisite crown jewel of the Brethren.

Skyla thinks she's special because of her father and while, yes, he is a high ranking Elder, that's not the reason. She is so goddamn valuable because up until her, there hasn't been a female born in the Elder families in over two hundred and fifty years.

At first, no one thought anything of it. Men are more useful, more powerful. At least that's how they saw it. But then, after having child after child, all being boys, the Brethren became curious. They started actively trying for girls, even going as far as going to fertility clinics all over the world in the last fifty or so years. Every time it's a boy, never a girl.

It began a sort of crazed quest for many of the families. They wanted to know why it wasn't possible. Other members of the Brethren didn't have a problem, it was just the Elders.

Obviously, you already know what they're thinking. They are cursed. I'm not sure how much I buy into all of that stuff. I think the trials were a distraction from a power struggle they wanted desperately to win. What better way than do the worst thing you could do back in the late seventeenth century? You accuse those you don't like or see as a threat, of being a witch.

My phone buzzes in my back pocket, and I step away from the man after applying his second tourniquet before answering it.

"Yeah?" I answer.

"It's Skyla, man," Liam says. "The stalker left her a note and rose in her class. She thinks it could be Andrew Hutchinson."

Anger sparks inside me, followed by irritation. Hutchinson? I cleared him weeks ago. He was an initial suspect for me as well, what with his infatuation with Skyla, but after a deep dive, I came to the conclusion that he was harmless. Guess I'll be needing to look into him more thoroughly.

"Do you have him?" I ask, already packing up my bags. My job is done here anyways.

"No. We can't find him. Was hoping you could help us with that."

I nod wordlessly, keeping my gloves and mask on as I open the office door and step out into the foyer. It's a nice house. I'm sure the blood will come out of the carpet, eventually.

"You have her?" I ask, making sure to keep my words vague as I slip out of the house and head for my bike that's stashed a block down the road.

"Yeah, we got her. Wesley took her home. Ronan went with them. Asher and I are looking into shit here on campus."

"Good. Let me know what you find," I say as I hang up the phone.

Stepping out onto the front porch, I stop in my tracks when a shadowy figure moves towards me.

"Graves," I say stiffly, my hand going to my holstered gun.

That psychotic fuck tilts his head in amusement, his skull mask hiding the face of the well-known killer.

"Griggs, it's been a minute. Now, don't tell me you took out my mark before I could," he tuts, that amused lilt to his voice only amplifying how unhinged this man is.

Don't get me wrong, I can fucking slaughter someone with hardly a blink or moment's hesitation, but this guy...he enjoys it, has fun with it. Being in the same...line of work, we've run into each other over the years. My parents used to talk about the Graves brothers from time to time. Sometimes they would take out his mark before he could, other times, it was vice versa. Whoever his employer is, they seem to have similar enemies to the Brethren.

"Sorry, looks like you're getting slow with old age," I remark flatly.

A glint of silver flashes from his side, a long hunting knife firmly gripped in his hand. He hmphs lightly as we both stand still, watching the other, waiting. I'd like to say I'm not afraid of going toe to toe with most people. I know without a doubt, though, out of anyone in the world, I do not want to go against Zayden Graves. I might make it out the other side, but it won't be without a few dozen stab wounds as a parting gift.

Lucky for me, he seems as uninterested in a fight as I do.

"You don't mind if I tell my employer I handled it, do you?" he says on a laugh.

"Not as long as you don't mind me telling mine that I handled it."

"Fine by me, you saved me a load of laundry tonight. I have an angel to go see, anyways."

With that, he turns on his heel and walks off into the distance, disappearing into the tree line. I stand still, watching him every step of the way until I know for sure he is gone, before I begin walking to my bike. Now that I'm not faced with the hurdle of going head-to-head with one of the nation's most lethal hitmen, I have a new target in mind. One that is deserving of all of my wrath and then some.

Andrew motherfucking Hutchinson. You better hope I don't fucking find you.

Chapter Thirty Seven
Skyla

I'm finishing cleaning our plates from dinner before wiping down the counters. Vincent hasn't been by today, but he did text me to tell me that he loves me and that he's going to find Andrew. Ronan and Wesley hung out until Asher and Liam came home. Then they were gone, off to search for Andrew another way.

It's odd that one moment he was here, going to class, saying hi in the halls, and now he's just...gone. It definitely doesn't bode well for his case of not being guilty. Having a bold gesture like that in public and then going AWOL...yeah, it's not comforting.

Flopping down on the end of Liam's bed, I feel him lean over and smack my ass, giving me a mirth filled smirk as he does. I turn to face him, crawling towards him with a smile of my own. Since Liam's accident, Asher and I have practically lived in the living room with him. The stairs would be too hard for him, and I don't want him to feel like he's all alone down here.

His ribs are slowly healing, but still not all the way better, and obviously, he's still in a cast. It has definitely limited what we are able to...do in the bedroom, but of course, that hasn't stopped Liam. He's laying in the middle of the bed, and I come up to lay on his left side while Asher is texting on his right.

"You looking for trouble, sir?" I tease.

Liam's eyes light up as he nods quickly.

"Yes, ma'am. Please and thank you!"

I laugh at that, closing the distance between us as he cups my jaw. The kiss is slow and sweet, his tongue peeking out only once or twice to toy with me before he begins peppering my neck with kisses. I moan softly at the feel of it when Asher's head snaps away from his phone. He looks to me, his eyes darkening with lust as he scoots closer, leaning over Liam to press his lips to mine.

With Liam's mouth still on my neck and Asher's lips against mine, I feel like I'm in heaven. Being worshiped by these two godlike men is absolutely surreal, but for the love of all things holy, no one pinch me please.

I feel a hand slip under my chin before Liam pulls me away from Asher and back to his mouth. I go easily, enjoying the different feel and technique between the two. Asher mimics this move, both pulling me back and forth until Asher is kissing the left side of my mouth while Liam is kissing my right. I know the instant their lips accidentally touch because they both freeze, all of our eyes flying open while they stare at each other.

Surprise hits me when it's Asher who turns away from me, angling himself to Liam as he lifts his hand and cups his jaw, just as tenderly as he was with me. I watch as Liam practically melts against Asher, their tongues tangling together in a way that makes my pussy throb.

Slowly, they inch their bodies closer together until they are both plastered to each other. Asher's leg slides between Liam's, their sweats grinding against each other. I can't help but sit up a little, my eyes greedily taking in the sight of their cocks grinding together. A throaty moan escapes Liam as Asher grabs his hip, bringing him flush to his body.

Carefully, Liam maneuvers himself so that he's now straddling Asher. It's a delicate process with his cast, but somehow, he's able to make it work, and the lust in Asher's eyes tells me it was more than worth it for him.

I watch as Liam chances a new move, his hand runs down Asher's chest before resting on his cock, wrapping around the length as their mouths are pressed together. Asher arches into Liam's hold as Liam grinds himself against him, panting when they pull apart and look at each other.

"That feel good?" Liam asks cautiously.

Asher doesn't respond, just gives him a jerky nod. Liam grins at that, a wide, beautiful smile as he presses a kiss to Asher's neck, running his mouth down his shirtless chest before pausing just above his waistline. Liam's eyes glance down at it, clearly having a battle with himself internally when I speak.

"You want to, Liam?" I ask.

He looks to me, a tint of helplessness in his eyes as he nods before looking up to Asher. I look at him too, resting a reassuring hand on his thigh.

"Do you want him to suck your cock, baby?" I ask Asher.

He hesitates for a moment, his eyes flicking between the both of us as his jaw tenses and he settles on Liam.

"So fucking bad," he admits.

That's all the permission Liam needs. His hands are sliding Asher's sweats down and gripping his cock. It's as if he can't have him fast enough, like he's worried that he will change his mind. Liam wraps his mouth around Asher's cock and the way his mouth falls open, it's unlike anything I've seen.

His eyes roll into the back of his head, his hand coming to the back of Liam's head as he pushes him down further, groaning when Liam does so happily. My panties are absolutely dripping wet as I watch Liam take Asher. He bobs his head expertly, pushing him all the way down his throat before swallowing intentionally. It makes Asher buck against him, his teeth clenched together as he speaks.

"FUCK! Yes, again. More."

Liam runs his hands in circles on Asher's thighs, nodding at him before shooting him a wink as he does it again and again, causing louder moans to fall from his lips each time.

"Princess, come here," Asher practically begs.

I scramble beside him, ready to do, say or be literally anything in this moment.

"Ride my face, Princess. I want you both on me at the same time."

A shiver runs through me in excitement, and I scramble to my feet, pulling down my sleep shorts before coming up to straddle Asher's face. I don't even have time to be self-conscious or worry about crushing him. Instead, I settle all of my weight on him as I grab the headboard. Asher's tongue licks through me aggressively, leaving no time to warm-up, which is fine by me since my clit is quite literally pulsing.

Muffled moans sound from between my thighs, no doubt a reaction of him eating me and getting sucked by Liam. This moment is too hot, too perfect. I never want it to end. I turn around to watch, the feeling of Asher's tongue flicking against my clit as I watch Liam suck his cock while stroking his own. There are no words. Nothing compares to this.

I hear Liam moan first, the sounds echoing from around Asher's cock as he cums on the bed. Asher's hips begin mercilessly fucking Liam's throat as his fingers come up to me. His thumb swirls around my clit, giving me just the push I needed to fall over the edge.

I come hard, humping and grinding my pussy against Asher's face before I hear him also release. I can't help but turn for a moment to see Liam drinking down every drop of Asher before Liam's eyes land on me.

He sits up, gently crawling over Asher's body before he reaches up and into my hair, twisting it around his hand before yanking my head backwards. I follow his movements, my mouth opening in surprise as Liam spits Asher's cum into my mouth.

Before I have a second to process it Liam forces my mouth closed, tapping the side of my cheek.

"Swallow."

I do as he says, earning a wide grin from Liam.

"Good girl, doesn't our boy taste like heaven?"

Moving off Asher's face and to the side of him, I nod, looking down to see Asher's eyes wide and panicked. Oh no.

I expect this to be the part where he has another freak out. Now that the lust haze has lifted, he's going to push Liam away again. Surprisingly, though, Liam intervenes. He practically plasters his body against Asher's, bringing his lips to his.

"Mmmm, you and my babygirl mixed together? I could get used to this," Liam smiles, as he gives Asher another peck before moving to his ear.

He whispers so softly I barely hear him, but it's clear enough for me to understand what he's saying.

"Don't run, Ash. Please. Don't run out on me again. Stay...please," he begs softly in between kisses.

I watch as Asher's eyes close, his tense body slowly relaxing beneath Liam's kisses as he nods wordlessly. What looks like relief fills Liam, before he moves to lay on Asher's right side. Asher lifts his arm for Liam, taking us both by surprise, but Liam doesn't have a problem snuggling into Asher's chest. Asher does the same for me on his left and I mimic Liam's position, resting my head against Asher as I look at Liam. We share a soft smile between each other as Liam closes his eyes, one of the purest smiles I've ever seen, before I feel a kiss press against the crown of my head.

Looking up, I see Asher pulling away before giving Liam a matching kiss and closing his eyes. I'm frozen for several moments, doing my best to process how we all move forward. It's obvious that there is a pull between Asher and Liam, of course. Though, I'm not sure what that looks like exactly. Asher has, to my knowledge, always viewed himself as straight, though he is clearly grappling with his sexuality now. Liam has identified as Heteroromantic bisexual, though there is definitely something romantic about that smile on his face.

Whatever the situation is, they will figure it out, on their own and together. I'll support both of them in whatever they decide. I just hope it doesn't ruin their friendship because all of this aside, it's a beautiful bond. But as I've always stated, I have absolutely nothing against my boyfriends being boyfriends.

Chapter Thirty Eight
Ronan

My feet freeze as I blink several times, trying to make sense of what I just witnessed. Asher lifts his arm for Liam and he takes the offer easily, cuddling into his chest before Skyla does the same thing. They all look so peaceful.

I wonder how long this has been going on.

Not knowing if I should make myself known or slip out of the house, I go for the latter. I quietly sneak out the way I came before getting into my car, calling Wesley as I head out on the road.

"Hey, I'm almost there," he answers.

"Meet me at my place instead. They are...busy," I say.

"Busy like....busyyy?" he drawls out.

I grunt in response, which causes him to stay silent for a moment.

"So, why don't you join?"

I go to tell him that I think tonight is very much about the three of them, but I don't know if they'd want people to know, at least not yet. So, I keep it vague.

"We have work to do. Skyla is safe. So meet me at my place."

With that, I hang up the phone as I weave my way home. When I get there, surprisingly, Wesley is already waiting for me by the front door. Stepping out of my car and locking it behind me, I nod my head in greeting before unlocking the door.

Once we are inside with the door locked, it's like we both blow out a breath of relief and begin speaking freely.

"So, what? Didn't feel like getting laid tonight?" Wesley asks.

I smack the back of his head, shooting him a disgusted look as I shrug my jacket off my shoulders.

"Don't fucking talk about her like that."

Wesley's brows furrow like he's confused.

"I wasn't talking about her like anything. I'm just confused why you'd rather spend a night with me than her?"

The way he says it is laced with jealousy. I've noticed it pretty much from the start, but it's becoming more and more prominent. If he's not already in love with her, he's well on his way. There's no doubt about that.

"Careful, brother. You almost sound envious of my position," I warn.

His mouth opens to speak when he pauses before shaking his head and shrugging his shoulders.

"If your position is with me instead of her, then I'm not envious at all. Just thinking about how stupid you are."

I lift a brow in question as I move to my office, Wesley trailing after me as I fire up my computer.

"If you would rather spend time with her, then go. You know where she is."

Wesley makes a scoffing sound under his breath but doesn't say a word. I've already made several calls to Hutchinson, he's dodged all of my attempts swiftly, which only ratchets my suspicion. With Andrew disappearing into thin air and his father keeping him hidden, it's clear they are aware of something, if not responsible for the whole fuckin thing. If that little shit is the one who has been terrorizing Skyla since she arrived, I'll gut him like the pig he is.

I click on the app on my computer, pulling up the school's surveillance cameras. Over the next hour, Wesley and I pour over the footage, watching each angle, each wing, desperate to trace where the fuck Andrew has gone. Conveniently, the feed in Skyla's history class, Andrew's dorm and the parking lot were all cut today. How the fuck was no one notified about this sooner? Oh, yeah. Because Hutchinson is in charge of all surveillance and both him and his son are unreachable. How convenient.

"Fuck!" I snap, as I slam my fists against the keyboard.

Wesley shakes his head in frustration as he pulls out his phone, his fingers flying across the keys.

"What are you doing?" I ask.

"Well, we can't get a hold of them, right? Can't track them down on surveillance footage?"

I nod my head in agreement.

"Well, then we are gonna go to them."

"If you think I haven't already been to their house—"

"What about their safe house?" Wesley asks.

I frown at that. "What do you mean?"

"C'mon, like a tech security god/borderline doomsday prepper like Hutchinson isn't going to have an undocumented safe house should anything go wrong with the Brethren, the world or his son?" Wesley challenges.

I think on it for a second. Makes sense, pretty fitting to his character, with the little I know about him actually.

"How are you going to find something like that?" I ask.

Welsey continues typing on his phone as he speaks.

"I have made alliances with some of the most skilled hackers in the world over the last decade. What good would those relationships be if I couldn't utilize them from time to time?"

He finishes whatever he was doing on his phone before he pockets it and nods.

"And now?" I guess.

"We wait."

I curse under my breath as I shake my head.

"For how fucking long?"

Wesley gives me a flat look. "As long as it takes. My guys work fast, faster than you, me or any of those kids would."

Biting the inside of my cheek, I shake my head before begrudgingly nodding. It's not the answer I wanted to hear. It's not an answer any of them want to hear. If Wesley's contacts take more than a few days, I have no doubt Griggs will have already burnt the world down. For everyone's sake, I hope they are faster than that.

Chapter Thirty Nine
Skyla

The next morning, I wake up to the smell of bacon and something sweet. My eyes flutter open, landing on a sleeping Asher. I'm still tucked on his left while Liam is tucked on his right. Sitting up, he rouses a little before falling back asleep. Liam snuggles into him and I watch as Asher's hold on him tightens subconsciously. Seeing them like this has my heart tugging in my chest. They'd hate to hear me describe them this way, but god, they are so cute together.

Quietly slipping out of bed, I look to see Vincent asleep on the couch, his hoodie pulled over his face and boots propped up on the arm of the couch. It's as if he never truly relaxes, even when he's sleeping. Like he's one door opening or glass shattering away from jumping to attention and flipping that switch into kill mode.

Looking into the kitchen, I see Ronan at the stove, flipping what I now can tell is a piece of french toast as he pulls the bacon out of another pan. His eyes swing to me, a tired smile on his face.

"Good morning," he says.

"Morning," I smile, as I pad my way over to him.

He abandons the food in front of him, spinning to face me, as his arms wrap around my lower back. I can't help but sink into his touch, comfort washing over me as he holds me. His head leans down, pressing his lips to mine. My hand reaches up to cup his face, deepening the kiss as I do.

When we pull apart, I don't move away, instead softly whispering just over his lips.

"I missed you last night."

"Yeah? I missed you, baby."

"Why didn't you come over?" I ask.

His eyes move from me to the bed, before back to me.

"I did. Last night. You guys were...busy."

My cheeks flame, images from last night flickering in my mind. I wonder what Ronan walked in on. I wonder what he thought or what he's thinking now. Before I can ask though, he continues.

"Not going to lie, I thought Asher would have been the last person to fall for Liam's charm."

I raise a brow at him in question.

"You thought Vincent before Asher?"

He shrugs. "I could see Vincent enjoying causing Liam pain, and I think Liam would enjoy it too."

"Not a chance in fucking hell," Vincent calls out easily, clearly not asleep.

"You say that now, until you see how tight my asshole is," Liam says sleepily.

"Jesus, what a way to wake up," Asher grouches.

The sheets rustle before Asher stands on his feet, making his way into the kitchen. He doesn't meet anyone's eyes as he high-tails it for the coffee. I let him do his thing, doing my best not to stare but I'm worried about him. Worried about Liam. Maybe a little worried about myself.

Slowly, Liam gets to his feet with his crutches, smoothly making his way through the kitchen before he stops in between Asher and me. He places a quick kiss against Asher's bare shoulder, that instantly has him tensing before Liam gives me a matching one on my cheek.

My eyes watch Asher carefully, as his rigid shoulders slowly relax and he turns around to face us. His face is impassive and stoic, though I see a little bit of concern in his eyes. When I give him a warm smile, I watch as that concern begins fading and he returns it with a small one of his own.

"Did you make breakfast?" Liam asks Ronan. "Thank you, daddy."

Ronan scoffs, his face pinched up in irritation that makes me laugh.

"What's wrong? You love it when I call you daddy," I tease.

He looks down at me with a flat look as Liam cuts in, two pieces of bacon already shoved into his mouth.

"Yeah, and you're the oldest one in the group, AKA, daddy."

Ronan's hand smacks against my bare ass, the baggy t-shirt I have on barely covering me as he shakes his head.

"You're encouraging him and it's too fucking early for this."

I can't help but giggle as Vincent pushes to his feet, moving over to us like a zombie. He doesn't wait his turn or even ask anyone to move. Instead, he pushes through Liam and Asher before snatching me out of Ronan's grasp. His arms wind around me as his face buries into my neck, inhaling deeply before blowing it out and tightening his hold on me.

"Good morning," I smile, as my hand reaches up and begins scratching his head.

He makes the softest moan of approval as his lips murmur against my neck.

"Morning, Siren."

"When did you get in last night?" I ask.

"Five or six," he answers.

I frown at that, looking at the clock on the stove.

"It's seven."

He shrugs, still nuzzled into me, as my eyes come to Ronan before the others.

"Any news on Andrew? Did you guys find him?"

Vincent tenses in my arms before pushing up to his full height.

"No," they all answer, creepily in unison.

My face falls but I do my best to mask my emotions. Swallowing roughly, I nod. I'm doing my best to stay calm; for all I know, this could be a weird coincidence. Just because he's vanished doesn't mean the flower was from him, that all the notes and gifts were from him. He could be sick, really sick. Or on vacation with no cell service. I just...I can't seem to associate the sweet shy guy, with the same person that has been actively stalking me and threatening my guys.

Ronan's hand reaches out, cupping my waist gently.

"Wesley has some contacts looking into the entire family. We will track them down and get some answers, okay?"

I nod, my eyes sweeping around to see everyone watching me with pinched looks of concern.

Like a hurricane, Wesley blows through the front door from out of nowhere. I jolt in fear for a moment before my brain can process that we are safe and it's just him.

His eyes are wide, hair mussed as his eyes scan the room before landing on me. I could of sworn relief passes across his face before he makes his way to us.

"It's not Andrew."

"How do you know?" Ronan challenges him.

"Because I just spoke with him and his dad. They are at a safe house, off the coast of Italy currently."

"Why?" Asher asks.

Wesley's eyes come to his before going back to Ronan's.

"Because someone came up to Andrew in the parking lot yesterday morning. They put a gun to his head and told him he had to leave the country, immediately or he was going to be shot on site. He panicked, called his dad and the whole family ran."

Ronan frowns while Vincent speaks.

"Bullshit, he's just lying to cover his ass."

"Is he?" Wesley asks. "Or did someone think he would make the perfect fall guy? If they could conveniently get him out of here just as the stalker makes a bold move, all the attention goes to someone else?"

Liam and Asher shake their heads like they don't believe it when Wesley lifts his hand, dropping a black envelope onto the kitchen island.

"I was skeptical, too, until I got here and found this resting on the front doorstep."

Vincent is the closest and he makes quick work of grabbing it, his eyes scanning over it before he blinks and shakes his head. Liam and I are the next to read it, pulling it out of his hands as I read it out loud.

My Dearest Giselle,
You've hurt me again and again. It's always going to be them, isn't it?
I thought what we had was special, was real. They've clearly poisoned you, like a sickness seeping into your veins.
You need to be purged of their evil and cleansed by my hands. I'll fix it all and we can be together again.
Hold on, my love. I'm coming.

"What the fuck?" Liam guffaws when I finish.

My hands are shaking, stomach twisted into knots. This letter is so different than the others. It's not the same style, the same words. He's calling me Giselle. Why would he do that?

"Giselle, like your mom?" Asher asks.

I shake my head as I try to make sense of this.

"Does that mean the stalker thinks I'm my mom? Or that he knew her?"

"Maybe," Wesley answers. "Does anyone come to mind?"

How am I supposed to know? She died when I was three. If not for pictures, I wouldn't even know what she looked like.

My eyes come to Asher's, helplessly shaking my head. We continue to stare at each other for several seconds before we both seem to share the same thought at once.

"The man from the party," I gasp.

"Clark Lewis," Asher says, his jaw clenching tightly.

"Lewis? Dane's dad?" Liam asks.

"Yeah," Ronan answers. "What about him?"

"At the engagement party, Asher and I were leaving and this man stopped me. He called me Giselle and told me how I looked just like my mother. It was clear he knew her and….it couldn't be him, right?" I ask, turning to face Asher.

He stares at me before shaking his head and stepping up to me. He presses a lingering kiss to my forehead before pulling away.

"I don't know, but I'm gonna find out."

Vincent's fingers are flying across his phone before he nods.

"Got the Lewis address."

"I'm driving," Ronan says, as he presses a kiss to the top of my head and grabs his keys.

Vincent leans in, placing a quick peck against my lips before he follows after Ronan and Asher.

"We'll stay here," Wesley says as he looks from Liam to me.

"Wait, where are you guys going?" I ask, though I'm met with the sound of the front door opening and shutting.

"To get him, babygirl," Liam says as he winds his arm around my waist.

"And do what?" I ask.

He gives me a heavy look as Wesley speaks.

"To get answers."

"But what if he hurts them? He's clearly dangerous! We have to help them. We have to—"

"Babygirl, breathe. They are more than capable of taking care of him."

"Are you sure you understand who you're dating, little one?" Wesley asks. "Vincent is one of the most cold-hearted Eliminators that the Brethren has ever seen. A task no one thought he'd be able to achieve, seeing as his parents were full-blown psychopaths."

"And Ronan," Liam adds on. "He's all responsible and in control now, but he wasn't always like that."

"He wasn't?" I ask.

"Fuck, no," Wesley laughs solemnly. "Ronan has had a tough life. You see how fucked Christopher is, can you imagine what Luther was like? Ronan had a lot of anger growing up, a lot of skills. He might be just as dangerous as Vincent, at least when it comes to protecting you."

"And you should have seen Asher when we were sent on a job a while ago," Liam says hollowly, a shiver running through him as he does. "I've never seen him so...empty. Like he tucked the real Asher away and became this dehumanized killer."

Liam shuts his eyes and shakes his head as Wesley reaches out for my hand, gripping it in his own as he squeezes.

"Trust me, they will be just fine. It's Lewis you should worry about."

I do my best to ignore the way my stomach flips when he squeezes my hand and how my heart begins to race, when he shows no sign of letting go.

"Why is that?" I ask softly.

Wesley gives me a sad smile and shakes his head.

"Because if he is behind everything and they can prove it, they will shred him to pieces before he can breathe out a single excuse."

Fear pangs through me, not exactly sure why. They just made excellent points as to why the guys will be fine. Maybe I'm anxious about everything finally coming to an end, getting answers. Or maybe I'm terrified to get those answers. Regardless, I don't think I'll like the outcome of this scenario.

I feel Liam's eyes on me and when I look away from Wesley, I see Liam staring at our joined hands before his eyes come to Wesley. Dropping his hand quickly, I don't miss the flash of sadness on Wesley's face before he stands at attention, shrugging away any emotions that could potentially be read on his face.

"I'm gonna do a perimeter sweep. You two stay in here."

I nod, watching as he goes, his long legs closing the distance to the back door before he slips outside. His toned back strains against his black henley, his dark jeans hugging his ass in a way that leaves nothing to the imagination. Which is kind of incredible because, my god, I don't think I could have imagined an ass like that on a man, let alone this man. I don't realize that my eyes are still tracking him until Liam lets out a low chuckle.

"You got a little bit of drool, babygirl," he teases as he wipes at my chin.

I look over to Liam, rolling my eyes as he continues laughing.

"It's okay, I don't blame you. Maybe we can talk him into a three-some while we wait for the others?"

I scoff, though now that the mental image has entered my head I know it's there to stay.

Fuck.

Chapter Forty
Vincent

Sneaking onto the Lewis estate was easier than it should have been. Busting down the front door and throwing him into the trunk of Ronan's car, even easier. What's difficult is getting this motherfucker to talk.

We drove him to Ronan's house and unloaded him into the cellar. Ronan has never used the cellar before, and it shows. Cobwebs and rats cover every inch of the place. Conveniently, there is a room with a single dim light, no windows and enough space for me to...play.

My fist drives into his jaw, sending Lewis' head snapping to the side before spitting out a glob of blood. He lets out a whimpered groan as he shakes his head.

"P-please. I don't know what you want. I don't know anything."

"Cut the shit!" I seethe. "I'm not in the goddamn mood for your bullshit. Admit that you've been stalking Skyla, and I'll make sure to kill you nice and fast."

"Skyla?" he asks in confusion, his eyes moving to Asher and Ronan's before coming back to me. "Skyla Parris? Why would I stalk her?"

"I saw the way you looked at her at our engagement party," Asher cuts in, coming to stand beside me as he does. "You called her Giselle."

He shakes his head frantically. "It was a mistake. She looks so much like her mother. It caught me off-guard."

"Why would it?" Ronan asks. "What was she to you?"

"Nothing," Lewis answers quickly, causing Asher and I to share a look.

Wordlessly, he moves to the corner of the room where a five-gallon jug of water is before I grab a towel and wrap it around his face. Ronan moves behind him, tilting the chair backwards as Asher lifts the water jug up and over Lewis. The water begins to pour over the cloth, drawing out the suffering before I nod to Asher, and he pulls away. Ronan rights the chair and I pull the towel as he begins coughing up water.

"Let's try that again," I say. "Who was Giselle Parris to you?"

"Before," he rasps. "Before she married Henry, she was Giselle Thompson, and she was...everything. She was everyone's everything. There wasn't a man on campus who wasn't in love with her."

Hm, sounds familiar.

"And when Skyla came to town, you saw it as your second chance? Your redemption?" Ronan guesses.

"NO!" Lewis defends, his head swinging back and forth between us.

Frustration boils beneath my skin and I can't stop my forehead from swinging forward, cracking against his nose and exploding the thing across the goddamn room. He screams in pain as I grip his shirt and yank him closer to me.

"You're a fucking liar! Did you tell your piece of shit son about this obsession? Is that why he planned to hurt her? To rape her? I should have broken more than his goddamn legs."

Outrage fills his eyes as he looks up at me.

"Y-you hurt my son? He didn't fall?"

I scoff and roll my eyes. "Of course he fell. After a nice hard shove he fell all the way down those stairs. I scooped his bitch-ass up and took him to the hospital, though. I could have left him."

To my surprise, he fights against me. Ronan and Asher each rest a hand on his shoulders, pinning him into place. A grin spreads across my face as I watch him buck and curse me.

"You son of a bitch! You ruined his fucking life. He may never walk right again because of you!"

"No, that would be because of him. It was your piece of shit son who planned to rape the love of my life. A couple of broken legs was just part one of his punishment."

"The love of your life?" he frowns before looking up at Asher. "I thought she was Putnam's?"

Ronan and Asher shoot me irritated looks. Oopsies. Guess we really have to kill him now. Not like I wasn't already planning on it. Guilty or not, he's an Elder, which means he has more blood on his hands than any human ever should. His death will be celebrated one day. Though, I'm not fully convinced he isn't behind this. Or maybe it's him and Dane. Lewis clearly seems to hold some contempt for Henry.

I stand upright, slowly making my way over to my bag of goodies before I rifle through it. It takes me a moment to find what I'm looking for, but when I do, I hold it up like a grand prize.

"A meat tenderizer?" Asher questions.

I don't respond. Instead, I cross the room, whistling an eerie tune as I do. Lewis' eyes dilate in fear the closer I get to him, and I can't help but grin as I allow the darkness inside of me to take over this little inter-rogation.

"You don't seem to think highly of Henry Parris," I say.

"Wh-what makes you say that?" Lewis stutters, his eyes flicking back and forth between me and the cleaver.

My smirk lifts. "Intuition."

Slowly, I allow my left hand to trace every sharp point of the tender-izer, keeping my eyes on Lewis as I speak.

"Explain."

His eyes flick to Ronan and Asher before back to me, shakily shrug-ging his shoulders.

"He's a prick, no one likes him."

I nod my agreement. "True, but you seem to have a special kind of hate for him. So, elaborate. You had a crush on Giselle in school, yes?"

Lewis's teeth clench. "Yes."

"But she didn't return those feelings?" I guess.

His jaw tics, confirming that piece of information.

"Of course she didn't, look at you," I sneer, attempting to see if goading will pull him out of his quiet shell.

Still, he doesn't give in.

"That's why you're stalking Skyla, right?"

"I'm not stalking a little schoolgirl," he snaps defiantly.

Oh, it's going to be like that? Perfect.

"Left or right?" I ask.

"What do you mean?" he asks cautiously.

"Left or right, it's a simple question."

Lewis narrows his eyes at me before he says, "Left."

I nod at that, promptly grabbing his right hand, forcing it to lay flat against the arm of the chair he's in. Lowering my face to his, I smile in a way that I can tell turns his stomach.

"You're not the stalker; for argument's sake, let's say I believe you. Now, tell me something that will interest me, or I'll break your goddamn hand. You have a lot of bones. I can repeat this game as many times as it takes."

"W-what do you want to know?" he stutters, as I lift the tenderizer and crush it against his hand.

He squeals like a pig, moaning and shouting in pain, as Asher and Ronan hold him in place.

"Left or right?" I ask again.

Lewis is too busy whimpering and crying to listen, so I give him a little reminder to pay attention. My fist drives into his temple, sending his head reeling as he blinks roughly.

"Left or right?" I prompt again.

He blinks hard as he attempts to look at me before he shakes his head. A squeak catches my attention, and I watch as several dozen rats scamper off into a dark corner. An idea springs to mind, and I quickly drop the tenderizer, leaping over to the rats and grabbing one. I hold it by the tail as I gesture towards Asher.

"Tie his arms to the chair. Then grab me the thick gloves, metal bowl and blow torch," I rattle off.

Asher nods slowly but complies, tying up Lewis before fetching the items. The rat is going crazy in my hand, desperate for an escape. Soon, little guy. I can tell by the squeamish look on Ronan's face that he knows what my next move is, but like the good little helper he is, he grips Lewis's shirt, ripping it open to exposed his bare beer belly. Perfect.

I extend a hand for the bowl and Asher hands it to me before I set the rat down onto Lewis's stomach, trapping it in place with the bowl.

"Ah! Fuck! Get this fucking thing off me!" Lewis snaps.

Shaking my head with that unhinged smile I've perfected, I extend one of my hands, keeping the bowl in place with the other, as I gesture for Asher to glove me. He does so wordlessly before doing the other hand as well. Finally, I'm handed the blow torch and I bring it to the bowl before I pause.

"Did you know that rats can chew and dig through almost anything, especially when their life depends on it? Wood, plastic, even steel pipes on occasion."

Lewis squirms, his breathing labored and panting. My finger clicks the torch on as I slowly bring it to the bowl.

"I'd hate to see what this little guy is capable of chewing through when it gets a little too toasty in here."

The tip of the flame just grazes the metal when he screeches.

"Ah! Okay, okay. Giselle w-was a good girl until she was betrothed to Parris. Then her and Putnam started spending a lot of time together as well. All three of them were together."

I yank the flame away, looking at him curiously before I clock the confusion and shock on Ronan and Asher's faces.

"What do you mean?" I ask with narrowed eyes.

"Like they both fucked her. Putnam wanted her, hated that Parris was promised to her. Even tried to get Luther to switch their brides."

Ronan frowns at this. "Then what?"

"Then nothing," Lewis continues. "The wedding eventually came. Giselle married Parris. Isabel married Putnam. That was it until Giselle died. Everyone was devastated when we got the news. Christopher went off the deep end, took off for Europe or something for half a year."

Understanding passes on Ronan's face, like a piece of a puzzle clicked into place. Being smart, he keeps his mouth shut as we continue to listen.

"Who else was obsessed with Giselle?" I ask, as my eyes move to Asher and Ronan before back down to Lewis.

"I told you! Everyone. She was fucking perfect. Apparently, her daughter carried on her allure from the looks of it," he says, as he glances to all of us.

Ronan decks him, and I have to keep pressure on the bowl as he jerks in place.

"C'mon, Lewis. You're a smart man. Think. Who could be stalking Skyla? Mistaking her for Giselle, obsessing over her all these years later."

He shakes his head. "I don't know."

"Wrong answer," I grit out, before lowering the torch back to the bowl.

It heats up in no time, burning even through my gloves as he begins to scream. The sound of the rat squeaking as well as chewing and tearing flesh is audible through the bowl, as Lewis's cries for help fall on deaf ears. We all watch him squirm and shout. To my surprise, Ronan and Asher hold up well. Perhaps they have more potential than I realized.

"Give me a name and it'll all go away," I offer.

He can't speak though, he's in too much pain. Instead, he groans and screams, his body shaking in shock at being eaten and clawed alive.

"Vincent, enough," Asher says. "He's no good to us dead."

I look up at the youngest Putnam. "He's no good to us alive. He knows too much."

"So, what? You're just going to kill him? An Elder?" Asher challenges.

"Well, I'm sure as shit not letting him go. We'd all be dead by morning, isn't that right?" I ask the practically seizing Lewis. He doesn't speak, just moans and shakes as he stares up at the ceiling.

Ronan nods his head. "Vincent's right."

A few more minutes go by, before the squeaking stops and Lewis's sounds fade altogether. Ronan reaches down, feeling for a pulse before he shakes his head.

Rot in hell motherfucker.

Removing the torch and the bowl, it takes a moment before the blood-soaked rat scampers out of Lewis's body. A decent sized hole is now in the center of his chest, organs half chewed through and oozing blood. It's a gory sight, one that honestly rivals any I've ever seen. It was no doubt a painful death, but for a man that molested his six-year-old niece and got away with it thanks to the Brethren, it wasn't painful enough, in my opinion.

"What now?" Asher asks.

My eyes swing up to his.

"Now, it's time for you to have a chat with your daddy."

Chapter Forty One
Asher

I still don't think this is a good idea. When we grabbed Lewis, we thought we were finally going to get some answers. Instead, we walked away with a body to dispose of and more questions than ever.

My dad was dating my wife's mom? While her dad was?

I know how hypocritical it seems for me to be shocked, but my dad doesn't share, and he doesn't lose. Ever. If he truly wanted Giselle for himself, there is no way he would ever let Henry have her. And then for him to disappear for half a year mourning her? He didn't even shed a single tear when my own mother passed away.

That kind of care, maybe even love, is unusual for my father's character. However, it seems very typical stalker behavior. For him to obsess over something he lost, latch onto the first reminder of it, and never let go.

Ronan didn't want to say it, but we were both thinking it. The way that he's taken an interest in Skyla since she arrived is an added clue. I'm just not sure how he will react when I confront him.

Never thought I'd say this, but thank god Griggs is with me. Ronan is in his car, down the block a little ways. My dad doesn't need to get suspicious about why we've been spending so much time together, and he sure as hell won't open up when there is more than one person in a room. So, I'm going in alone. Though I imagine by the time I step inside,

Griggs will have already broken in and be in the shadows waiting for anything, really.

I tuck my keys into my pocket as the butler opens the door for me. I head straight towards my father's office, rehearsing all of the key points I'm going to bring up so I can trick him out of some information.

Though, as soon as I step through the foyer, a chill runs down my spine. The scars on mine and my wife's back will serve as a forever reminder of this room, of this house, of this...man.

As soon as my father's eyes come to mine through the open doors of his office, I lose my nerve, just for a second. A cold chill runs down my spine as he inspects me like a piece of gum beneath his shoe. Pushing it down, I roll my shoulders back, lift my chin and close the distance between us.

"Asher, you didn't tell me that you were coming," he says, in a tone that would be considered anything but pleased with this unexpected visit.

"My apologies. I didn't really know I was coming until I was here."

He frowns as he takes a seat behind his desk.

"Why is that?"

I pause for a moment, choosing my words carefully.

"Skyla has been talking about her mom a lot lately. She doesn't really know anything about her and she's desperate for it. I told her I'd do some digging if she complied in bed," I shrug in an asshole way my dad will love.

Sure enough, an amused grin spreads across his face as he nods.

"Nice negotiating skills, son. Just remember, these women are practically worthless. If they won't do it, someone else will. Or you can go for more...aggressive tactics. Double the fun," he winks, in a way that turns my stomach when I have to smile in agreement.

Oh, how did I spend my day? With my father telling me if my wife doesn't want to do something in bed, I should just rape her. God, he's a fucking piece of shit.

"Did you know her? You all went to school together, right?" I ask.

He nods slowly, a haziness coming to his eyes like he's reminiscing right this very moment.

"Well," he says, a soft clearing of his throat as he does.

"How well?" I ask a little too quickly.

He shoots me a suspicious glare before he responds.

"Very well. What is this really about?"

"I told you. I—"

"Yes, and as you can tell, I see through your lie. Now, tell me why you're really here."

There are a couple of ways that I could play this. If I double down on my denial, maybe I could get out of this. Then again, maybe I should tell him the truth; he might be able to help. Maybe I'll leave out the whole 'we killed Clark Lewis' thing.

"Skyla has a stalker," I say, testing the waters with that sentence.

I study him like a hawk, waiting for any indication or reaction. He looks taken back for a moment before he tilts his head to the side in intrigue.

"A stalker? Since when?"

"Since the beginning of school," I answer.

"Why didn't you tell me sooner?" he accuses, like that should have been my first instinct.

"I didn't know until right before the ceremony. After that, I didn't feel it was necessary. I thought it was just someone messing with her head."

"But it's not?"

I shake my head. "No, the stalker is behind Liam's car accident and they—"

"Why would he hurt Liam if he's after Skyla?" my father asks curiously.

Fuck.

My mind scrambles with any reasonable answer I can give. I draw a blank across the board, though. Understanding seems to dawn on my father's face, and I swallow roughly as he stands, rounding the desk to stand in front of me.

"You sharing your wife, son?"

I read him as best as I can, or at least I try to. I can't be seeing what I think I see, though. He isn't angry or disgusted. Instead, he's engaged, maybe even a little proud? I decide to lean into this, carefully.

"When we're bored," I shrug nonchalantly. "Somehow, the creep snuck into the house, took a picture of us...together and left a threatening note right before Liam's accident."

My father's lips purse in displeasure for that last piece. He begins pacing the room as he speaks.

"What do they want? Do we know?"

I shake my head. "Besides the obvious, her?"

"Who have you eliminated as a suspect?"

"Well, that's kind of why I'm here. I didn't know if..."

For a moment, I pause, forcing him to stop mid-step. His head swings over to me, eyes looking me over.

"You wanted to know if I was stalking your wife?"

I don't respond, but I don't have to. So instead I wait, I watch, and I save it all for later.

An amused chuckle rips through him as he shakes his head.

"Little boy, if I wanted your wife, I'd take her. I wouldn't waste my time with games."

That's more on par with the man I know, but still...I can't help but be suspicious.

"She got a letter this morning, addressing her as Giselle."

His eyes narrow at that, amused smile nowhere in sight.

"Where is the letter?"

"Back at the house. Why—"

"What did it say?"

"Uh, fuck. I don't know. I don't have it memorized. Basically something about how she doesn't have to worry, that he will come for her soon."

My father frowns, his mind racing as he nods.

"Keep me apprised of this situation. I assume you're setting up a watch for her?"

I nod.

"Good," he says, as he sits down and dials his phone, avoiding eye contact and thus silently dismissing me.

As I walk down the front steps to my car, I replay it all in my mind. His reactions, his words, his body language shifts. It all rings true for someone who was surprised, but my father is the master manipulator. He's such a compulsive narcissist. I have no doubt that he believes his own lies.

The fact that he knows Liam and I share her is...concerning. I mean, I suppose not since he seemed in full support of it. Only because he assumes it's to use her for our pleasure, not because we love her and want her happy. Also, never mind the calculated eliminator and my uncle, that are also in this happy little family. Yeah, that wouldn't go over as well.

Looks like we need to do a little research and see who else was close to Giselle Thompson.

Chapter Forty Two
Skyla

Wesley has his laptop open on the kitchen island, a pinched look on his face while I sit on my phone. It rings and rings, but Steph doesn't answer. Instead, it goes to voicemail.

"Steph, hey, it's me," I say, not even trying to hide the shake in my voice as I re-read the letter for the twentieth time. "Can you call me back? I need to talk to you, about mom and other...stuff. Please call me back as soon as possible."

I hang up the phone as Wesley speaks, keeping his eyes on the screen.

"Don't you think you're going to worry her with a voicemail like that?"

"Shouldn't she be? Shouldn't I be?" I ask.

His mouth flattens into a thin line as he runs a hand through his hair.

"Maybe," he admits, pouring himself a glass of whiskey.

I nod. Thought so.

"Shouldn't the guys be back? Where is Liam?" I ask, suddenly feeling an intense sense of paranoia.

"Liam is upstairs, working on his essay that's due tomorrow. The guys have only been gone for two hours. I expect them to be gone for longer than that. You need to relax."

"How can I relax? Everything is so fucked," I snap, tossing my hands out by my sides before letting out a rough breath. "I'm sorry," I say softer this time. "I'm scared, confused, and desperate to know what is going on. I'm so tired of living on edge, and now that this clearly involves my mom in some way, I just...I need answers."

He nods. "I know, we're trying. We're close. You've been so strong through all of this, just trust us? Hang in there a little longer."

"Why should I?"

"Excuse me?" he asks.

"Trust you? I mean, of course I trust the guys, but you...you don't owe me anything. Why are you even here?"

Wesley frowns at that. Slowly, he stands, rounding the kitchen island before coming toe to toe with me. He looks down at me, tilting his head to the side so he can hold my gaze more easily.

"Why do you think I'm here, little one?"

I swallow roughly, butterflies that have no business existing begin fluttering through me at the nickname.

"Out of loyalty to Ronan, right?" I ask, wetting my lips as I do.

Wesley's blue eyes snap down to the movement, tracking it slowly before they come back up to my own.

"If my loyalty to Ronan was in the forefront of my mind, I wouldn't be standing inches away from the woman he loves, thinking all the things that I currently am."

My heart thuds out of rhythm, and I find myself speaking before I can stop myself.

"What are you thinking?"

He watches me for a moment or two before lifting his hand to cup my jaw. The feel of his calloused hand against my skin sends a delicious shudder running through me as my breath upticks.

"You really want to know? Once I tell you, there won't be any going back for either of us."

My eyes move back and forth between his, not sure where to settle when he closes the distance between us. If I wanted to stop it, he gave me enough of a delay, but I don't move a muscle.

When his lips touch mine, my stomach flips and my pulse races.

The soft, pillowy feel of him against me has me wanting to sink into him and never come up for air. His tongue peeks out, swiping against my own once as his hand tightens on my jaw. He pulls away too soon for my liking, resting his forehead against my own as his chest heaves.

"That. That's what I've been thinking about. Every minute of every day since I laid my eyes on you."

"Wesley," I whimper breathily.

"I know, little one. I know. Even if we only exist in this moment, I'll take it. A stolen moment with you is worth a lifetime with anyone else."

He dives back in, either because he doesn't want to have to hear me reject him or he just can't help himself. Either way, I can honestly say I'm not mad about it, which probably makes me a terrible person.

This kiss is more passioned, less gentle. His teeth nip against my lower lip, sucking it into his mouth as his hands run up and down my body. They settle beneath my ass, lifting me into the air and resting me on the edge of the island. My legs part instinctively, and he steps between them, burying his hand into the back of my hair as he pulls slightly, deepening the kiss as our tongues tangle.

All of the feelings I've attempted to push away for Wesley, come rushing into me like a freight train. Every stolen look, accidental touch, melt-worthy word. Every single moment overwhelms me, and all I can find myself able to do is wrap my arms around him and hold on for dear life.

His mouth tears away from my own, peppering my face and neck with kisses as he slowly lowers me to lay on top of the island. He plasters his body against mine, the feel of his hardening cock grinding against my pussy as he thrusts forward once.

I'm so lost in this, in him, that I don't hear Liam come into the room. At least not until I look to see him sitting at a bar stool, stroking his cock as he watches Wesley and I. Wesley seems to notice him in the same moment, his body stilling and mouth pulling away from me.

"Walcott," Wesley greets stiffly.

"Don't you dare fucking stop. I can practically smell how wet she is for you all the way over here. Make her cum at the very least," Liam says, as his hips jerk slightly, his fist working faster as his eyes flick between Wesley and me.

Wesley's eyes come down to me, wordlessly checking on me. This is so Liam though, that I'm not surprised. I shrug my shoulders shyly.

He gives one more look to Liam before he presses his lips to mine.

"So, he likes to watch?" Wesley guesses, his mouth moving against mine as he speaks.

"Very much," Liam answers for him. "Both of you, honestly," Liam says, as he sinks his teeth into his lip, very obviously checking out Wesley.

To my surprise, he doesn't grouch at Liam like anyone else does, doesn't tell him to get fucked. Instead, Wesley tears his eyes off mine, running them over Liam assessingly before his eyes pause on Liam's pierced cock. Something akin to lust fills his eyes before he tears his gaze away.

"Careful flirting with me. I've been with more men than you ever have; that's a guarantee, and I don't back down from a challenge."

I can't help it. My pussy literally pulses at that as Liam's mouth drops. Shock is written all over his face, but right beneath it is excitement. I don't mean to, but a whimper escapes my lips as my head flicks back and forth between them. Both sets of eyes land on me and Wesley grins.

"Would you like that, little one? You want to share one of your men with me for the night?"

I nod enthusiastically. Too enthusiastically probably causing a chuckle to rip through Wesley. His eyes come back to me, an adoring shine in them.

"Maybe another time. Right now, I need you."

My heart tightens in my chest as his mouth returns to mine. Those soft lips practically pulling every worry, fear and hurt from my body, absorbing them into his own as his mouth dances across my skin. His tongue darts out, tracing a lazy line between my breasts before reaching the neckline of my shirt. His hand fists the cotton material, balling it up as he lifts it to expose my bare stomach.

Sweet kisses are placed all over it as he works his way down further and further until he's at the waistline of my leggings. Releasing my shirt, he takes my leggings in both hands and rips them off me so fast I almost fall from the island. He's there, though, stabilizing me while discarding my leggings and panties to the corner of the room.

"Jesus christ," he curses with a shake of his head as he rests his forehead against my upper thigh.

"What?" I ask.

"She's fucking gorgeous, right?" Liam asks, his hand jerking a little faster. "Prettiest little pussy you've ever seen?"

"So fucking pretty," Wesley murmurs against my skin.

His tongue peeks out, running slowly through me and making me shudder in the process. Those dark blue eyes come to me as if checking in with me, but they don't leave as he does it again and again, pulling a moan from my lips.

"Fuck, that's so hot," Liam groans from the side.

Wesley's eyes come to Liam's a sensual smile displayed across his face.

"Enjoying the view, Walcott?"

Liam sinks his teeth into his lower lip and nods, his eyes lingering on Wesley.

"I'd love to see more of this view."

Wesley chuckles, trailing a finger through me before pushing inside, curling up and hitting my g-spot in record time. What the fuck, does he have a GPS tracker on that thing or what?

Together, his tongue and finger work together in perfect synchronization. I can't help but tighten my thighs around him, resting each leg over his shoulders as he pulls me closer to him.

"Wesley," I gasp as his nose rubs against my clit.

"Mmmm, I love my name on your lips, little one. Say it again," he says.

His tongue swirls up to my clit, licking and sucking on it in a way that steals my breath straight from my lungs.

"Oh my god. Holy shit! Wesley," I whimper.

"You like that, babygirl? Is he eating that sweet little pussy so good?" Liam asks as he moves closer beside me.

"Yes," I moan. "S-so good."

My eyes move down to see Liam's eyes on Wesley, his hand jerking his cock faster and faster as he does. There is a lust-drunk look in his eye, like he's imagining Wesley's tongue on him instead of me. Maybe that should make me jealous or even turn me off, but instead, I'm desperate to see that image myself.

"C'mere," Liam says as he holds his cock up to me. "Open up."

I do as he says, feeling his cock stretch my mouth and push down my throat. Running my tongue along his piercings, he curses and grips my jaw tightly as Wesley nips at my clit. I moan and squirm, and with one more swipe of Wesley's tongue, I'm coming.

Liam follows closely behind me, letting out a string of curses as he coats my throat with his release. I swallow him down until he rubs my cheek lovingly before pulling out of me, tucking himself back into his pants.

When I'm able to finally catch my breath, I look down to see Wesley fisting his cock, his face still buried in my pussy as he lets out a low groan that has me clenching again already. Oh my god, I don't think an orgasm has ever sounded so sexy in all my life.

Wesley slowly pushes himself to stand, a satisfied smirk on his face as he reaches for a paper towel. He cleans himself as Liam helps me up. I feel a soft kiss press against the side of my head and smile up at Liam. He shoots me a quick wink before my eyes come to Wesley.

"Well, that wasn't exactly how I anticipated my first time with you going," Wesley chuckles lowly.

"It was better, right?" Liam teases.

Those blue eyes come to me as he takes half a step closer, his hand reaching up to cup my jaw as he nods.

"Most definitely."

Butterflies flutter through my body as I look between the two of them and even see them trade a few curious glances towards each other. I'm not one hundred percent sure if Wesley was just teasing Liam earlier or if he was serious. It's not like we've exactly had the kind of relationship to discuss his preferences or his past.

Wesley pulls away from me, moving to the stove as Liam leans into me.

"Did we just get a new boyfriend?" he whisper asks.

"I think so," I agree, as I watch the god-like man at the stove.

Wesley hears us based on the silent shake of his shoulders, but he doesn't turn around.

"Do you think Asher will be upset?" I ask.

"I fucking hope so," he laughs. "Jealous hate sex is some of my favorite."

I laugh at that, raising a brow to Liam.

"You already thinking about having sex with one of my boyfriend's?" I ask teasingly.

Liam grins at me.

"Like you wouldn't love front row seats to that show."

I would. I so fucking would.

Wesley moves towards us, a mug filled with cider in his hand as he gives it to me. I accept it happily as he bends down, stealing another kiss from me. When he pulls away, he grins.

"So, how long am I allowed to keep kissing you? Just so I'm aware."

"Uhm, as long as you want, I guess?" I smile shyly.

He grins and shakes his head.

"Not sure you should have said that. There is no getting rid of me now, little one," Wesley chuckles. "Need a drink?" he offers to Liam.

Liam looks at him, licking his lips seductively as he shakes his head.

"I have a different drink in mind if you're offering," he smirks.

Wesley's eyebrows lift as I take a sip of my cider, shaking my head at them. I can't tell if he is impressed by Liam's boldness or turned on. Maybe both?

Liam and Wesley banter for a few minutes as I sip my cider, casually sitting on my kitchen island with no pants and not a care in the world. What a life I live.

Like a freight train though, a wave of exhaustion slams into me. All the stress and worry of everything going on in my insane life, combined with the incredible release from an orgasm that has months of sexual tension behind it, given to me by someone who should technically be off-limits, has me ready to pass out right here and now.

I know some of the guys won't be happy about it, and when I say some, I mean pretty much everyone except Liam. Maybe if Wesley gives everyone mind-blowing oral, they will let him stay. Look at my slutty mind go. It's a pretty fantasy, though.

Chapter Forty Three
Skyla

A rough jerk shakes me awake. My eyes are heavy and my body sluggish. God. I don't even remember falling asleep. One minute, we were in the kitchen, post-orgasm bliss and the next...lights out.

God, I must have been so exhausted.

When I'm finally able to pry my eyes open, I freeze. What the fuck.

I'm not in my bed, not in Asher's, not even in Liam's. I'm in a car, the backseat of a car and it's pitch black outside. Based on the way the trees out the window look, I'd guess I'm flying down the road. Either on a highway or speeding down backroads.

I go to lift my hand when I notice I can't. My hands are tied together with thick rope, my legs also wrapped tightly at my ankles. I'm dressed, so I guess that means I was able to slip on my leggings and panties again before I fell asleep, but where the fuck am I?

It's hard to see anything, but occasionally, a light will illuminate the cab. It's easy to tell that this isn't any of the guy's cars and fear grips me like a vice. Oh my god. It's him. He's finally got to me, hasn't he? How did he get in? How did he get to me? How did I not wake up? Where are the guys? Oh my god. What if they're hurt? What if it's too late for them...what if it's too late for me?

My body is shaking, adrenaline and terror filling my veins as I strain to look around the seat. I see a large body in the front seat, a black jacket and black gloves on his hands as he steers. A streetlight is coming up, and I know that at least the mystery of who my stalker is will be solved. Unfortunately, it's being solved in one of the most dangerous ways possible.

My stomach turns, my breathing quickening as the car is illuminated for only a second or two. It was long enough, though, and the shock of it all nearly takes my breath away. Him?! How could it be him? How could he? How could I have not seen this coming? Oh, my fucking god.

"Y-you," I stutter. "I-it's you? Y-you're my m-my stalker?"

He turns to look at me, a sinister smile spreading across his face as he takes me in.

"I told you it wouldn't be too long, my love."

Thank You

Thank you so much for reading Descent!

I know, I know ANOTHER CLIFFHANGER?! Good news, the trilogy is now complete! The third book in the Gallows Hill series, *Demise*, is waiting for you.

Once you complete the trilogy and are ready for some more smutty emotional damage, make sure to be a good girl and check out my other books below!

Gallows Hill Series—a dark academia reverse harem
Damnation (Prequel)
Deceit
Descent
Demise

Standalones
Graves—an MFM stalker romance
Deliverance—an FF secret society romance (spin-off from Gallows Hill)
Gratify—a forbidden age gap
Jagged Harts—an MMA enemies to lovers

The ONS Series—interconnected forbidden romances
One Night Seduction
One Night Scandal - Coming Soon
One Night Surrender - Coming Soon

The Alphaletes Series—interconnected football romances
The Loyalties We Break

The Walls We Break
The Hearts We Break
The Rules We Break

Reviews mean everything to indie authors, so if you could take a moment to leave a review, I would be so thankful!

Review on Amazon & Goodreads
Find me on Instagram, TikTok, Facebook, and my Facebook Reader Group

Make sure you are subscribed to my newsletter and following me on socials to stay up to date on any upcoming releases, special announcements, and giveaways!

Acknowledgments

This book. At times it tested me, excited me and just straight up turned me on. It was a labor of love, frustration and some vibrating tools. Without all of these amazing people, though, it never would have happened.

To Sara, thank you so much for being by my side every step of the way. Some books are harder than others but they never feel impossible with you on my side. I'll message you at two in the morning with an unhinged idea or plot twist and I can practically see your eyebrows raise and your smile spread as you say, "Ohhh okay. I love it." Even if you don't love it, you know exactly how to make me feel seen and I love you for that. Thank you will never be enough to explain how grateful I am to have you as my PA, my alpha and my incredible friend.

To my Betas, Kreature, Brittany, Sheyla, Courtney and Mel, thank you for all you do! Beta reading can be so tricky and it's hard to find the right readers to an author and vice versa. I'm so grateful for all of your help, insight and amazing words of encouragement. I know you all love this book as much as I do and honestly, that means more than I could ever express!

To my editors, Lynsey and Slasher, thank you so much for all of your expertise. I write quickly, not well haha. Without you, this book would have undoubtedly been a grammatical nightmare and so I think I speak for all of the readers when I say, thank you!

To my street team and ARC team, thank you for every post, share, comment and words of support! I truly believe that any amount of success any of my books bring me all come back to you all. Without your support, advocacy and overall spamming, a very miniscule amount of people would even pick up my books! It's because of you all, putting your faith into me and my stories, putting your reputation on the line for me. I'll never be able to thank you enough.

To my readers, thank you for being here! Whether the Gallows Hill series was your introduction with me or you've been here from the start with that god awful mafia series (We won't talk about it haha). Thank you for trusting, supporting and falling in love with these characters right beside me. If it wasn't for you all, I'd have no joy to do what I do. You all have made my dreams come true, and then some. I hope I get to meet or at the very least speak to each of you one day so that I can personally thank you for supporting me.

Truly, deeply, passionately in love with all of you,
Katelyn